TELL ME EVERY LIE

Also by Ellen Hagan

Watch Us Rise (with Renée Watson)
Reckless, Glorious, Girl
Don't Call Me a Hurricane
All That Shines

TELL ME EVERY LIE

ELLEN HAGAN AND
DAVID FLORES

BLOOMSBURY
NEW YORK LONDON OXFORD NEW DELHI SYDNEY

BLOOMSBURY YA
Bloomsbury Publishing Inc., part of Bloomsbury Publishing Plc
1359 Broadway, New York, NY 10018
50 Bedford Square, London, WC1B 3DP, UK
Bloomsbury Publishing Ireland Limited, 29 Earlsfort Terrace, Dublin 2, D02 AY28, Ireland

BLOOMSBURY and the Diana logo are trademarks of Bloomsbury Publishing Plc

First published in the United States of America in June 2025 by Bloomsbury YA

Text copyright © 2025 by Ellen Hagan and David Flores
Illustrations copyright © 2025 by Bex Glendining

All rights reserved. No part of this publication may be: i) reproduced or transmitted in any form, electronic or mechanical, including photocopying, recording, or by means of any information storage or retrieval system without prior permission in writing from the publishers; or ii) used or reproduced in any way for the training, development, or operation of artificial intelligence (AI) technologies, including generative AI technologies. The rights holders expressly reserve this publication from the text and data mining exception as per Article 4(3) of the Digital Single Market Directive (EU) 2019/790.

Bloomsbury books may be purchased for business or promotional use.
For information on bulk purchases please contact Macmillan Corporate and
Premium Sales Department at specialmarkets@macmillan.com

Library of Congress Cataloging-in-Publication Data
available upon request
ISBN 978-1-5476-1495-0 (hardcover) • ISBN 978-1-5476-1496-7 (e-book)

Book design by Jeanette Levy
Typeset by Westchester Publishing Services
Printed and bound in the U.S.A.
2 4 6 8 10 9 7 5 3 1

To find out more about our authors and books visit
www.bloomsbury.com and sign up for our newsletters.
For product safety–related questions contact productsafety@bloomsbury.com.

To Araceli and Miriam—
Tayo ang pinipili nating maging tayo.
We are who we choose to be.

TELL ME EVERY LIE

SUNDAY

JP

This is the kind of story that starts with a lie.

Not a white lie like "I lost your number" or "My battery died."

Not weeknight lies to Tita Dalisay like "I already took out the trash" or "I'll be home by nine."

Not guidance counselor lies like "These are the best years of your life" or "Every teacher is here to help you" or "High school prepares you for the real world."

When you think about life, or at least when I think about mine, lies are always in orbit of what we want to be true. Junior year, I lied about being able to write in Tagalog because I wanted Model UN Club to see me as a global citizen. In middle school, I lied about having a girlfriend back in the Philippines because I wanted a girlfriend. When I was six, I lied about my mom and dad loving each other because I wanted them to love each other. But they had already moved to different cities, opened separate bank accounts, and started celebrating all the holidays apart. There are a lot of things I want to be true that just aren't. And maybe a lot of things that are true that I wish weren't. This summer, I'm gonna lie my way out of other people's pity, out of failure to start, out of the truth tied to my legs like a cinder block. I'll lie all the way to brilliance, exceptional son, praiseworthy college freshman, kind cousin, overall good human being. But hell, I'll even lie my way to just feeling fine. If that's what it takes.

"Boy Reyes," Tita Dali calls from the front seat. "How long has it been since you've seen your mother?"

I pause at the simple question. "Maybe six months? Last Christmas," I say. "That sounds about right."

"That is too long, John Paul," Tito Alvin says from the driver's seat. "She carried you in her belly for nine months. A man should always visit his mother."

A man? I think to myself. *How am I a man? I graduated high school less than forty-eight hours ago.*

I'm sitting in the back seat of my aunt and uncle's fancy all-electric SUV with my cousin Tiffany, who's eleven. She has spent the better part of the past two hours glued to the screen of her lux, gold-cased iPhone. I can hear the treble of electronic K-Pop leaking from her wireless earbuds. And Cass, her nine-year-old little brother, is passed out to my right. His face, fingers, and fancy glasses are covered in a high-contrast mix of earthy Nutella smear and neon Cheeto dust.

We started out on the road late morning, eventually trading the art deco co-ops of Morningside Heights for the winding pines of the Catskill Mountains. The air is different here upstate. Clean. Fresh. Definitely cooler than the city, but nowhere is cool in late June.

Tita Dali has the AC on blast. "It is bad manners to perspire, Boy," she reminds me for the five millionth time. Dalisay

Corazon Abrigo hasn't sweat since she was little girl back on Luzon. Her modern Imelda Marcos (wife and fixer of Dictator Ferdinand Marcos) updo is held perfectly in place by no less than six products. Everything about her—clothes, nails, skin—is immaculate. Dali is the kind of person who always looks like she's going somewhere important.

Tito Alvin's family are the famous Abrigo textile importers from Manila. They started off trading polyester and cheap linen, but Alvin's focus on trends and optimization have transformed the family business into an exclusive import/export house for Japanese cotton. Those ads on YouTube for ultra-heavyweight motorcycle denim? That's all Alvin Abrigo.

He presses a switch on the console and opens the moonroof.

"This makes the air *doble* pure, *doble* fresh, JP." AC and an open window—despite the all-electric vehicle, my family's commitment to the environment is dubious.

After crossing over the George Washington Bridge and taking in the lush greenery of the Palisades Parkway and I-87 north, we're on our way to the Majestic Mountain House in Monument, New York. "It is one of the top three spa resorts in the continental United States," Tita Dali tells us. "Your mother works so hard for you, and she deserves some of the rest and relaxation."

It is true that my mother works hard. It is also true that I don't see her very much—usually a few days around Christmas and a week in the summer—because she's always on the move. As a traveling nurse, she's lived in Boston, Stamford, Newport, and at least fifteen other cities in the last dozen years. And every summer for as long as I can remember, we go on some version of this trip where she's supposed to join us. Two years ago, my dad and I took the train from Moynihan Hall for the big family meetup in Philly. Dad, the cousins, and I beat the X-Men arcade game in the back of Atomic City Comics on South Street. Last year, Dad had to work, so I took a Megabus on my own to meet my mom and her family at a casino-spa-resort in Atlantic City.

Four months ago, my dad died. I had to move from Queens to Manhattan to live with my Tita Dali, Mom's sister, and Tito Alvin and their kids. Uptown is like another planet for me. I've gone from sleeping on an IKEA pullout couch in a Jackson Heights living room to an organic latex queen bed in a guest room with herringbone hardwood floors. Where instead of seven keys that open two gates and three doors to get into my old apartment, Mr. Inday—an immigrant from Visayas—opens the front door and calls the elevator that opens into my Tita and Tito's living room. Mr. Inday carries groceries and manages deliveries. Sometimes when I come down early in the morning, I find him singing along to Tagalog love songs from his phone. I can almost hear the soapy sounds of "Ikaw Ang Lahat Sa Akin" as we start up the single-lane road to the mountain.

A gentle breeze flows through the moonroof, bringing sweet smells of tree sap and fresh flowers. Cadmium-green road signs encourage us to "Proceed slowly and gently" on the steep, winding pavement.

Cass, somehow recovered from his sugar-and-MSG crash, tugs on my sleeve and points out a family of deer.

"They're called *Cervidae*," boasts Tiffany in an annoyingly loud voice.

Then, silence. For the next ten minutes, the road is the only sign of human touch on the landscape. Tall trees, berry bushes, wildflowers, bird chirps, and the celestial blue of the sky make me forget all about Mr. Inday singing kundiman, about Uptown Manhattan, FilAm Queens, my father, my mother, and everything else in the world.

Am I lying to myself? Trying to forget about everything that happened back in the city? This week I just want to be someone else. Feel other feelings. Feel the world open up. Want to find myself in a different story. So, yes, this is the kind of story that starts with a lie.

Not a stupid lie like "Of course I'm listening" or "Let's stay in touch."

Not a cover-your-ass lie like "The trains were crazy" or "I thought I already sent that email."

No matter what anyone tells you, leaving things out is the worst kind of lie. The kind of lie that starts everything full-on wrong, off tilt, south of south. But sometimes we need to leave things out. Sometimes the worst lies are the only way forward, the only way to feel . . . just fine.

MIA

THE MAJESTIC MOUNTAIN HOUSE

YOU HAVE ARRIVED

HERE, YOU ARE FAMILY

WELCOME HOME

I read the signs to myself as we walk across the grounds from the Majestic Kids' Club, through the botanical gardens blooming with butterfly bush and bee balm, and wind through the tree houses built into the pathways and on the sides of the walking and hiking paths, toward the nine-hole mini golf course and around Lake Majestic, making our way into the grand dining hall. This is our routine every single Sunday afternoon, when the staff takes their lunch break with the new guests. For Jasmine and me, who run the Kids' Club, it's our first chance to greet the new families and kids, who are starting their week fresh. We want to make a good impression, so we show up early.

"Come on!" I call to Jasmine, who has stopped at the dock

and is holding a handful of fish food and trying to get them to come to the surface.

"But I love these little guys," Jasmine says, referring to the loads of rainbow trout that have been stocked in the glacial lake ahead of the summer season. "This one is my favorite," she says, making eye contact with a massive trout that has clearly already been overfed.

"I don't want to be late," I say, tapping my watch.

"Summer hasn't even officially started and you're already on one thousand! Calm down. Can you just take it easy this summer?"

"Are you kidding? No, I can't just relax. You know that. I have some very specific plans to get the hell out of town, and they don't include us taking it *easy*."

"But if this is our last summer together, then it can't just be all work. You have to have some fun, Mia. Remember fun?!" Jasmine laughs. She sighs as we approach the wraparound porch at the back entrance. The dozens of old-school rocking chairs are already full of new guests who are looking out on the lake. They are imagining their most ideal vacation week. They are trying to envision perfection, and we are here to provide that. I take this job seriously, even if it means secretly rolling my eyes at their every single request.

"I like to call them goats instead of guests," Jasmine told me and Ellis two summers ago when we all first started. We were sixteen, and babies when I think back on it. I was drawn to the two of them, who were easily the coolest of the kids working at the resort.

"What? Why goats?" Ellis and I broke out laughing just the same, both of us bleating and hollering.

"You know it fits. And besides, I can say 'goats' quietly

under my breath, and none of our managers will ever know the difference. We can even bleat every once in a while so we'll know exactly who we are talking about." She laughed and at the end it trailed into an adorable little bahh-a-a-ah.

So that's how we came to start calling them all goats. *The goats at Table 13 want yet another round of sparkling mineral water with just the tiniest squeeze of lemon.*

The goat coming into the Kids' Club is bringing a baby goat with a temperature of 103. Just heard that from the doc's office. Get your masks ready.

The goats are vicious today. It's hot and they are all very disturbed by the sunshine streaming onto the resort.

Oh, look at those sweet goats who don't know how to lift their own suitcases.

Some of them got to be called guests—the ones who didn't treat us like we were completely invisible. The ones who called us by our names and asked about our families, because this place is a community, and we often see the same families summer after summer.

I nod hello at the new guests and enter into the Majestic Hallway. Everything is labeled and called Majestic. Sometimes it's shortened to MMH for the staff, but it's subtly drilled into both staff and guests that this place is MAJESTIC. All you need to do is look around to be sure of that. We snake through the hallways lined with photographs from the past; this place being founded in the late 1800s as a recreational guesthouse on over four hundred acres surrounding the lake and the great Catskill and Majestic Mountains. It is easy to see how someone could land here and never want to leave. But for me, it's even easier to see how someone could be born here, feel endlessly stuck, and do everything in their power to get out.

"Jasmine, seriously, we're gonna be late!" I call back to her. She's looking at the photos, while I'm trying to hustle up the Majestic Grand-freaking-Staircase when I run right into one of the guests.

"Excuse you," he says after I stumble into him. Classic. He's got on a loose tie and suit jacket. His hair in a buzz cut. Chiseled jawline. Attitude. He might as well have a sash that reads: *I'M GOING TO HARVARD IN THE FALL*, because that's exactly where he's going.

"I'm so sorry," I say, and hate myself for apologizing. "Were you looking for the dining hall? It's that way," I point, and try to disappear.

"You should watch where you're going," he says. "Or maybe I'll watch where you're going." He smiles at both of us before he turns to walk away.

"Ew. What was that?" Jasmine asks as we watch him.

"Rich clown," I whisper.

"Come on, they're not that bad," Jasmine says, giving me a look.

"You're the one who told me to call them goats! And I'm not saying all the guests are rich clowns. I'm just saying most of them are."

"Oh, smart-ass Mia and even smarter-ass Jasmine," Wolf says, coming up behind us. "Tell us how you really feel." He pushes as he puts his arms around our shoulders. I shrug them off.

"Shut up, Wolf," I whisper back at him. I regret thinking Wolf was hot when we first started, and regret even more making out with him that first week. He's a total jerk who showed his true colors as soon as I said I wasn't interested. His favorite pastime since is giving me crap. We walk faster down the hall, toward the keeping room off of main dining, where the staff hangs out before going to introduce ourselves and welcome families and guests. It's part of the Majestic hospitality tradition. "All I'm saying is that most of them are so full of themselves that they have no idea what's going on outside their own little worlds."

"Is that why you spent all last summer trying to hook up with one of them?" he asks.

"Shut up, Wolf," Jasmine says now. Louder.

We can see the guests starting to stream in. All of them in attire, per the requirements based on long-standing traditions: No swimwear; no ripped, torn, or frayed clothing; no robes; no hats or caps while dining. Suit jackets and resort wear encouraged. They took out the labels for men and women when the staff requested a more inclusive update.

"What are we talking about?" Ellis asks. He has joined up with us and the other crew that are now walking into the side room.

"To be clear. I did not try to date anyone last summer, despite your ideas. You don't even know me," I add. "Besides, I wouldn't date anyone here. Ever. Thank you very much."

"Come on. Not even that guy?" Bee asks.

Bee is my nemesis, if you could call it that. She's on staff with the music crew, who teach lessons to small groups and play in the classical quartet at dinnertime. She points to the buzz-cut clown who gave us a hard time in the hallway. He looks into the doorway and winks at me.

"Nope. No thank you. Never. Not ever," I say.

"I call bullshit," Wolf says. "You couldn't get one of these rich-kid assholes to fall for you if your life depended on it. Who would notice you anyway?"

Charming.

"Are you saying she couldn't do it?" Jasmine snaps.

"Oh, please!" Wolf fires back. "A Richie Rich falling for Little Miss Shutterbug? Look, Mia, you've got a cute face, but if you think guests see anything other than your uniform, you're dead wrong." A crowd of coworkers has started to gather around us. "Trust me, I've hooked up with my fair share of guests. None of them ever remember my name."

"This is something you're bragging about?" I clap back.

"I'm not bragging," Wolf replies. "We're not important to these people. I mean, sure—they need us to carry their bags, valet their fancy cars, and serve them chichi meals. We're like an ant farm to them. Worker bees."

The crew is silent. Wolf isn't wrong. We haul, we polish, we serve, we *yes sir* and *yes ma'am* and *yes-yes-yes*. We are uniforms that smile and say *enjoy your journey with us*. I dig deep for a reset. Guests are rich and they enjoy their stay because of our work. But they're not better than us.

"They have money and they're on vacation," I start. "I'm at work. I'm here to make my money and keep it moving." Nothing could be more true. I've got exit plans. Big things are happening for me. Of course, big things have big price tags.

"You wanna make your money?" Wolf challenges. "I dare you. All-caps DARE YOU to get a guest to fall in love with you."

"Keep your voice down, Wolf. You're beyond unprofessional," I start.

"I'll give you all the tips in my pocket," Wolf honeys, patting a wad of sweaty bills in his front pocket. "Dare you. Dare you to get one of these punks to fall in love with you."

"You know what? I bet she can do it," Jasmine adds. "In fact, Mia, I'll give you fifty bucks when you do."

"Oh, I like this," says Bee, turning from me and looking square at Jasmine and Ellis. "I'll put fifty on it. No way you're gonna win, but I'll definitely pay for the show. How about the rest of you?" Bee asks.

One by one all the hands in the room go up. There are twenty-one of us young staffers this summer. I do the math quick in my head: $1,050. Add Wolf's tips and I'm on my way to California and into the photography program that I never thought I could afford. I'd even have a little money to spare. I can do this. I might have to do this. But what do I know about dares? When someone gives one, I never take it. That's the way it's always been.

Dare you to swim across Lake Majestic in the middle of the night. Nope. Don't wanna drown.

Dare you to hike through the death-defying Eagle Rock blindfolded. And fall three hundred feet to my death? No thank you.

I am what you might call risk averse, safety first, a rule follower. Always trying to be the opposite of my family, of all I've ever known. Trying to keep it all together, hold it all down, but where has that gotten me? I'm still stuck, and the same old, boring me. Maybe this summer, I can convince one of those goats that I am totally someone else. Wild, uninhibited, spontaneous. Living right on the edge. Unafraid of . . . everything. Maybe I can be someone else completely.

"But how are you gonna prove it?" Wolf asks, bringing me back to reality, laughing at this deal. "This can't just be the honor system if I'm handing over all my tips."

"I'll prove it," I say, looking over at Jasmine and Ellis for an idea.

"Ohhh, I know," Bee starts, and I'm already nervous about what she's gonna say. "Whoever you get to fall in love with you has to be recorded saying it." She is so smug.

"Well, how am I supposed to do that?" I ask, already thinking that I should bow out of this deal. I will just work more hours and save more, but of course I know that won't really work, with helping my aunt and all the extra stuff I'll need when I get there.

"'That's for you to figure out," Wolf says. "We can't do everything for you, now, can we?" Wolf and Bee laugh together, coconspirators trying to get me.

Screw them. I can figure this out. "Fine then, yes. I will get someone to fall in love with me and get them on record saying it to me by the time the week is over. Easy," I add again, trying to convince myself. "I can be seen. Just watch me."

"And what if you don't?" Bee asks. "Then what do the rest of us get if that happens?"

"Then she'll have to pay each of us fifty bucks," Wolf adds. "Sounds fair to me."

I look over to Jasmine, who shrugs her shoulders at me, and Ellis, who shakes his head no. They don't believe I can do it. Fact is, I'm not totally sure I can either, and I will absolutely be sunk if I have to pay everyone. But I'm resolved. So, I grab Jasmine's hand to head over to main dining.

"Challenge accepted," I say.

JP

We have to get to the dining hall. But, nawawala ako, I am lost.

The Majestic Mountain House is a monstrous historic hotel with over six hundred rooms and suites, two indoor pools, four outdoor pools, a roller rink pavilion, twelve hiking trails, horse trails and stables, an eighteen-hole golf course, a nine-hole mini golf course, and the list goes on and on. This place is like that hotel from *The Shining* with, as Tita Dali keeps sharing, "one of the top three spas in the continental United States." The spas in Jackson Heights were little five-seaters for gel nails, eyebrow shaping, and blowouts. The list posted here in quill-inked calligraphy offers a full novella of services—many with bizarre monolithic marketing like "Ancient Asian Foot Calm Compression" and "Himalayan Salt Stone Restoration" and "Gua Sha Facial Sculpting."

Twenty minutes ago, we checked into our suite—two deluxe rooms connected by a shared living space. My aunt and uncle have a room to themselves, while I'm sharing the other with Tiffany and Cass. The adults are out of the suite on a walk to stretch before lunch, and I've been put in charge of getting the kids ready and downstairs for our reservation at 1:30. This is easier said than done. Tiffany has figured out how to lock one of the connecting doors, while Cass has taken to jumping from bed to bed on our side of the suite.

"Tiffany, please open the door," I plead while simultaneously trying to wave Cass down from his Floor Is Lava game. There is no response, so I'm guessing she's scrolling through crappy dance videos with her noise-canceling headphones blocking me out. It takes a full fifteen minutes to get Cass changed out of his Nutella- and Cheeto-crusted clothes and into something fresh. "Ugh!!! It's 1:25! We've gotta get down to the dining hall in five minutes!" I exclaim.

Tiffany magically appears wearing a summer-dress-and-sweater combo.

"My mom hates it when we're late. It's time to go, JP!" Tiffany orders. It's in this moment that I realize that I haven't changed clothes and won't have time to. My dress shirt, embellished with Cass's Cheeto prints, is going to be a problem. I rummage through my duffel bag, pull out an oversize black hoodie, and cover it.

I'm zipping my sweatshirt up when my eyes catch the top-floor view of Lake Majestic out the window. The waters are clean and clear. Blended forest greens and the deep purple of wildflowers call me to calm.

"JP, resort wear!" Tiffany breaks my moment of grounding. She's reminding me of the dress code for the dining hall. *Guests are encouraged to dress in suit jackets or resort wear.* I cross over to my aunt and uncle's room and find no fewer than twelve formal jackets and suits in the closet. I pull the first one off its felt hanger and throw it on over my hoodie. This thing is huge.

"You look like a beige kite," snaps Tiffany. Her cutting tone shakes me to the core. I would never dress like this. I look and feel ridiculous. Cass laughs as both cousins pretend to be the wind blowing my comically large blazer around. I sheepishly roll my left arm out of the jacket, then pause. Old-school John Paul Reyes would take the jacket off. He would accept the simple truth that this ultra-layered look requires the confidence and swagger of a different character. But today I can be new-school JP. Cool, smooth, rich.

In one sweeping move, my body stands up straight and my arm snaps back into the shiny sleeve. I pop my collar to the ceiling. A half smirk washes across my face.

"Whoa," Cass exclaims. "That was cool."

In a mad dash, we tear out of the suite. 1:27—we're inside the elevator on the sixth floor. The doors close and the breathless panic of loss sets in on all our faces. Cass forgot his Switch, Tiffany forgot her phone, and I misplaced the room key that would give us easy access to the aforementioned pacifiers. So much for new-school JP.

My mind races forward in time. *This is easy*, I say to myself. *I can pick up another key from the front desk after lunch.* One problem solved. I turn to Tiffany. Her face is sunken in disappointment. She will be so sad to miss fifteen-second makeup tips and dance tutorials, but she will survive. My eyes lock with Cass. Heavy tears are already falling. His breathing is all over the place. He's about to lose control of himself. I kneel down on the floor of the elevator, meeting my cousin in height. We hold hands.

"Cass, look right at me," I say calmly. "We're going to take three breaths together."

At every meal for as long as he can remember, Cass has taken his chicken fingers and buttered pasta with a Nintendo. I've never been allowed to use a device while eating. My dad was very strict about this. But, like cousin Cass, we had our constants. Cass's grip on my hands tightens on the exhale of our second breath.

My mind flashes back to a winter meal with my dad. Our little round kitchen table covered with steaming bowls of arroz caldo with fresh shavings of ginger and garlic, leftover biscuits from Popeyes, and a microwaved plate of green beans over adobo-soaked rice—his favorite. The sweet and savory blessing of spices and cheap, canned veggies slows time down. Dad closes his eyes before we eat, takes a deep breath, and says, "Amen."

The elevator door opens on the ground floor. I'm shaken out of the food memory that could have taken place on any Thursday of my eighteen years of life. But this is a memory from this year. The face of my Tatay fades as a now-calm Cass and a foot-tapping Tiffany pull me by the sleeves out of the wood-and-gold box and into the ornate lobby of the hotel.

"We're late now. Where is the dining hall?" Tiffany snaps impatiently.

"Hello," a calm voice interjects. "This is the ground floor. Please follow me up to dining on the first floor."

My body follows the quick turn of my head to a young person, maybe just slightly older than me, dressed in a hospitality uniform. We have the same eyes, medium-brown face, and large earlobes. A laser-cut name tag on their uniform reads *Caloy, they/them*.

"This way, please. The stairs are faster than the elevator."

"Salamat po," I say.

"Very formal," they reply.

"Waland anuman po." We share a quick nod, both of us relaxing a bit.

"Taga-saan ka?" asks Caloy. I tense up again. We spoke a mix of Tagalog and English in my house when I was little. When my mom left, so did my Filipino tongue. I can say a lot of basic things. I know how to be polite. I easily understand Caloy's question, but I watch their enthusiasm fade slightly as I respond somewhat sheepishly in English, "I'm from Queens. My mom is from Baguio. And my dad—my dad was from Queens too. His mom was from Pasig and his dad was Irish."

"Well, welcome to Majestic Mountain House," Caloy offers gently as we all climb the stairs.

Switching to full English is a common custom Filipinos offer FilAm kids who either only know the basics or don't know the language at all. It's moments like these—and I've had more than a few—that make me want to learn more words, or at the very least practice my Tagalog.

"Very good to have you here. Please enjoy your meal." With that, Caloy opens the hand-carved ten-foot door to the dining hall. We enter to the sounds of calming strings, the tinkling of glass drinkware, and at least three types of forks in conversation with heavy plates.

Tita Dalisay appears from nowhere, scolding me for my lateness. "This is not a diner in Jackson Heights, John Paul. Here you must be on time, every time."

She's right. This is not a diner in Jackson Heights. If I were on Roosevelt Avenue, I'd be ordering lamb samosa and spicy pancit at Meera and Elvie's Toro-Toro—an Indian-Filipino cafeteria that sells out of everything by two p.m. I'd grab Spider-Man comics from Arturo's Deli and read them cover to cover with ube jam at the bar at Krystal's Diner. I'd be hanging with my newly-graduated-from-high-school friends and we'd laugh about how bad we all are at basketball in spite of our Dunks, rereleased Jordan 4s, and Air Force 1s.

Looking around the dining hall, I guess there must be two hundred tables. Service workers in all black carry trays of fancy drinks and freshly baked breads to visitors in floral prints, suit jackets, ties, pastel polos, and empire khaki. I do not fit in here.

Tiffany and Cass pull me toward the kid's buffet. For the third time in as many minutes, I trip over my own foot. Embarrassing. I hope no one saw that.

MIA

I walk into the main dining room and immediately see one of the goats who must think he's all that trip over his own two feet while trying to make it to the kid's buffet. Is he thirteen or eighteen? Does he belong in the kids' or adults' section? His hair looks wild, as if brushing it was a total afterthought, and is that a hoodie underneath his "resort wear"? Classic rich-kid rebel. Too good to follow the dress code. I know his kind.

But when he looks up, there's the one second—feels like a million seconds—that my eyes meet with his and I find myself trying to catch my breath. His eyes are everything. Deep. Intense. And is he smiling? At me? Or just in my direction? Or just because? There is no breath in my lungs, but my face rolls up into a smile. He's not gonna fool me with his now seemingly sexy tousled hair or his freaking eyes that are still locked on mine.

Wait. Am I smiling lopsided at a total stranger? Is he even looking at me? If he is, does he think I'm some sort of weirdo? *Why did I take this stupid bet in the first place?!*

Just then, the two little kids who are trailing behind yank

him toward the food. I'm so shaken by locking eyes with him that I completely forget that I'm supposed to be introducing myself to the new families—that I am still on the clock. I make my way over to the buffet as I watch him pile his plate high with chicken tenders, mac and cheese, pigs in a blanket, fried shrimp, and Tater Tots. At the last minute, he adds a piece of lettuce and a single slice of tomato to the top of the food mountain. *Is that for him or a five-year-old?*

I turn around to head for one of the tables to say hi when I lock eyes with him again. This time he's walking right toward me. And no, I do not believe in love at first sight. That is for romance novels and cheesy teen YA rom-coms. That's not real life, but then if that's true, why can't I seem to get any real oxygen in my brain? And why is my heart jumping out of my chest? And why am I still staring directly at him while two kids pull on his arms and his plate falls to the floor in cinematic slow motion?

"Here, let me help you," I say, rushing over to him.

"No, no, it's cool. I got it. Don't worry, I do this all the time."

I look at him and desperately try to hide my smile.

"That's not what I meant," he starts again. "That's not even . . . not what I do. I do not drop plates on the ground at fancy resorts, like, all the time. That's not . . . something I do."

We get the plate situated and both stand up. I am surprised that I still can't catch my breath. His smile stretches across his face. He takes one hand and covers his eyes for a half second too long. Shakes his head. Is that actual self-awareness? Unlike the other King Babies spread out around the dining room being spoon-fed by their moms and aunties and grandmothers. All telling them how wonderful and brilliant and special they are.

"I'm Mia," I say, holding out my hand, which is way more awkward than I mean for it to be. I move it to a high five position, but that's even worse, so I just nod my head a whole lot and try to match the wattage of his freaking smile.

"John Paul . . . er . . . JP. My friends call me JP. You here for the week?" he asks, and clearly has not clocked the red polo I'm wearing or the name tag that reads *Mia, she/her* near my shoulder.

"No, I, um . . . I work here. I run the Majestic Kids' Club. I'm Mia," I say, pointing at the name tag now. "On Sundays, we welcome new guests. Welcome," I say again, not fully able to find all my words and feeling the eyes of my coworkers on me now.

"Oh, that's cool. We love it here," JP says. "Come here every summer with my family." I nod, trying to remember if I've ever seen him or heard his name over the last few years. I am pretty sure I haven't, but I pretend otherwise."

"Well, welcome back! I knew you looked familiar to me."

He nods. So sure of himself. There it is. That cocky affect that all the best goats have. Just graduated and here again for the summer, relaxing and taking it easy before college starts and they're off to study—spoiler alert—finance, law, economics, premed, money. If this was any other time or place, I'd walk away, let this just be a moment to forget, but a bet is a bet, and something about him has me standing still, moving in slow motion.

"Well, if you want a tour guide," I say, "just let me know. I've been working here since I was sixteen, so I could show you around if you wanted. I kinda know everything about this place."

"Oh, really? After all these years coming here, I still feel like I know nothing. Clearly don't even know how to hold this plate," he says, and stumbles backward, almost dropping it all over again. "See, I was telling the truth . . . happens all the time. But yeah, yeah, I'd love that."

I tilt my head and stay looking at him. Study his thick black hair and the way it waves around his head. His dark eyes studying me right back. "How about we . . ."

"Oh, excuse me. Just making sure everything is good over here," Layla, my manager says, eyeing me close. "Mia, I think it's almost time to get back to the Kids' Club."

I look at her and nod. *Be friendly, but not too friendly. Be attentive, but not overbearing. Never spend more time than is needed with guests. You are here to serve.* "Right. On it." I turn back to JP. "Enjoy your journey with us." It's the line we are supposed to say over and over, like the Majestic Mountain House is some bizarre ship we're all sailing through the sea on.

"And to you also. And also with you," JP says, and when I look at him, he has that same scrunched-up smile on his face. Has he not learned how to smile yet?

I give him the biggest, toothiest grin I have and turn away, knowing we are just beginning the journey I am about to bring him on. Yeah, this kid is gonna fall so easy.

"See you soon," he says, and keeps his eyes on me while I walk away. I know it. Can feel it and want it more. I turn around and wave one last time. He's standing there, still watching, holding the same plate that's about to drop out of his hands all over again. *What in the hell am I getting myself into?*

JP

You're blank, kid, I scold myself. *What in the hell was that?!*

Nerves shot, I wander an awkwardly long way to the table where Tito Alvin and Tita Dali are sipping fancy cocktails. My body crashes down in a dining chair that is somehow both antique and modern.

"Boy, you took so long," says Tita Dali, "we ordered for you. You will have the steak."

I nod my head and silently command my open mouth to close. But my mouth has some kind of direct line to my thoughts and suddenly spills, "Mia, she/her . . ." My stupid face is performing a dramatic reading of a name tag.

Tita Dali cocks her head to the side. "Who is Mia?" she asks.

"Mia is a pretty girl with dark eyes and coily dark hair," Tiffany reports. "She wears a red polo shirt, runs the Kids' Club, and helped JP after he dropped his plate at the buffet. She can also talk and smile at the same time."

Without her face buried in the blue glow of a phone, Tiffany is quite attentive. And her observations are mostly accurate. Mia can, all at once, smile and talk. She runs the Majestic

Kids' Club in a red polo. Her hair is dark and coily. Her eyes, brown.

Pretty is a word that I stopped using junior year. Ms. Mendoza, my humanities teacher, warned that the popular use of the word was designed to create a "hierarchy of desire to manipulate the marketplace of fashion and cosmetic products." It's a word that gives a higher value to a constantly changing set of corporate-prescribed visual aesthetics. I don't use the word *pretty*, but I know why Tiffany does when she's describing Mia.

"John Paul, close your mouth," orders Tita Dali.

I swallow hard and take a deep breath. No, I don't use the word *pretty*. I don't know what the right word is for when you share four sentences with somebody and you can't get them out of your mind.

After lunch, I find myself back in the suite. A set of floor-to-ceiling glass doors lead out to a small covered porch with two rocking chairs. My nerves have the best of me. I rock eight times in one, stand, go to the other, rock another eight. Then repeat. And repeat. And repeat. *Was she just being friendly? Does she like me? Like me like more than a guest? Like me like a summer fling?* I feel like I'm assuming too many things and asking myself too many questions. I have no answers. Just anxiety mixed with uncontrolled smiles and numbing cold in the pit of my stomach.

I am struck by Mia. I want to hear her laugh and lock eyes again and see her cool confidence. Soon. Like, sooner than soon. Like sooner than now! *Why didn't I shake her hand? Or at least do the high five?* Redo. *Should I drop my plate tonight at dinner and hope she's watching?* Wait, that doesn't make any sense. Maybe I'll stop by the Kids' Club this afternoon. I want her to show me around the endless maze of the Majestic Mountain House—learn more about one of the top three spa resorts in the continental United States.

In therapy, I've learned to control some of this anxiety with breathing. Dr. Kumar taught me an exercise—seven perfectly balanced inhales and exhales in sixty seconds. I try this several times and fail. Too many breaths. Too much rushing on the inhale. *This is stupid*, I tell myself. *You just met this person. Calm down.* The calm down mantra isn't working. The breathing thing isn't working. I can feel an attack coming on. I raise my arms above my head, locking my fingers together behind my neck. I inhale slowly. Hold. Exhale. Repeat. Twenty-four breaths later, I'm back in control. I'm going out. John Paul stays here. I'm JP from now on.

Everything is hustle bustle. A whirlwind of sunshine-friendly resort wear. Men in smoking jackets follow staff cigar aficionados and sommeliers to the north tobacco hall and the south cocktail porch. The fitness obsessed wear superhero uniforms and sneakers with uncreased, fresh foam soles to appointments with chiseled trainers at one of two indoor or three outdoor gyms.

Yet again, I confuse the ground floor for the first floor. Caloy, seeing me fumble for the second time today, points with their eyes to a terraced staircase while directing a team of five bellhops moving seven bell carts. There's so much action here. So many people and so many moving parts for a place promoting rest and relaxation.

I'm down the mahogany stairs and out the fifteen-foot door

of the east entrance in less than thirty seconds. As soon as I'm outside, there is the smell of jasmine, the sound of breeze over tall trees, and the glow of summer sun still several hours above the horizon. I ground myself with three perfect breaths and head out to the trails. I need to walk. To move. To shake off and sweat out whatever this thing is on my back.

Walking is always perfect. When I'm going nowhere it gets me somewhere. Everywhere. When I lived with my dad in Jackson Heights, we just walked. Under the train tracks on Roosevelt Avenue to Adelmo's, our favorite Sari-Sari store. We'd buy dried wheat noodles, fish sauce in double-weight glass jars, banana ketchup, shrimp chips, and overripe pineapple—pick any three for a Wednesday night dinner. We'd walk to Johnny Chang's Red Dragon DVD—Queens's one-stop shop for bootleg Donnie Yen and Dingdong Dantes movies. The Exclusive San Miguel Barber Shop—one of the last places left in the city where you can get a shape-up and hot towel shave for ten bucks.

In Queens, people walk. We walk phosphorus-lit streets and avenues and roads—all with the same number in front of them. If you want a good tres leches cake, you need to know the difference between the bakeries on 34th Ave and 34th Road. They aren't the same. Walk to shop. Walk to eat. Walk to the all-ages karaoke bar and the corner record store for re-released Pilita Corrales CDs.

"John Paul, no one in Pilita's band knows how to read music. They play everything by ear," Dad tells me at our Christmas party last year. "Can you imagine how much talent they must have?"

I can imagine. I can because I have. I have because we've

had some version of this conversation every year for as long as I can remember. My dad loved Pilita because "This is the music that my Ermat played at all of her holiday parties. I miss her so much, John Paul."

During Christmas and Easter every year, my father mourned the loss of his mother. Even though she was not and is not dead. She's eighty-three and the pinnacle of health, and she retired three years ago and moved with some friends to California. A Filipina *Golden Girls*–type thing. Her secret to a long and healthy life? Walking.

I cross the halfway marker post on the Baby Eagle 2k trail. The elevation of the mountains fills my lungs with crisp air that smells like river and sky. The evening blue above holds me in an embrace of calm and peace. My breath is in perfect sync with my steps.

My mind remembers my father's excited voice, "We should visit your Lola, John Paul. Maybe take a train cross-country. Save a little money and have some adventure."

I pause a sec, then, "I dunno, Dad. Sounds expensive. And trains take a long time."

"Ah, John Paul . . . Sometimes it's fun to take your time. Let your mind wander. Get a little lost. And, yeah, we're always kind of broke, but we can save here and there. And trains are cheap. We can cancel cable, take the money, and buy a ticket."

"One ticket? That doesn't make any sense, Dad. You going solo?"

"John Paul, you barely look twelve. You know Amtrak runs specials where kids ride free?"

"HEY!" I snap, my eighteen-year-old voice cracking with the indignity of both baritone and soprano.

"JP?"

Wait, who said that? In an instant, I snap back from holiday memories with my family. I've finished the Baby Eagle 2k trail and made it down the mountain again. In a burn, I've sweat through my Batman tee, underwear, and shorts, all while hearing the voice of my dead father in my head. Even my feet are soaked. Wait. I'm standing ankle-deep in water? My eyes slow-crawl back to focus. "Mia?"

"Hey again," she calls out. "Everything okay?"

"Oh, shit!" I shout as my body and mind simultaneously snap out of whatever the hell trance I was in. My MJs—the last pair of shoes I bought with my dad last fall—are wet toast. My stomach bottoms out like a roller coaster going hard in reverse. I feel my throat closing up, the corners of my eyes filling, my breath leaving me.

MIA

Is he about to start crying? Over his shoes? "You good?" I call over to him. He is ankle-deep by the docks and I am pretty sure the rainbow trout are already going for his feet. I take one more quick look inside the Majestic Kids' Club to make sure everything is in its place, lock up, and jog down the little sloping hill to where JP is standing. I look at my watch. 6:17 p.m.

"My shoes," he says when he sees me. "I was walking on one of the trails and just . . . got lost."

"You got lost?"

"Not for real. Just lost in my head. In my thoughts . . . and next thing you know . . ." He points to his shoes, which are soaking on his feet—wrecked in mud and grime.

"Don't worry. We can fix this. Come on," I say, and lead him back up the hill and unlock the door again. "Welcome to the Majestic Kids' Club—also known by the staff as Club Kid." I open the door, and the smell of animal crackers and cleaning solution hits us instantly. "Follow me," I say, and lead him through the hallway and into the main room, which is meant to mimic the lounge in the guesthouse with its tall, sloping ceilings and dozens of skylights and cozy seating and play areas throughout. We walk toward the bathrooms in the back. "You okay to take your shoes off?"

"Oh, you don't have to . . ."

"It's cool. You're definitely not the first kid to ruin your shoes in the lake. We fix them here all the time."

"Yeah, but I'm not really a kid, so . . ." He looks up at me. We both smile and I'm not even sure why. There's something about him that makes me want him to stay, to say more. *Don't get attached, Mia. Don't be so dramatic. A dare is a dare. This is work for you. Focus. Clean his shoes. Talk. Flirt. Get him to like you. Finish the job.*

"Oh, no. I didn't mean you were a . . . I know you're not a kid. You must be . . . how old did you say you are?" I ask. If he is in fact thirteen, it will be very awkward to reverse this dare. "And what grade are you in . . . ?" I trail my answer, hopeful.

"Just graduated," he says, unlacing his shoes.

"Oh, me too," I say, relieved.

He's about to hand them to me when he stops. "Could you just tell me what to do? You really don't want to be touching my shoes."

I laugh and point to the massive sink outside the bathrooms. "Okay, okay. You got this. Just take out the laces and any inserts and run them under cold water. Lake water has all sorts of contaminants and dirt. Grit and harsh chemicals and bacteria . . ."

"Oh my god. And people swim in that lake? If it's not good for shoes, it can't be good for people, right?"

"No, no. It's fine. You just . . . don't think about it. There's actually a lake swim we all do. You should come with us this week." He nods his head like he has already decided, but then smiles and I feel sunk all over again. "Go ahead and rinse them out. Totally. And then here." I grab a handful of paper towels. "Stuff them with these and let them air-dry. That's the part that takes the most patience. Air-dry means *air-dry*. No hair dryer or direct sunlight if you want to save these. And it seems like you do."

"Yeah, but I have plenty of other shoes, so . . ."

Of course he does. Money, money, money. Enough to travel with an entire cart of shoes. You ruin one, you have a backup. "No problem," is what I actually say. It's not too late to get someone else to fall in love with me, is it?

"So, this is Club Kid, huh? It looks cool as hell."

I laugh. "That seems like a stretch."

"No, seriously. Look at this place! If I was a kid, I would be so into this." He walks barefoot back into the great room, pulls a book about animals off the shelf, and sits down in one of the beanbag chairs. "I could stay here all day." Look at him. Comfortable anywhere. Shoes off, walking around like he owns the place. So casual with it. Like he's got nothing to do. Nowhere to go. And of course, he doesn't. On vacation. Relaxed. Easy.

"Check this out," I say instead of asking him to leave, which part of me wants to. What was I thinking, making this stupid bet? I walk over to the performance area and open the trunk full of costumes. "You can be anyone you want to be here."

"Ohhh, see, that's cool," he says, and runs up the stairs to the raised stage. He peers into the trunk and pulls out a firefighter's jacket, a stethoscope, a pair of long black gloves that he immediately pulls up both arms, a hot pink tutu, and a clown wig. "Perfect. Everything I've ever wanted. Your turn," and he points to the trunk now.

I pull out a cowboy hat, a bright red cape, and a horse mask that has a long mane of hair that trails behind it.

"What is that? That is terrifying!" he shouts, and we both start to giggle, looking at each other—mirroring the chaos we're wearing. "That's not a costume, that's a nightmare. What kind of play is this?"

"It's a total nightmare," I agree, and suddenly we're both moving around onstage like we're underwater, dancing and grooving, and I can't tell if this is nerves or anxiety, but it's ridiculous and silly and just then, I realize I'm supposed to be flirting with this guy and trying to get him to fall for me and I'm not entirely sure why I'm wearing a horse-head mask to get him to want me, so I take it off and see that we're both sweating and breathing hard now.

"So I see there's a lot of weirdness that goes on down here, huh?"

"Totally. I told you. You can be and do anything you want here."

"Just like a dream . . . *err* . . . nightmare. Just like being eighteen and graduating from high school," he says, and looks down as he starts to take off his costume pieces.

I stop for a second, not sure what to say. I definitely can't tell him I got accepted into a prestigious art program across the country and have a totally messed up family and no actual money to get there. That is not the story he is looking for. "So, you're not sure what's next?" I say instead. Figure the best way to hook him is to get him talking about himself. My aunt June always says *interested is interesting*. What she means is that asking questions and flattery are the way to anyone's heart—at least that's what I've always assumed.

He pauses and looks at me. He's still wearing the long black gloves as he pushes his hair away from his face like he's deciding what to do next. "Oh, I was just joking. College, of course. I'm headed to Brown in the fall. It was between that and, uh . . . Yale, actually."

Brown and Yale. *What a rich-kid loser* I think, but bite the inside of my mouth and nod along instead. He is exactly who I thought he was. Suit jacket over hoodie, world-class vacation with his rich family, infinite pairs of shoes for when you ruin your first pair, and of course—Ivy League in the fall. I wouldn't have picked any other way. "That's sooo amazing. Congratulations! Those are some pretty awesome schools to choose from, huh?"

He seems almost surprised by my enthusiasm, so he keeps on. "Yeah, thanks. I'm pretty excited actually." *Why does he keep saying 'actually'?* "And just happy to know what I wanna study."

"What's that?"

"Finance," he says, shaking his own head up and down like he's trying to convince himself. That tracks completely. Ivy League for "finance" or whatever that actually means. Money, of course. He has to maintain the lifestyle he is most comfortable with. Yes, this all makes sense. I chose the perfect mark.

"I love that you already know what you want to do with your life."

"Yeah, I've always been really interested in how the markets work," he says, and I have no idea what he *actually* means by that, but I keep nodding. Keep pretending. "How about you? Plans for the fall?"

"Oh yeah," I say. "I'm headed to California after the summer is over. A photography program in LA. I love Monument, of course," I lie. "But I've been wanting to head out west to see the rest of the country, just to mix it up." I try and sound breezy, casual. As if getting there will be the easiest thing in the world. And it will be, if I can convince JP to fall in love with me.

"Wow. So you have it all figured out."

"Totally," I say. "These are some of my snaps here." I point to the walls that are covered in documentary photos and portraits of the kids over the last few years.

"These are awesome," he says, studying them and getting up close. "You took all of these?"

"Made them. Yeah. I don't like to say 'take a picture.' Like you're stealing something from somebody. I make photos. We're in it together, you know?"

He nods and looks at me for a second too long. I can feel my face flush. I look down at my watch—nearly 7:30 p.m. I can smell the fire starting down on the main lawn and know it's time to get out of here. I'm supposed to be photographing tonight's s'mores making. Now that I'm eighteen, my manager promised more hours if I wanted to document some of the events, and I don't want to be late. He sees me look and starts to fumble for his shoes, which are still soaking wet.

"I should go, right? Thank you so much. I really appreciate it . . . you. Thank you."

"Anytime," I say. "And you need something to wear back to your room, right?" I walk back to lost and found and find him a gigantic pair of slippers. They have dinosaur heads on them. I don't wanna humiliate him, but Brown and "finance" make me want to embarrass him just a little. "Put these on. And we can walk by the fire to get s'mores on the way back if you want."

"Oh! Yeah. I want to," he says. So simple. So easy.

"Me too."

JP

My borrowed brontosaurus slippers have us walking a little slow, but Mia doesn't seem to mind. She leads the way to the bonfire, turning back every so often with a smile. I'm racking my brain for things to say, but I'm stuck on trying to organize all the little untruths from Kids' Club. John Paul Reyes doesn't have the cash for City College, let alone the Ivy League. But I could totally be JP *Abrigo*—son of the shipping magnate, ready to glow up the fintech scene and show up to class in a self-driving car.

Just before we come off the trail, her left wrist brushes against my right. The hair on the back of my neck stands straight up. The night air is sweet with cinnamon and warm oak. The crackle and pop of the firepit is its own vibe. *Say something smooth, JP!*

"I don't think I've ever actually had s'mores." Mia looks at me like it's my first time on planet Earth. Smooth JP is clearly on the bench.

"How have you *never* had s'mores?" she asks indignantly. "They're a top-five dessert. One of the best things you'll ever eat." Mia's eyes are smiling. "In the summertime, my mom and dad would slow cook lamb and onions and toss them over rice with tomato and cucumber. For dessert, s'mores. Always s'mores. The perfect summer night treat!"

"That sounds awesome," I spark. "Family meals—they're the best. I can tell that you and your folks are tight."

Mia looks away. "I love my mom and dad so much," she reflects. "They raised me here in Monument. It's a beautiful place to grow up. But summers are different now. During the on-season, I live in staff housing, so I don't get to see them as much." A solid beat, then her eyes lock into mine. "Are you gonna roast some marshmallows or what?"

Mia shuttles me over to the buffet covered in a red-checkered tablecloth. Handwoven baskets lined with delicate paper doilies hold Jet-Puffed marshmallows, Hudson Valley chocolate bars, and an endless supply of house-made graham crackers. She hands me a skinny stick. "What's this for?" I ask earnestly. Mia shakes her head and points toward a group of five-year-olds roasting white clouds of sugar over open flame. She pokes a puffy marshmallow atop my stick and says, "Do what they're doing."

Mia steps back, pulling a nickel-plated camera from her shoulder bag. Adjusting a set of oversize dials, she looks through a little window with her right eye. Her focus set on the smiling kids at the edge of the firepit, she presses a button and advances a thin lever in one smooth action. Mia steps forward with confidence and makes another frame—this time closer to her subjects. Her eyes dart back to me and, with a sharp tilt of her head, I am directed to make some dessert.

My first attempt starts strong. I carefully move my marshmallow toward the orange glow. The round edge begins to brown. I press the stick farther into the flames until the delicate marshmallow combusts into a yellow fireball. Quickly pulling the stick back, I blow the torch out to reveal a bitter, black knot. Defeated, I toss the charcoal nugget into the firepit.

Mia, camera slung across her body on a thick leather strap, encourages me to try again. I pierce another marshmallow to the end of my stick and approach the fire slowly. My second attempt is overly careful. I pull back every time I think I'm getting too close to the flames.

"Need a hand?" Mia asks. "I'll help guide you." Coming in behind me, she glides her soft palms over my forearms, settling the full weight of her hands on my wrists. With little brushes of her fingers, I rotate the treat slowly. The edges gently caramelize as the belly of the marshmallow softens. The process only goes for a minute, but I could stay right here forever. "Done!" Mia declares, pulling me back from the flame.

With the excitement of a child, she sandwiches the toasted delight and milk chocolate between two graham crackers. Smiling wide, she raises the confection to my mouth.

I taste everything she promised and more. I greedily take the s'more in both hands.

Her brilliant eyes smiling into mine, Mia takes a step back. She raises her camera to me. Click.

MONDAY

MIA

My alarm goes off at 5:30 a.m. Everyone else is still asleep. It's dead quiet and the whole bunk feels like it's under a spell with only the sounds of finches and cardinals outside our windows. Four bunks in all, eight bodies crowded in together. My phone buzzes gently on the table next to the lower bunk. I roll the covers off and try not to make too much noise. I take my caddy and a change of clothes to the outside showers. This is steady. This is routine. This is what I do every day. No complications. No differences. Follow the rules, stay in line. Wake up before everyone else to clear my mind. Empty my brain.

Once I am outside, the day feels expansive, open, unending. I put my gear in the last stall. I'll come back to get ready after my run. The grounds are empty at this hour—mostly animals and the earliest of risers. Me. Sweatpants and tank top on, I lace up my tennis shoes. The first run of the day is essential. It's what keeps me sane, what stops all the thoughts from running wild in my head.

Stretch. Lean. Pull shoulders back. Loosen hips. Roll neck. Dip. Pump. Twenty-five push-ups. Twenty-five sit-ups. Punch.

Exhaust. Twist. Turn. Swing. Repeat. Repeat. Repeat. *Wear out the body so the mind will follow.* I have been saying that mantra in my head all year. Graduate. Get out of town. Disappear and exist somewhere else. Away from here. *Wear the body out so the mind will follow.*

I start slow up the mountain. Keep my head down. If I see people I know (and I usually don't), nod, be friendly, keep it moving. If I see families that I have worked with at the Kids' Club, nod, be friendly, keep it moving. There is a system here. A way that things need to run. A set of rules to keep everyone in their place and everyone accounted for. I still remember three years ago at one of our very first staff meetings. Layla, our manager, sat us all down and went over the rules. The ones that kept us in line, the ones that we were supposed to adhere to as much as possible in order to make things run smoothly. We go over them as a team every year so that no one will forget. They stay scrolling through my head now as my legs pump through the woods.

Look and present your best self. Yes, I smile, think of the face I need to put on, the ways I need to show up: neat uniform, teeth brushed, fresh breath, hair combed. Nothing out of place.

Flow with the crowd. You do not want to call attention to yourself. You want to blend. You want to float, you want to be there whenever anyone needs anything at all, but you do not want to be in the way. Be like the lake. Like the swimming pool with underwater music piped in. Flow. Flow.

No substances of any kind unless prescribed by your doctor. You want to be in physical, mental, and emotional health at all times, though often the staff sneak in alcohol and weed for after-hours, so lots of people break that rule, but not me. Never me. I haven't touched any substances for my own reasons. I remember that rules are often broken—but never in plain sight, always behind the scenes, quiet as can be.

Always say yes. That's another rule. Or *My pleasure*, or *Of course, that is no problem. Yes, absolutely we can do that. Yes, we can make that happen. I am on it.* We are yes people. We are here to serve the guests, and what they want to hear is that it is no problem. They do not want to hear about our problems. It's sunny, we bring the shade. It's rainy, we bring the umbrellas. We bring the relief and the breath of fresh air. We serve. We service. We wait on. We absolutely deliver.

And finally: *Don't bother or irritate or fraternize with the guests.* Meaning . . . do not date or hook up with anyone who is paying to be here.

I keep my legs pumping and think about my own obsession with following the rules, with keeping things in line, with paying attention to what I need to do in order to survive. My mind stays working overtime, trying to figure out if making that bet was genius or completely idiotic. If I am supposed to run farther away or run closer. Toward freedom? Toward disaster? I keep running, faster and faster. The air is charged. I feel shifted when I run like this. Blood coursing, heartbeat in my head. Trying to run away from the past. If I do not run fast enough or far enough, I will get caught in the web of this town. Caught in the stories of my parents, who are trapped in their history, and stuck helping my aunt with her life rather than starting my own.

Lamb and s'mores for dinner? Sitting down with my family at all?! I love my mom and dad so much?! That last one is true, but the rest of what I was saying to JP last night was total bullshit. It started and I couldn't make it stop. Inventing the kind of life a guy like him is used to or would be into. I couldn't get the words back in my mouth after I got started. And now, maybe that could work. I have put so many other people first, but I am letting that go. That's not who I want to be. I try to release it. Release them, my fear, my anxieties. This dare is for me. I know this. It is my ticket, my way out, my way of distancing myself from the past, from everything holding me back. So what, I'm telling a few small lies. If that's what it takes to get to the finish line, then I'm doing all the right things.

And then I see JP up ahead, sitting by himself on a massive rock. *What is he doing up this early? And why is he alone?* I stop myself from going to him. Even though it's only a week that he's here, I have to play the long game and stretch this out, so I leave him alone and cut my run short. There will be plenty of time to figure out what gets JP up so early.

I decide to head into the Mountain House for a cup of coffee. Gina runs the breakfast buffet, and she knows my schedule, knows that I'm up early to clear out all the mess in my head.

"Hey, kid. Good run?"

"Yup. So beautiful up on the mountain. And it's just me and all those tourists who think getting up at five a.m. is healthy or whatever."

"Oh, and that's not you?" Gina asks as she pours a coffee with milk and two sugars.

"Just gotta clear this up," I say, pointing to my head, "before another wild day starts and I lose track of everything and then get to bed and can't stop thinking."

"I got you," Gina says, and hands over the coffee. We both know me coming to the dining room to be fed is not something that management looks kindly on. This is the main space, the grand room with expansive views of the lake and Majestic Mountain. It's for the paying customers, the ones who have the funds for a view like this. So I take my coffee with me to go on the trail back to the bunkhouse.

Breathe in. Breathe out. *Wear out the body so the mind will follow.* In. Out. Rest. Repeat.

"Mia? Hey, what are you . . . It's so early," he says.

I stop in my tracks. There he is. He has made it down the mountain and has his own cup of coffee in hand. JP. In another world, another dimension, he is someone I would have ignored, would have told that this is my time, and no one interrupts this quiet, this steady, but I have a mission here. Have to get out of town, and somehow this kid is my ticket, so I bring my best attitude to this moment.

"JP! Hey. Hi! Yeah, I am up this early. Yes, I am definitely what you would call an early riser."

"Yeah, no. I see that. Are you? Going for a run?"

Sherlock Holmes, I see. Oh my god, be nice, be nice. "Ah, how'd you know? Yes, yeah I am. I kinda find that in order to deal with little kids all day, I really have to take some time on my own, so I generally just try to get out here and, you know . . . But what are you doing up so early? You're supposed to be on vacation. Sleeping in, getting up late, and all that."

"Oh, I never sleep in. Gotta be up early too. About to get a copy of *The New York Times* and *The Wall Street Journal*," he says, and even though I can see a comic book peeking out of his tote bag, I don't say a word. Yup, the kind of guy who wants people to know how well-read he is, how much he knows, how smart he is, how much it matters. "I like to read the hard copies. Something about a real paper, you know?"

"Of course," I say. "So much better than online, right?"

"Exactly."

"Exactly."

"Hey, I was still thinking about those s'mores last night, lying in bed."

"You were? Wow! So, what you're saying is . . . I basically changed your life, right?"

He breaks into a smile. He is somehow easy to talk to. And if I don't think too much, easy to flirt with too. And maybe even easy to convince him of who I am without revealing too much.

"I didn't say all that," he says. Oh, back to being cocky. Ivy League. Out of my league. Great.

"Well, we still have a whole week. Maybe I'll have you thinking about more than s'mores while lying in bed at night." *What am I even saying?*

"Yeah. I'd love to see you try." *What is he even saying.*

"Game on," I reply. Smile even wider and wave as I walk away.

JP

"Magandang umaga," I greet Caloy walking into the Majestic Mountain House.

"Good morning, JP," they reply. "May I help you with anything this morning?"

Caloy's question is welcoming and hospitable, but their eyes have clocked the red flush across my face. Mia just hit on me. Hard. Said, and I quote, "I'll have you thinking of me in bed tonight." Okay, that's not exactly what she said, but I'm faded and more than a little anxious about what to say or do next. Mia is used to real rich folks up here. Rich. Rich means confident, resourced, well-read. Me? John Paul Reyes is mid-confident. Resources? Shaky. Well-read? Being a regular at half-price back-issue day at Midtown Comics gives more *thrifty nerd* than *Richie Rich*. I'm a Queens kid staying in a rich family's guest room. If I'm going to be cool, smooth JP Abrigo, I'm going to at least have to read the rich-people newsletter. I swallow hard and ask, "Is there anywhere I can find a copy of *The New York Times* or the *The Wall Street Journal*?"

Caloy gestures to the Reading Room.

I scan and dismiss dry stories about stock valuations and living off dividends before landing on a headline that stops me in my tracks—"Mothers: America's Backbone." Holy shit. It's Monday. My mom arrives today.

I rush back to the suite to shower. It isn't until I wipe the steam off the mirror and make sure my hair is tucked neatly behind my ears that I realize the entire space is empty. Maybe Tita Dali and the family took an early hike? A note on heavy linen-textured hotel stationery says to meet at 8:30 in the dining hall. The words *DON'T BE LATE* are underlined three times. Tita Dali has never been subtle. It's 8:09 and I'm on the first floor—not the ground floor—early. With some time to kill, I walk the long hall, bouncing between the nerves about seeing my mom and the heart-clanging swag of Majestic's own Mia.

As I move south down the sun-drenched corridor, I'm drawn to all the oversize family portraits lining the walls. To the east are paintings from the turn of the century. Victorian, Romantic, and Realism styles abound. To the west are all beautiful family photographs. Family names are etched into shiny gold plates below each image. The classic script style transforms the names into beautiful little poems complete with hyphens and semicolons—*The Anderson-Williams Family; Lauren & David with children; Riley & Ryder from the Village of Piermount.* And *Evelyn & Jackie Green; loving mother & child–Inwood, Manhattan.*

I'm completely taken with a black-and-white photograph at the end of the hall. A closer look reveals the print is more caramel than straight-up BW. I can tell by the clothes and the background that it was made recently here at Lake Majestic, but the style makes it feel like it came out of one of those old, accordion-looking cameras. In the photo, a couple—in their sixties? Filipino?—stand together with their adult child set slightly forward and center. The family is holding hands and looking into the camera with a warmth that only comes from real closeness. The picture is brilliant in its simplicity. All the people are in sharp focus with background fading into swirls of butter. Nothing feels set up or posed, but the people in it are looking warmly right into the lens. It's like the photographer saw something in them and the family saw something back.

The Mendozas: Peter, Remmy & their loving daughter, Josie, from Hudson, New York. Photograph by Mia Malik.

Mia Malik? These must be her photos—

"JP, you're on time," Tita Dali says softly as she places a hand on my right shoulder. I turn from the photo wall as Tito Alvin pats the upper part of my left arm, ending with a gentle grip. Their faces are somewhat sunken, their eyes down toward the floor. I know what they're going to say before they even know how to say it.

"She's not coming, is she?"

We're all quiet walking into the vast dining room. A string quartet of young people is playing a bright and also sad-sounding something or other as Tiffany and Cass run to the grand buffet of pastries, muffins, and fresh-squeezed citrus juices. My little cousins get their own table this morning. Tita Dalisay, Tito Alvin, and I sit at a four top with one empty seat.

"She called this morning, JP. The hospital was short-staffed, so they asked the nurses to stay. She might make it later this week," Tita Dali gently explains. "It's good money. Time and a half plus a bonus. Very good money."

Money. Money is messy—explosive, even. Talking about money and my folks is like closing a fist over a stick of dynamite.

When they were together—and even after they parted ways—my parents just saw dollars differently. My mom was always the high earner in the family. She worked crappy jobs and ran at least a half dozen side hustles—all while going to school to become an RN. My dad cobbled a bunch of little gigs together before settling into something that paid enough of the bills to free up nights and weekends. Her emergency fund could protect rent for three months; his could barely cover three slices of pizza. What really made them so different about money was how far they could see into the future. Dad lived for the day. Drip coffee and buttered pandesal for breakfast, saltine crackers and peanut butter for lunch, some kind of adobo-drenched FilAm Frankenstein deal for dinner. Everything else went to rent and ConEd.

"She started with ten dollars in an old can of Bustelo," Tita Dali says, reminiscing, her eyes studying the foam atop her coffee. "Remember her dream, John Paul."

"It used to be your dream too," I snap. Across the table—past the lattes and avocado toast, the sterling salt-and-pepper shakers and the porcelain egg cups, past the hand-polished forks and impossibly bright white tablecloth—my aunt and uncle look down at their plates. They have nothing to say. Maybe there's nothing to say. A long silence.

Before Alvin came along, Tita Dalisay and my mom shared a wild vision of moving back to the islands and living it up in a house in Baguio. Tita Dali dropped the dream when she married Alvin, whose family had money. Their business is a cash register. But my mom is keeping the dream alive. She bought some land a few years back but hasn't built anything on it yet.

"I'm sorry," I start, trying to soften my tone. "That wasn't fair, and this isn't your fault."

Tito Alvin raises his kind eyes. "This isn't fair, and this isn't your fault either, John Paul," he says. He exhales a long breath. Then more silence.

"It is only Monday. Even though your mom is not here, let's try and have a nice vacation," Tita Dali says. "Your uncle and I have a spa appointment this morning. Why don't you take Tiffany and Cass to the Kids' Club? Then you go out and explore—do your own thing."

I nod, letting out a long breath of my own.

It takes three napkins to get the gourmet Pop Tart filling off Cass's face. Tiffany, impatient as always, taps her foot staccato. As we make our way out of the dining hall, Cass pulls me hard by the hand, and I accidentally bump into the cellist as she's packing up her instrument.

Rising up from the floor, she stares at me, unfolding bright red lips over a very forward, white-flame smile. "Oh, you're Mia's new friend, right?"

"Yeah, that's me. I'm sorry for bumping into you. I'm JP," I reply awkwardly.

"Well, JP," she says while looking intensely into my eyes, "I'm Bee." Without breaking eye contact, she slowly raises a pointed finger to the name tag on her all-black jumpsuit.

"Bee, she/her," reads Tiffany.

"Pleased to meet you, JP," Bee says, keeping her eyes on mine. An uncomfortable silence follows. She is not breaking eye contact and seems to be studying me. All of me. I'm so uncomfortable now, my mouth has gone completely dry.

She cocks her head slightly right and adds, "If you ever get bored with Mia, let me know. I play every afternoon and evening with the quartet. Are you interested in playing music?"

"Uhhh . . ."

"I also give private lessons if you're interested in that."

"Did your parents name you after an insect?" Tiffany fires off.

Bee blazes a quick look down at Tiff and inserts, "What an adorable little girl!" She sets her all-black-everything vibe back on me.

I feel like I'm about to get chewed up and spit out. *Is she waiting for me to say something? Jeez, this is uncomfortable. I've gotta get out of here.* "It's nice meeting you," I say clumsily. "Have a nice day."

"Enjoy your journey on the mountain, JP," she unrolls as I take the kids by their hands and bolt for the exit. The tension of the moment has me short of breath.

"What the hell was that?" Tiffany asks. "When did girls start liking *you*?"

MIA

I show up at Kids' Club fifteen minutes before everyone else and unlock the door. The smell of cleaning solution hits me hard. We make sure to wipe everything down in a very intense way because we know what the little ones are capable of. I prep the front desk with permission slips and parent release forms, check that the bathroom is in tip-top shape, and do a quick walk around the main space. I clock the trunk of costumes and think about JP in that tutu and the dinosaur slippers he went home in. Definitely not too cool to be silly or dress up or play. That is for sure. And not too cool to try s'mores. But then, too cool this morning? Hot and cold. I have to be better at reading his signs and figuring out who he is. I make sure the play kitchen is stocked with pretend fruits and vegetables and line the dolls up just so. Check the board games in case of rain and take stock of our snacks and treats for special occasions.

I do one final sweep of everything and then Jasmine arrives, followed by the three new club staff. They are young, for sure, but quick learners.

"Hey, everybody. Let's circle up real quick before we open

the doors." I can already see a line forming outside. "We want to run through our list of activities for the day." Jasmine hands everyone sheets of paper. The list is printed fresh each day on double-weight stationery.

"Remember, Monday is the most important day of the week for us," Jasmine starts. "This is when we establish trust with our young campers. We get to know them, play some name games, comfort them if there are tears, and just try to have as much fun as possible."

"This is their vacation too," I add, "and we know they are missing their families when they first get to us, so it's our job to make them feel relaxed and at ease." I smile over at Jasmine. The more we work together, the better we get—fine-tuning what to say to new coworkers. "They see us having fun, and they'll have fun. Promise."

"Our activities today include lake-inspired arts and crafts—we'll be making papier mâché fish and creatures from the deep; a nature-walking tour through the creek bed at the edge of Laurel Trail; croquet on the main lawn; and prepping for the carnival this evening. Sound good?" Jasmine asks.

We all nod. As soon as that's done, we open the door, and it is an onslaught.

At the check-in desk, we listen as every kid arrives with their own set of rules and circumstances.

"Little Lizzy only eats her cheese puffs ONE at a time. Can't give her more than that. She throws up just about everything. Don't you, Little Lizzy?! So really, you need to feed her ONE at a time," the mom repeats, eyeing me close. She waves her tennis racket in the air, gesturing to everything in the room. "She is so particular. I have no idea where she gets it. Ha, ha!"

Ha, ha? Who says the actual words ha, ha *out loud?*

"Dustin only likes the color pink. No other colors are allowed near him. Do you understand?" a father says while adjusting his visor and rapidly checking his watch. "His rules, not mine. Go figure!"

I understand Dustin to be an exact replica of his father, and before the day is done, I am going to introduce him to the entire rainbow. Open up Dustin's world to all the possibilities.

"Jessa is obsessed with her Jenny Jump Up doll. Takes her everywhere. When Jenny jumps, Jessa jumps, and when Jenny and Jessa jump at the same time, they get jelly beans! Yes, they do! Can one of you sweet kids give my sweet Jessa her jelly beans?"

Why in the world is everyone talking in so many exclamation points? Of course I will do what is asked of me. No exclamation mark needed. Yes, I will feed Jessa and Jenny jelly beans. And yes, I understand that Jenny is in fact a doll, but no, Jessa does not think of her as a doll and so neither should I. Clearly Jessa has no human friends, which only makes me feel sad for Jessa, and so I will do anything that is needed to make her feel like she has a community here, like she has people who want to know her story.

"Luna loves nature so much. Please plan to engage her outside for no less than four of the five hours. This place is just so stunning, and we want her to have as much time as possible in the outdoors." This from two moms nodding back and forth as they spew directions at me. They want their kid to spend as much time outdoors as possible, but without them.

That seems to be the key for everyone spending time at the club. I nod again. I understand. I will do the best I can with the very specific rules for these very specific goats, I mean children.

"Still room for two more?" I hear, and look up from my paperwork. JP. Again. We will see if he is a guest or a goat this morning.

"Oh, hi! Hey. How's it going? You all ready to sign up?" I ask, and all three of them signal yes. "You two can head on back and I'll get everything sorted."

"Thanks so much," JP says. "They are super excited to hang here."

"They seem sweet. Your family looks so perfect," I say, looking back as he writes the names *Tiffany* and *Casper* on the forms. "Your brother and sister must really look up to you," I add. "I always wanted an older sibling to kinda watch out for me and protect me. That's cool they have you."

JP looks up for a minute and seems like he's about to say something, but then he stops and goes back to filling out the forms.

"And also very cool that your mom and dad brought you to Majestic Mountain House. You know, there's a bunch of stuff you can do on your own at the resort. Archery, nature walk, history tour, paddleboarding. The list is endless," I finish. "I mean, if you're looking for something to do to fill the time."

"Yeah, I have a couple of good books I'm trying to get into, so I'm glad to drop these two here," JP says, looking up at me with a question on his face. *What is he thinking? Those books he's talking about are definitely comic books. What's he trying to prove?*

"Cass and Tiff," JP calls out into the playroom, "can you two just, uh, come and see me for a second please?" He looks at me again. "I just wanna give 'em one last hug and talk about the plan for this afternoon. Um, it's good to see you again. And I'll see you at pickup, right?"

I nod and leave him to it.

JP

"Okay, come over here and do not make a scene, just look at me with love in your eyes, got it?"

"What the hell are you talking about?" Tiffany asks, clearly excited that she can curse now that she's without any parental figures.

"Just look. Mia thinks that you are my brother and sister," I say, smiling at them and then nodding toward Mia, who is watching me with what feels like great interest. She has an awesome and warm and loving family who all sit down to dinner together and eat s'mores by a damn fire, and so if she thinks I also have an awesome and warm and loving normal family, then I am going to go full nuclear on her and show that my family is not only loving, but also wealthy, and has it all the way together. Gonna prove it to her.

"Why would you do that?" Cass asks, looking over his shoulder and doing the same smiling and nodding that I have been doing.

"Because he likes her . . . no, no. He loves her!" Tiffany whispers, but loud enough for me to shush her and pull the two of them outside the door.

"Look, don't worry about why I am doing it, just do it for me. Just say I'm your older brother, okay? Besides, my dad just died, so can you at least give me this?"

"Oh my god, you can't use your dead dad to get things."

"What? I have never used my dead dad once." I stop. "Okay, well, this is once." My dead dad. The words don't stop me in my tracks anymore, but they stay lodged somewhere in my chest, an imprint or weight. I'm someone who had a dad once and now I don't. Take a breath in, let a breath out. "Could you just do this for me, and we don't have to make some trade or barter? Can you just be my cousins and do me this favor?"

"Your cousins? Why, we're not your cousins, JP. What are you talking about, *Brother*?" Tiffany lays it on thick. Cass is still looking back through the doors at Mia.

"I like her," Cass says, and moves to give me a fist bump. "Good luck out there. If you need me to be your brother, then you got it."

"Yeah, yeah. Me too. Whatever. You probably need all the help you can get. And maybe I should help you pick out some clothes later too," Tiffany says, eyeing my whole entire look. She cuts me down exactly like Tita Dali.

"Yes, of course. My fashion rests in your hands, dear Sister."

"Okay, don't push it. We'll do it," she says, and looks over at Cass, who nods along.

"Thank you. I owe you." It's that easy to invent an entire family for yourself. Make your real one disappear and your imaginary one appear right in its place.

Walking away from the Kids' Club, I'm asking myself so many questions. *Why did I set my cousins up to be my sister and brother?* Because Mia thought they were. *But that doesn't make any sense! You could have fast-corrected that. Why didn't you?* Because Mia thinks my aunt and uncle are my parents. *Dude! That's absurd. She's not talking to you because of who your parents are.* Yeah, well, maybe I DON'T WANT TO TALK ABOUT WHO MY PARENTS ARE. I don't want to have to explain to another person that my dad is dead and that my mom is a workaholic who skipped his funeral, skipped my high school graduation, and is currently skipping the one week a year she's supposed to spend time with me. *Dude. That's a lot.*

I cross my arms tight and sigh. *Keep it together. You don't need to think about any of this right now.* I look out toward the water. Vacationers are smiling and moving quietly in canoes along the lakeshore. A father raises a toddler onto his shoulders at the bay beach. A mother and her kids are laughing and carrying on as they struggle to stand up on paddleboards. They fall in unison, splashing into the calm waters, bobbing up seconds later and climbing back on to go again. I'd like to try paddleboarding sometime.

Just then my stomach lets out a bendy, low-to-high-pitched note. *Ruhhhhhhh—ooo.* The bad jazz is audible proof I didn't touch a thing at breakfast. *Why didn't I eat?* I decide this is why I'm being cranky with myself—probably doesn't have anything to do with me flat-out lying to Mia and pressuring Tiff and Cass to become accessories to the crime. My stomach groans again. This time so loud that a hiker passing on the trail looks quizzically in my direction. I have to eat something. Don't want to go back to the dining hall for fear of running into Bee. Where else can I grab food?

Back on the ground floor of the Mountain House, I ask this

question to Caloy. They walk me north along a corridor of realistic landscape paintings through a set of ornate stained glass doors. The smell of good coffee and cotton candy fills the air. "This is our soda fountain and gift shop, JP," Caloy says with a gentle tone that lets the sweet fragrance and bright colors of the space speak for itself.

To the right, the gift shop. There's the branded resort swag that lets the rich guests from Pennsylvania, Jersey, and New York advertise that they stayed here and can afford it. There's also a bunch of small displays with wares made by local artisans and craftspeople.

"The soda fountain is this way," Caloy gestures. "You'll find snacks, refreshments, and any sundries you might need." We both nod and smile as Caloy makes a polite exit.

The blackboard menu over the lunch counter is meeting me in my moment. Wildberry muffins with Irish butter, house-cured bacon with organic eggs and Havarti cheese on French toast, blue corn popovers with Hudson Valley honey—I'm so hungry I don't know where to begin.

"May I start you with a coffee?" asks a friendly voice. I saddle onto a chrome stool at the rounded corner of the bar as a teenage worker comes into view. His name badge reads: *Ellis, he/him*.

"Yes, please," I answer. "Thanks."

"No problem. I'm Ellis, by the way."

"John Paul . . . I mean, JP," I say. Editing myself, my whole identity changing, shifting. Trying to remember who I say I am.

As Ellis pours house blend into a heavy Eisenhower-era mug, I feel like I've stepped back in time. The counter separating us is a beautiful starlight color. Little specks of rose gold and antique silver dance fractals in the Formica. The napkin dispenser to the left is stuffed full of one-ply squares—the kind that are useless unless you clean with six at a time. There's a stainless steel bin with metal cutlery and paper straws to the right. A place mat with a treasure-map-style view of the resort in front of me. Even Ellis's uniform is throwback—a striped soda jerk apron with matching bow tie, and a fresh, ship-like paper cap at an angle.

"What year is it in here?" I ask.

Ellis smiles. "Sometimes it's 1952, but I like it better when it's 1962," he replies.

"Why '62?" I ask.

He places the steamy coffee directly in front of me. "Medgar was still alive, Kennedy was president, and Stan Lee was writing the first X-Men comic."

Heavy. In US history, we learned a lot about the grimness of 1963. Medgar Evers was shot in June, JFK in November. Kirby and Lee's X-Men #1 dropped sometime that year. "Wait, didn't X-Men come out in fall '63?" I ask.

"September," Ellis says, not missing a beat. "That cover had so much movement, but it was also pretty weird."

"Yeah," I say, like a light bulb lighting up. "It has Magneto blocking Scott's optic blast and Bobby's snowballs with a magnet shield, right? I thought he could only block metallic stuff."

"The better question is why Iceman would be throwing snowballs at an arch-supervillain," Ellis adds. We both chuckle the chuckle of comic book nerds. This is an out-of-place experience usually reserved for sidewalk sales at musty comic shops or the first day of cosplay at Comic Con.

As I tear through a plate of farm-to-table salad and miso

soup for breakfast, Ellis and I talk nonstop. Golden Age DC vs. Silver Age Marvel; the civil rights movement in Mississippi circa 1963; Ferdinand Marcos becoming president of the Philippines the same year; political comic books and the fight against fascism. Somehow, we keep going back to the X-Men. "The strangest thing about being a Black reader of the OG X-team is that the comic was supposed to be about being Black, about being different, but all the characters are White," Ellis notes. "I was reading this post about it on BlackNerdProblems.com. Storm, the first Black mutant, doesn't even show up until 1975."

I know what Ellis is talking about. All the comics I like best challenge dominant culture with ideas and groups that are different. Race is always something that's implied in these books, but rarely—if ever—discussed outright.

Ellis steps away to make some very complicated coffee drinks for a gaggle of golf-shirted business class dudes. "Five lattes, please," Businessman #1 orders flatly. "Double shots in all, whip on three, extra whip on two, regular caramel pump on one, extra caramel pumps on four."

Without skipping a beat, Ellis assembles the drinks with an impossible combination of elegance, grace, and speed. Before the men can finish discussing pharmaceutical stocks and new IPOs, Ellis is calling out the contents of each cup and handing them off. The men take their drinks, awkwardly pick through the vintage penny candy jars, and head out of the shop.

Ellis refills my coffee cup. "You're pretty easy, JP. I don't know a lot of kids that take their coffee black. Actually, I don't know any kids that drink straight-up coffee."

"I dunno," I say. "I don't think coffee should be too

complicated. Especially in the morning. My dad and I used to split a four-cup pot before work and school."

"Have you ever tried a latte?" he asks.

"They sound nice, but I don't think they're for me."

"Look, it's almost eleven. Morning shift is ending. You wanna hang in the library? There's a bunch of sick comics and graphic novels up there. There's even a new one about a big brawler from the Philippines. Tulk or Tulka-something?"

"Yeah, I heard about him," I say. "He's from the future. He won't technically exist in the canon until 2099." We laugh again.

Ellis rocks his head back. "C'mon, JP. Let's go."

MIA

"But, Mia! I have to poopy!" Lana is yelling now. Top of her little lungs. "Poopy, poopy, poopy! Now, now, now!"

"I know, buddy, I know, but I just have to feed your sister these cheese puffs ONE AT A TIME. You heard your mommy tell me that, right? Or else she will . . ."

And then, it happens, and suddenly a stream of vomit hits me across the chest of my perfectly ironed red Kids' Club polo and I am fully covered.

"What in the . . ."

My boss, Layla, is standing at the opposite side of the room, watching the way I do or do not control the situation. Lizzy has a huge smile across her face as if she is so pleased to have just erupted all over me, and Lana is *still* yelling that she has to go poopy. Now! So, I rush to my feet and pick Lana up as fast as I can and run straight toward the bathroom to set her up with her favorite book: *The Poop Tales*. Poop seems to be a really big theme for this kid. I close the door and tell her I will be sitting right outside and to call me if she needs any help, and then I look down at my shirt, covered in a kind of electric-lime-green slime. *What in the world did this kid eat today?* Layla smiles in my direction as she makes her way out and to her other rounds at the resort.

"Nice job back there. Always on your toes, Malik. I love to see it. Grab another shirt from the back," she says before heading out.

I look at my watch and then catch the line starting to form at the door. I run to the back room and throw on one of the extra shirts we keep lying around for this exact type of situation.

"Poop, poop, poop some more," I hear Lana singing at the top of her lungs.

"Buddy, I'm just gonna start to get kids ready to go. You stay in there and take it easy," I call to Lana. Wipe my brow and try to fix my wild hair in the mirror. The first person at pickup is JP, looking fresh and relaxed. Of course he is. He is on a luxury vacation and had nothing at all to do today except to chill, take it easy, and catch up on his comic books.

"Hey, how'd they do today?" he asks, walking in and surveying the chaos. The toys, board games, books, and costumes are strewn around the room. I have not had time to do our cleanup song. "You doing okay?" he asks. "Do you need some help? I know where the costumes go." Maybe he's trying to be funny, but I don't want him to think I can't do my job or don't have it together. I always have it together, or at least look like I'm trying.

"No, no, I'm good. We just had a really good time today, so I'm all good," I say again. Trying to convince myself. What I don't tell him is that all day my mind was clouded. With the way his arm felt up against mine, his silliness last night, the way he was so easy to play with, and then his aloofness today at the docks. Still trying to figure him out. But what I fixated most on today was what it would be like if my family really was the way I described them. But of course, I don't tell him any of that.

"Look, I have a few other things to do here to close up, and not sure what you're doing tonight, but if you're interested, there's a carnival happening on the main lawn."

"Oh yeah. I am definitely interested," he says, and looks right at me.

I can't tell if he is talking about me or the carnival, but I feel myself blush.

"A carnival, huh?" he follows up. "With ring tosses and rides and clowns? That sort of thing?"

"Oh, well, no clowns, sorry to disappoint, but yeah, games and pony rides, a hayride on the small side of the mountain. All fun and games. Guests are all invited, of course, and I'll be there making some photos and filling in at the face-painting station, but I get breaks throughout the night, so I can try to win you a Majestic Stuffed Bear, or a Majestic Stuffed Dolphin, or a Majestic Stuffed Giraffe. You get the idea."

"I do. Yeah, of course. That sounds totally Majestic. I am one hundred percent positive that my mom and dad would love for me to take Tiffany and Cass to the carnival. Is there food there?"

"Definitely. Imagine all the best cookout food. Ribs, hamburgers, hot dogs, Italian sausages, corn on the cob still in the husk, every salad you can imagine—potato, macaroni—and pies too. Blueberry, peach, and oh my god, I forgot my absolute favorite dessert: Majestic Mountain Crunch, complete with maple honey, walnuts, and a thin layer of fudge in vanilla ice cream. It will make you dream of coming back to the mountain."

"So what you're telling me is that there's not much food to eat, and even if there was, you're not so into it," he says, laughing. And it's his smile that makes me blush even more this time.

I punch him in the arm. "It's a bomb-ass cookout. And you do not want to miss it. Besides, you'll also get to meet some of my friends. By the way, I heard you spent the whole day with Ellis. He texted me this afternoon, not that we were talking about you or anything, it's just he said he met this cool guy and the cool guy happened to be you." I know how to flirt when I need to.

"Oh man, Ellis is so awesome," JP says, clearly not caring at all about Ellis's and my top secret texting. He calls to Cass and Tiffany, who come running and give him big hugs. "We will definitely see you tonight," he says.

I watch the three of them walk away. The kids clearly love their brother—a lot. Maybe I should ask them for some information on ways to win over JP Abrigo. As I check the other kids out and start to straighten up the space, I think about what I know about him. So far all I've got is that he has a family that loves him, he's headed to Brown in the fall, he's clumsy as hell while walking, game to wear costumes if asked, a recent s'mores virgin, and secretly a comic book fan. It all feels pretty typical to me. But the difference is he doesn't really talk endlessly about himself. That seems different. The last guy from the resort who tried to ask me out *only* talked about himself. I made it known I wasn't interested, but he showed up around me that whole week and took the time to tell his entire life story, place of birth, origin, background, favorite band, places he traveled, trophies he'd won, and on and on, and so by the last day, when he finally asked me what my job was at the resort, I had to laugh, had to pretend it didn't matter that his story was seemingly way more intriguing than mine, which it was not.

So yeah, maybe JP is different. All I know is that something has to happen tonight, and it has to be good, has to convince JP that we have more in common, that we have a deeper connection, that we're meant to be.

The crowd is full, and the kids—loaded up on sugar and high from the cotton candy truck, the caramel apples, and every game that offers candy prizes—are already wild and they all want me to watch them play and dunk and race and cry. Yeah, crying is the worst one as they stumble and trip and look for the last person who took care of them at the Kids' Club.

"Mia, Lucy stole my turn at the ring toss. Can you yell at her?"

"I think this is something you should talk to your mom or dad about, okay?"

I am playing the ultimate game of dodge-the-kids as I make my way to the face-painting table. It's loaded with paints of all colors. Brilliant purples, fuchsia, lime- and teal-green, all of them popping and coming alive. There is a list of things we can paint, an agreed-upon assortment of flowers, animals, and cartoon characters. We already have a long line of kids, and even some adults, who are ready for their transformations. My specialty, and what I have worked to perfect over the last three years at my post, is a bouquet of flowers across the cheek. But this year none of the kids want that. They all want to be very specific animals, with an emphasis on wolves and cheetahs, so I settle in next to Ellis, who is a true visual artist, and we get in sync.

"So, just to clarify," Ellis says between cheetah faces, "JP is good people."

"How do you even know that? You basically just met."

"Yeah, but there's something about him. He's laid-back and just . . . He's cool. We spent the whole morning talking comic books."

"Comic books? And that makes him cool? When I saw him, he tried to convince me he was reading *The New York Times* . . . cover to cover."

"Well, he probably was, because we didn't just talk comic books, we talked racism and all the messed up parts of reading them when you're not White. It went deep . . . fast. He's not playing around either."

"Oh," I say, and sink back into my face painting. This is big for Ellis to say. He is a self-proclaimed Black Nerd who knows everything about Black superheroes and racism in comic books. The fact they connected on that level means something. When I told Ellis and Jasmine (whose family is Dominican) that even though I present as White, I think of myself as mixed race, they both just nodded like *duh*. And *okay, moving on*. They accepted me and don't care if I talk about my confusion or my anxiety around race or color or if I talk about my parents being gone and not feeling like I belong. They just listen. They just care about me. They just laugh and talk trash about whatever they want. That's why I love them. They're my people. And it sounds like maybe JP is our people too.

"Well, thank goodness then. Otherwise I am definitely not getting out of Monument, and you know I have to get the hell out of Monument."

"It's not that bad here," Ellis says.

"Easy for you to say. You're leaving for college in the fall. Also, it's only beautiful because you didn't grow up here and you don't know all the chaos that's around this place for me." I take a deep breath. I know Ellis means well. "Can we drop it please? I'm leaving, and JP is my way out of town, so we can't fall too hard for this guy, okay?"

"Ooh, you are tough. Just do me a favor and don't hurt poor JP too badly."

And as if we are calling his name, JP shows up at the back of the line with his brother and sister. He waves at me, and I wave back, smiling, despite the conversation with Ellis.

I'm not trying to hurt "poor" JP. And besides, he is definitely not poor or sad or broken. He's all good. Fact is, he's great! He won't even know what's happening to him. He will really think we're falling in love, and nobody is going to get hurt.

By the time JP makes it to the front of the line, I have done quite enough kitty cats and dogs and lions. I give Cass my signature flower bouquet treatment and Ellis gives Tiffany a cheetah. They thank us with high fives.

"We're going to get Mommy for the ring toss to win Majestic Teddy Bears," Cass says, and hugs JP. JP hugs Cass back, and even though he's so much older than his siblings, their connection feels close, warm. Unexpected.

"You're up," I say, and motion for JP to sit down.

"Oh no, this is just for Cass and Tiffany. You don't have to worry about me. I don't need my face painted or anything like . . ."

"Just sit," I tell him, and move the stool closer to me so that when he sits we are eye to eye, and my heart rate picks up fast without me even realizing it.

His gaze is steady on me.

I start to fumble my paint. I drop lemon yellow, and we

both move down to pick it up, our arms and hands touching, and I don't know if it's electricity or heat, but I feel it, the energy, there's something unexpected there. We smile hard at each other when, suddenly, someone bear-hugs me from behind and rips me up and off my chair.

"Hey there, Malik!" cackles an annoyingly familiar voice. "Missed me?!"

"Put me down!" I yell. My feet hit the ground hard and fast as I tear free from the hold. Before I even turn, I know who the grabby little shit behind me is. Ugh. My face goes serious quick, my tone pissed, and I look him right in the eye. "Wolf, do not pick me up. Do not enter my space like that. Don't—"

"C'mon, Malik! Lighten up—it's Majestic Carnival. Everybody's having fun. You remember fun, right? Have a little fun with me!"

I don't shift, budge, or change my tune. "Do not touch me, Wolf. Do you understand?"

He pauses for a short beat. "Fine, Malik. Whatever."

I realize that JP is standing now, facing both of us. His focus is my focus. His posture my posture. From goofy to business time in under three seconds. In this moment, he's not a goat or a mark or my ticket out of this town. Not standing in front or behind, JP Abrigo is ally guy. Wouldn't it be nice if more folks knew how to do the ally thing?

Trying to quickly reclaim alpha status, Wolf turns to JP and asks, "Who's this guy? Do I know you, man?"

Before Wolf can finish his questions, JP's right hand is extended for a formal handshake. "I'm JP. I'm a friend of Mia's."

Wolf slaps JP's hand on-the-side style and rolls up a toothy grin. "I'm Wolf," he inserts smugly. "I'm sure you've heard of me. I used to be a good friend of Mia's. Like, a good friend that's a boy. Like a boyfriend." He shifts his stance to play up his height.

I'm laughing my ass off inside my head. To be clear, Wolfgang Schafer-Schmidt is a quippy, insecure jerk who started at Lake Majestic a couple of years before me. He spends his downtime trying to impress girls with his infinite knowledge of muscle cars, Scorsese movies, and Catskills bourbon distilleries. I wish he wasn't the same guy I made out with when I first started work here.

"You know what, Wolf? JP and I were just headed out, weren't we?" I ask, motioning JP along and confirming with Ellis that he can take over the rest of the line, which is starting to dwindle.

JP

Who the hell is Wolf? And why did he say he was Mia's boyfriend? I think to myself. *Stop. Stop. You're not supposed to think that way. You're cool, smooth JP now. Oh my god, but seriously.* I want to ask Mia about it, but she's already pulling me away from the crowd. Away from the chaos of the carnival. The games are still dinging and whirring in my head.

"I wanna show you around," Mia says, and now that I'm holding her hand I realize that I would absolutely follow her anywhere. "Forget the carnival for a while. You have so much more to see!" she tells me.

I race to keep up with her, the breeze floating around us, smells of hot dogs and hamburgers still in the air. She seems to effortlessly dodge everyone she works with to find a way to a trail marker at the edge of the manicured grounds.

She drops my hand as we go single file into the path snaking up the rocky side of Majestic, the side only the super athletic tourists go up. I do not tell her that I can't do it or that I am scared I'll lose my footing or my breath. I just follow her and push on, pumping my legs, working up a sweat, aching, trying my hardest to make it to the top, to a place where no one can hear us and where no noise or chaos can interrupt us.

Does she want to be alone with me that bad? If yes, then I need to up my game, so I follow faster. *And if she wants to be alone with me, then does she want to kiss me? Am I second-guessing myself? Yes, yes you are. But you also better hope she doesn't find out you're a total liar who invented an entire other family to impress her. You fool.* I follow close so no one can watch what I am trying to do, but also so no one can judge me, and every time I think about what I am trying to pull and who I'm trying to be, I run faster, trying to outrun who I am. Shake that person off me. I keep going, hustling, stretching, weaving up the mountain.

"Wait up!" I call, and we finally stop at one of the tree houses that are built into the cliffs so you can sit and watch, so you can be away from everyone and a part, somehow, of everything.

"Are you on the track team or have you been training for a freakin' marathon or what?" I watch her slow, and then she moves just slightly out of the way and there is this view that is unlike anything I've ever seen before. She knows what she is doing. They do not call it Majestic for nothing. It catches my breath and a hold of my heart somehow too. The Catskill Mountains rise up like a massive wave in the sky, jutting and heaving up, peaking right in front of us. I can't stop staring. I feel like someone else up here, maybe even the someone else I am trying to be.

"This," Mia says, throwing her arms out wide. "I wanted to show you this. Needed you to see what this whole place is all about. The grounds are good and they require gardeners and landscapers and groundskeepers and all that, but this . . . this is just, I don't know . . . just here and whatever God or gods are around or whatever universe or vision you believe in, it's gotta be real, right? I don't even know what kind of religion I follow—but look. Look at that."

And we both do, and she takes a quick breath and suddenly reaches her hand toward mine and I think: *Oh my god, is she holding my hand right now? Are my palms sweaty? I hope they're not sweaty.* But I tell old John Paul to shut the hell up and inform new JP that we are in it for real now, so I grab on to her hand too and it's that same electricity or lightning or the bubbles inside a can of soda or fireworks or anything that lights up, that lights me up inside, because that's what it feels like. Deep breath—in and out.

"I get it," I say, steadying my breath, slowing. Methodical. In and out too. "I do. I wanna hold on to this somehow."

"I know. I always wanna hold on to the picture of the mountains in my head. Hold it there for whenever I get stressed or just need to see nature like this, and . . ."

"That's not what I mean. That's not the picture I want to hold on to," I say, looking at Mia the whole time. "It's you," I say, finding this new courage inside me. I pull her toward me, hold the back of her neck in the palm of my hand, and put my mouth so close to hers that I am breathing in, her breath inside mine, and it makes me feel like I might pass out or lose consciousness and does new me have all types of game because I feel like I am full-on electricity. I almost pull away to check myself or this moment, but before I can her mouth is on mine, and her lips are so warm I want to disappear inside them. My hands, both of them now, on the back of her neck. She holds on to my shoulders—steady, wide—the way it feels like she is anchoring me, this moment. I kiss back harder, realizing I want her more and more, and we stay this way. Kissing, elevating, moving toward one another.

MIA

His kisses make me feel dizzy, lopsided. They are surprising and warm, shooting heat all over my body.

I try not to get lost in them. *This is just a game*. I can't start feeling things, can't get caught up in the way his lips feel so soft against mine or the energy coming from the palms of his hands, or the way my breath is getting caught in the back of my throat. My throat. He has his hands on my neck and they're hot. *Is JP hot?!*

He pulls back for a moment and looks at me, really looks at me—right into my eyes—and my stomach roller-coasters and beatboxes and rearranges inside my body and I can't take it anymore, so I kiss him again harder. Hungry for him and needing to make all these thoughts disappear. His lips are so soft and find their way to my neck, and then just as fast as we started, we pull back—both of us, as if on cue.

"Damn," he whispers, putting one hot palm to his mouth.

"Yeah," I say back, trying to avoid the smoke of his eyes. *The smoke of his eyes?* What is happening to me?

He looks at me for a beat longer, like he can't quite figure out what to say next, so I make the next move for him. "Come here," I say, taking another couple of steps closer to the cliff. He holds his hands out like he's trying to stop me from moving. "It's okay, I do this all the time," I lie. But I have to look unafraid up here, have to prove I can take a risk. The edge of the mountain feels like the edge of the world and the view here is unmatched. "Check it out," I say, gesturing out at the mountains and the lake way below, even though he said that I was the vision he was looking for. *Does JP Abrigo have game?* Who am I up here on the mountain with anyway? "I wanted to make sure you didn't miss this," I say, trying to figure out what my strategy is here and trying to get to know JP at the same time. But when I look back, he has not moved one inch closer to me. "You okay?" I ask.

"Yeah, I'm good. I can see it from here," he says, trying to lean forward.

"But if you come closer, you can actually see the lake below too," I say, trying to steady my own nerves as I look down.

"Uhh . . . will I sound like a total chicken if I don't walk over there?"

"Noooo . . . but . . ." And then I can't help myself, I start to cluck and bawk. No, JP Abrigo is not a goat, he's a chicken!

"Come on! It's not that I'm scared, it's just . . ." He takes the tiniest step forward. "It's just that I am petrified. Terrified of heights and of cliffs that overlook large bodies of water."

"But I'm right here. And I've done this hundreds of times. You're with me. You don't have to be scared," I say, and mean it this time. If I can convince myself I will be okay, then maybe I can convince JP too. I hold my arm out and he slowly takes another step toward me. His palm against my hand. I can feel his breath warm beside me.

"Can we at least sit?" he asks, and we do. Slow and gentle so we're far enough back for him to feel comfortable. It makes me wonder why I am so eager to get to the edge of the world in the first place. "It looks fake or like a painting. It doesn't even look real," he says, and we both stare out at the lake, which looks just like glass, all smooth and shimmering. JP goes quiet beside me and says nothing for a few minutes. Just closes his eyes and stays that way for long enough that I find myself wanting to kiss him all over again.

"But it's definitely real. And you gotta do the lake swim while you're here. It's the best! It's seriously one of the most amazing things you can do at the resort. Legend has it that if you make a wish before you jump in the water, then make it all the way to Big Rock on the opposite side of the lake without stopping, your wish will be granted."

"Where's Big Rock again?"

"Right there," I say, and put my hand on his shoulder and lean forward. "If we get a little closer, you can see it. Plus, you get to be right there in the heart of the lake. They say a lot of things are magical at this place, but that one is really true."

JP smiles, finally. Doesn't look quite so nervous. "I bet you've always been cool," he says.

"Well, not always," I say, playing with him now. Realizing this might be even easier than I thought it would be. "But you gotta do it. You gotta say yes. Take a risk. Wednesday is my day off. We could meet up? I'll show you how it's done." And then he looks at me and shakes his head.

"What?" I ask.

"Nothing, it's just. I'm not the kind of guy who takes risks that often."

“Really? You’re too busy with all your reading material, huh?”

“Yep.”

“Okay, well, then what kind of a guy are you?”

“I like to keep things safe. Stick to the plan. My life has always followed a plan, a course of action. I’m not the kind of guy that walks to the edge of the cliff. Definitely not close enough to fall off, but . . .”

“But what?”

“But you’re wild and free and comfortable right here. Right on the cliffside, right where anything can happen and . . .”

I can’t help it, I reach up and kiss him again. Put my palm on the back of his neck this time. Smell sweat and feel the grass move softly along my legs. He tastes like salt, and I can feel myself start to let go. Chasing this feeling. If he thinks I am living on the edge and taking all the risks, then this is the Mia Malik who is gonna show up for the rest of the week. Not just taking risks out here in the woods, but doing so in my real life too.

Finally, he pulls back. “Did you say your day off is Wednesday?”

I nod. “That’s right. Meet first thing in the morning? I’ll show you everything you need to know about Majestic Mountain.”

JP Abrigo smiles, and I resist the urge to kiss him again. Maybe I’m the one who needs to play it cool, and I am closer than before to everything I want. I remind myself that JP is no different, even if he seems quirky and cute and maybe even sexy? He’s still the same deep down. The kind of guy who thinks he’s made of gold, partly because he is. All rich and know-it-all. All of them playing it safe because their lives are simply given to them. Entirely set up and glimmering. Wealth and power following them around. They haven't been asked to do a damn thing on their own. Everything handed to them. Polished and shining. So yeah, I'll show JP how to live on the edge. Otherwise, I stay stuck in this town that only wants to see me fade away. I can't let that happen. Not this time. Not ever.

TUESDAY

JP

Yellow gold rises over Majestic Mountain just before six a.m. I'm awake—blue electricity in every part of me—watching the slow morning sun swell anamorphic over the peak. From my balcony, the sky is blush pink and warm white as I play, over and over, that kiss from last night. I have never felt *anything* like *that*. Before it happened, I remember feeling cold in the pit of my stomach; chilling fear—climbing each of my ribs—and jumping to my throat. Then, in one explosive moment, our eyes met, our mouths ravenous and honeyed and together until satisfied. I felt flame coming off her lips, her skin; the warmth of her breath in my lungs. The fear? Gone. The cold? Done for. For months, I've been trying to feel nothing, and—suddenly—I can feel everything.

Tap-tap-tap. The jump scare of Cass knocking on the porch door reminds me that I'm not alone. Not that I want to be alone. I wonder where Mia is this morning. Maybe she's on a run; maybe she's having coffee in one of the five hundred rocking chairs they have all around here. I close my eyes and catch the sun on my face. I can still feel the weight of her lips on mine.

"JP, we're going to the pool today!" exclaims Cass. He holds up a note from Dali that reads: *Take kids to breakfast then meet @ pool by 8:45.* Nothing in all caps, but the time has been underlined twice. After a brief struggle getting Cass to wear his swimsuit under regular clothes, we're on our way down to the dining room. The resort looks different today. Overnight, spaces have transformed with red, white, and blue ribbons; American flags; and tiny replicas of the Declaration of Independence. July 4, 1776—America celebrates its independence from the colonizers of England. July 4, 1946—the Philippines celebrates its independence from the colonizers of America.

I order coffee and fruit salad while Tiff and Cass compete at the buffet station to see who can pile more candy on their waffles. Breakfast for these kids is just cloying. I slowly sip my coffee and start humming the familiar song playing. *Dah-doo-da-da-da-doo— What is that?* I turn toward the sound and see Bee—staring right at me—plucking the strings of her cello to ~~Nirvana's~~ David Bowie's "The Man Who Sold the World." My mom and dad both had a copy of Nirvana's *Unplugged* album on CD, but I always liked the Bowie version better. I sampled it last year in my music production class for a house track. And speaking of scary, Bee's unblinking gaze is really starting to creep me out. I turn back to the table to find my breakfast has arrived. We eat quickly and start to head out. I can feel Bee's eyes on me as we approach the exit. In a flash she's standing right in front of us. "JP, I'm off at noon today if you want to hang out," she says.

I spout a slew of excuses: *busy, headed to the pool, not sure what the day entails.* So much that I'm not sure what I've said to Bee to get out of the dining hall; I'm just happy to not have her all up in my face.

Tiffany shakes her head disapprovingly as we move north through the main lobby. "You don't have to spend time with people that you don't like," she counsels. "You don't have to talk to them. You don't have to have anything to do with them."

I nod knowingly. The stress starts to roll off as we make our way through the wide spa corridor to the pool area, where a kind face welcomes us.

"Greetings, JP," Caloy says. "Is this your first time at the pool?" I nod and smile as my eyes take in an impossible sight. "Our guest aquatic area is one of the finest in the world. One heated Olympic pool for health and fitness and one sixty-foot saltwater dipping pool with adjacent hot tubs and underwater music." I've never seen anything like this. Tranquil earth sounds and the smell of lavender and eucalyptus fill the space. Enclosed in a cube of frameless glass, it feels like we're outside. Looking up, I can see the clouds and sky alive in the morning sun. All the lighting fixtures in and around the pool are tuned to match the warmth of the natural light.

"Jump in, JP!" yells Cass as he cannonballs into the salt water. I can see Tita Dali and Tito Alvin smiling and waving from one of the hot tubs.

Caloy walks me to a set of chaise lounges reserved for the family. "Is this to your liking?" they ask, somewhat rhetorically.

"I've never seen anything like this, Caloy. It's like a more beautiful, much fancier version of Astoria Park pool."

"That's a beautiful pool too."

"Yes," I reply. "I went there a lot as a kid."

I learned to swim at the Astoria Park pool. Mom and Dad

taught me together. They would stand a few feet apart and have me doggy-paddle between them. With each stretch they would step just a little farther apart from one another, raising the stakes. When I was five I went from swimming a yard to nearly the entire length of the pool. I wasn't fast then, and I'm definitely not fast now, but my mom and dad were so proud. I felt like we spent the entire summer there. I miss those days.

"Spend much time in the city?" I ask.

"I used to have family there. They still live there. But they're not my family anymore." Caloy exhales sharply, frustrated for sharing something personal about themselves.

"Family is complicated," I respond softly. They nod. "Sometimes what family wants isn't possible because of who we are. I don't always know who I am, but I'm trying to get a good handle on who I am not."

"Very good, JP," Caloy says with a smile. "Sanay swertehin ka. Enjoy your journey on the mountain."

As they exit, Tita Dali and Tito Alvin arrive at the chaises covered in plush Majestic Mountain House robes. "Not swimming today?" Alvin asks.

I shrug, settling into a poolside seat. My aunt and uncle sip iced lattes through bespoke metal straws as they sit down together.

"We were wondering about your plans for next year, John Paul," Tita Dali starts. "I know you might start at CUNY, but if you can get your grades up, maybe you can transfer to a real university."

My brain locks the convo out. Tita Dali is going to talk and talk and monologue on and on about how important it is to go to a "good" school. I don't even know what that means. I don't even know what I want to study.

"You could study the premed," Dali says for the seven gazillionth time.

"No, he has a good head for business or prelaw," counters Alvin.

I nod along, tuning out again. Here's the deal—*I don't want and can't afford to go to any college, private or otherwise, despite my fake acceptance to Brown*. Dali is obsessed with the Ivy League because a bunch of her in-network Filipina hive married rich White guys from there. Whatever I study at City College is already going to cost me serious money. I've saved some, but nothing even sufficient for the first year. Maybe I have enough for a semester. I had a plan with my dad to live at home, pick up some morning classes, and find a second-shift gig to afford second semester. I'd work summer youth employment and grab an evening job to pay for the following year. Repeating this cycle and depending on expenses, that could get me through college in five or six years.

Some folks take out loans, but my family has a bad history repaying them. When he died, Dad still owed Tito Alvin three thousand dollars. My mom's been paying that one back. On top of that, she has her own student loans and a high-interest personal loan at Metrobank in Manila. I don't want to owe anything for school. I especially don't want to get into debt over a degree that may or may not help me with whatever it is I'm supposed to do with my life.

High school history teacher, comic book writer, backup dancer—my future education and future career remain undeclared. "I don't know if I should be spending time and money on something that I don't understand," I tell Dali and Alvin. They look at me dumbfounded.

"Boy Reyes," Tita Dali declares. "Your tomorrow is right around the corner. You might not understand this, but I can assure you the future will always cost time and money."

Time and money, I think to myself. I don't have much of either.

"What do you want for yourself, John Paul?" Alvin asks.

I just want to see Mia Malik. Can't get her out of my head. Her mouth on mine last night; our date tomorrow. Less than a week left here. No money to my name. I don't think I can go all day without seeing her. Gotta find a way to see her. No fancy diploma is gonna help with that.

MIA

"Bee? Are you kidding me?" I am sputtering. "Bee was hitting on JP? What, like, she asked him out? That's ridiculous. I don't even think she's into guys. I don't think she's into *anyone* except herself. You have to be kidding. Unless . . ." It suddenly hits me. "She's just doing it to mess with me. To sabotage me. That's it, isn't it?"

Jasmine agrees. "I do believe we have a saboteur in our midst."

"Yeah, her and Wolf"—I'm fuming now—"who acted like he owned me yesterday, pulling me out of my seat like the dumbass jerk he is, and right in front of JP too. It was soo awkward, and now I have to deal with punk-ass Bee. What?!"

"Tell us how you really feel," Jasmine says.

Ellis laughs. "Just doing some truth telling," he adds. "They're playing games anyway. Don't worry about all that stuff. Focus on what needs to get done."

We are sitting in the staff mess hall, the main area where everyone who works at Majestic goes for their meals. This morning, scrambled eggs, biscuits and gravy, and a big fruit salad. I go up for seconds, and the big old insect herself is loading up her plate.

"Well, look who it is," I start, knowing I need to confront her before it gets out of hand. I don't know JP well enough to know if he would be into her too, if he's a player or not, but I have to let Bee know it is not okay to interfere with my plan.

"Oh, hi, Mia, how's it going? Kids' Club treating you okay? I just have no idea how you handle all those bratty little snots all day. I could never," she says.

Yes, we all know she's in the upper tier of staff, or what we call *The Talent Pool*. I hope she drowns in her pool of talent, but I do not say that.

"Yes, it's definitely a lot, but I love them, I do. It takes a very kind and patient person to run the club, so . . ." I say, bowing slightly. I can play this game too. "By the way, I heard you introduced yourself to JP yesterday. What's up with that? What's your plan there?"

"Well, I just figure it is a free resort and a free city and a free country and I can do . . . whatever I want, whenever I want. Is that a good enough reason for you? I like him. I find him very interesting. Just like you do."

"Okay, fine, but you know he's the one I chose for the bet. Everyone should know that now. You're in on the freakin' bet and you know I'm trying to get out of town, so could you just lay off, please?" I ask, trying to reason with her.

I have no idea why I am begging her to stay away. If I can just trust that JP really likes me, then I have nothing to worry about, and if the kiss from last night tells me anything, it's that he does. He went for it, but maybe it's not just me that he's into. Bee is certainly beautiful. That's true, even if also kind of creepy with her whole Goth Wednesday Addams vibe. Maybe he's into that. Maybe he's a liar, maybe he took a bet from *his* rich and full-of-it friends to hook up with workers at the luxury resort, some bet about the townies he'd be surrounded by. Maybe he's an asshole in disguise. But the more I spend time with him, the harder that is to believe. I turn my attention back to Bee, expecting her to respond to my request, but she's just standing there, smiling at me.

"May the best person win," she says instead, giving me a wink and walking over to collect her cello. Of course she plays a cool instrument that also makes her look hot in that *Corpse Bride* kind of way.

I shake my head and loosen her hold on me. "Thank you. It will be me!" I shout as she is walking away. "Don't worry about it!"

"I'm not even thinking twice," she says, much cooler and calmer than I am being.

I try to stop second-guessing myself. I am in this to win. I don't have time to consider Bee and her journey or how she even fits into this puzzle. I committed. I'm in it now, have a goal, and if last night is any indication—the warmth of his hands on me, his mouth against mine, the smell of his neck and hair, his body tensing beneath my touch—I've got him, or I am on my way to getting him, and that's really all that matters at the end of the week anyway. It's only Tuesday and guests don't check out until Sunday after breakfast, so we still have five and a half days and what feels like all the time in the world this morning.

"Hey, we gotta get going," Jasmine reminds me. "Come on."

I snap back into it. Busy day today. We're with the kids from ten to six p.m. I put my game face on, and we head out.

JP and his brother and sister are sitting at one of the miniature tree houses, already waiting for us to open, when we get to the front door of the club. JP leaps out of the seat like he's about to lift off when he sees me.

Yeah, I think, *maybe he is as into me as I imagined he was.*

"Hey, hi, how did you sleep?" he asks first thing, and his little sister obviously rolls her eyes.

"Oh? Um . . . good, great. Tiffany, Cass, how did you two sleep?" I ask, all three of us giggling now.

"That was a weird question, wasn't it?" JP asks.

"Play it cool," Tiffany whispers, but loud enough for me to hear her.

"Shut up," he whispers back. "Anyway," he looks at me again. "What's on the schedule today?"

"Ohh, we have such a fun day planned. Are you all with us for both sessions?" I ask. Generally kids come for the morning from ten a.m. to one p.m. and then if their families are still enjoying the spa or alone time, they come again from two to five p.m. with a late pickup of six p.m. if there are any who need it. There are always a few who need it.

"Yep. We're here all day today," Tiffany says. "Mom and Dad have lots of plans . . . without us."

"Well, perfect, because we have lots of plans without them too." I smile. Most times kids want to be here, but sometimes there are tears and what the kids want most is time with their parents. We try and provide as much fun and play as possible to distract them. "This morning we're headed to the pavilion for a roller-skating party!"

"A what?" Cass asks, concern floating across his face. "But I'm not good at skating."

"Sure you are," JP says. "Remember when we went to Skater Rock last summer? You were awesome!"

"Correction, *you* were awesome," Tiffany says, looking right at JP. "Cass could barely stand up on his skates."

"I'm sorry, let me get this right. *You* were awesome?" I ask.

"What? You think I can't skate?"

"No, no . . . I believe it, I just . . ."

"John Paul, can you please come with us?" Cass begs.

"It's JP," JP whispers again. "But, uh . . . I don't know, can I?"

I nod. "Sure. Anyone can skate. It's open for all. And you can show me your moves."

"Oh, I have moves."

"Great. You can prove it, then. See you around eleven?"

"I'll be there," JP says, and smiles like he has a secret I'm about to find out. *He skates?* What else don't I know about John Paul or JP Abrigo?

JP

The pavilion is buzzing with visitors young and old. Casual skaters move counterclockwise around the rink, smiling and laughing and taking little breaks as needed along the outside edge. Rollerbladers and advanced gliders do tricks and perform four-wheel ballet on the inside fast lane. It's 10:45. I'm early. Across the hardwood to the west, a copious amount of guests line up to borrow skates. I walk over along the outside of the rink to join them when suddenly, a young woman in a red polo spills an assortment of child-size skates out in front of me.

Cool and professional, she kneels down and starts packing the loose roller boots back into an oversize bin. "Need some help?" I ask. I bend over, trying to catch a few stubborn skates from rolling away.

"Thank you so much. Wait, are you JP?" she asks. I nod, sliding a mismatched pair of unicorn and lion boots over. "I'm Jasmine. I'm friends with Mia. We work together at the Kids' Club. She said you might be joining us today." The thought of Mia mentioning me to a coworker and friend has me cracking the biggest smile. In seconds, we've packed two dozen pairs of roller skates into the bright yellow tub. "Thanks for your help," Jasmine says, quickly scanning the collection. Narrowing her eyes, she declares, "I think we're missing one."

"This one?" a familiar voice calls out. Ellis steps forward with a lone purple skate in one hand and a five-gallon water cooler in the other. "Ellis!" Jasmine exclaims. Her eyes light up like Christmas. "What are you doing out here?"

"I'm pushing in for a hot sec. Layla has the soda fountain crew rotating water and snacks up here," he replies. He hands Jasmine the loose skate and places the cooler atop a low table at the edge of the rink. "JP!" Ellis fist-bumps me. "Are you skating today?"

"Absolutely," I reply. "Might take me a while to get some skates though." The line at the loaner counter has grown threefold.

"One of us can sneak him around the back," Jasmine tells Ellis. She takes the loose skate and tosses it into the bin. Her wide eyes locked on Ellis, she holds up two fingers like scissors. He playfully drops a rock fist on top. Then she covers his fist with a paper-flat hand for the win. She nods at Ellis and tells us both she'll catch us later. As Jasmine struts off with the container of skates, she shoots a quick wink over her shoulder right at Ellis. Ellis and I turn to look at each other. My eyes are bigger than pizza pans and Ellis's jaw is on the floor.

"My guy," I start. "She really likes you." Ellis, trying to hide the blushing embarrassment on his face, waves me to come over with him behind the skate counter. "Do you like her?" Ellis is trying and failing to keep the answer to himself. Dude is shining brighter than the sun. "You do like her," I tease. The moment feels so pure and middle school. "This is awesome!" I say a little louder than I should.

"Look," Ellis explains. "This is all very new. Too new to talk about. Please be cool." My mouth fires excited question after excited question. "JP, you are embarrassing me. If you do not stop, I will find your biggest level-ten secret and expose it to the world." I zip my lip and hand Ellis my air-dried Jordans. He quickly disappears through the service entrance behind the counter and emerges with a pair of black leather skates with candy-orange wheels.

By the time I'm laced up, Mia and Jasmine have the entire crew from Kids' Club on their feet and making moves. Some kids are excited and comfortable to skate on their own. Others balance against the wall or use skate walkers to keep steady. Tiffany is having the time of her life—cutting up and backward skating with Jasmine and a new group of friends. Cass holds hands with Mia and sings along to the retro pop music pumping through the PA system. They both wave as they pass by.

Stepping out onto the floor, I'm nostalgic for City Skatium—the East New York rink I've been going to since I was a little kid. On my seventh birthday, I learned to backward skate and my parents cheered for me. They weren't together, but we all had a great time that day.

I build up my speed and catch up to Cass and Mia on the outside lane. I do a left-right crossover and spin 180 to a full stop facing them.

"Don't stop!" Mia shouts. I clumsily push off into a backward skate. She laughs at my less-than-elegant launch.

"You can't just stop in the middle of the lane, John Paul!"

Cass scolds. He reaches out to me with both arms. I take his hands and pull him forward. I guide Cass through a crossover, and we switch positions—me moving forward and him in backward skate. He's new to this move, but my cousin is a natural.

Mia glides past us—pumping her legs and leaning forward Roller Derby style. She is lightning—zipping and weaving her way through slowdowns and pockets of novice skaters drifting into the fast lane. She makes a full lap before we're anywhere close to the next turn. Like a hurricane, she shreds over from the fast lane back in front of us, 180-jumping into an Olympic front to back transition. "Whoa . . ." I mouth in slow motion. Cass breaks away from me and does his own version of the trick. Though wobbly and unsure, he sticks the landing. Mia applauds and gives him a fist bump.

Jasmine teaches everyone how to shoot the duck—the poorly named maneuver of squatting low with one leg straight out in front of you. The DJ plays an old Motown song and calls for couples' skate. I get to hold Mia's hand for the opening verse.

"Now it's my turn, JP!" shouts Tiffany.

"Then mine!" belts another kid.

This goes on and on. Mia Malik is everyone's favorite.

MIA

"So, what's next?" JP asks, helping all of us put the skates away.

"Next?" I ask. What is this kid's end game? "Let me get this right. You meet us early at the pavilion, hang out all morning and show off your, uhh . . . spectacular skating moves, and now you wanna, what? Have lunch with us and then join up for arts and crafts?"

"Yeah. That's exactly what I wanna do."

"But you don't work here, JP. You could be off doing anything. There's horseback riding, wildlife tours, calm heart meditations, guided mountain biking, there's—"

"Stop. Look, I know there are about a billion things I could do with my time here at Majestic. I have been reading about them every morning on the bulletin outside the front desk, and my mom and dad have been listing them off during every meal we have, but will you be at any of those activities?"

"Well, no, because I have to work, so . . ." He looks at me like I'm totally missing the point. *Oh.*

"I didn't really wanna skate with a bunch of kids or my brother and sister, and I don't really wanna have lunch with that one kid who has a really runny nose, and I promise you that I am definitely crafty, but what I want . . . is to be with you."

"Oh, I . . ."

"You don't have to say anything. Just let me know how I can make that happen?"

"John Paul! John Paul!" we both hear, and stretch our necks to see the direction the voice is coming from.

"Do you go by John Paul or JP?" I ask, starting to get confused.

"JP. Definitely JP," he says quickly, and then catches the eye of his mom, who is speed walking toward us.

"I finally found you, John Paul. We have been calling and texting, you know," the woman in front of me says. She is immaculate. Her hair and makeup perfect and her tennis skirt pressed and sweatshirt tied over her shoulders just so. Everything in place. His mom is impeccable. I should have known. I take inventory on myself—my hair a mess of waves escaping the rubber band meant to hold them in place, my shirt untucked, and not a lick of makeup—not even lip gloss. I hadn't planned on seeing either JP or his mom today. I tuck my shirt in and smile at both of them.

"Hello, Mrs. Abrigo. My name is Mia. I am one of the coleaders of the Majestic Kids' Club," I say. "It is our pleasure to work with Tiffany and Cass. They are absolutely wonderful." At least I don't have to lie about that part. "And JP even helped us out today at the roller-skating pavilion."

"Well, isn't that kind of him." She looks disapproving, but I keep my smile plastered on my face. "Lovely to meet you. Cass and Tiffany adore the Kids' Club and have said only kind things about you all and their fellow campers. Thank you." So proper. So put together. Everything in place. How does she do it? And how did a person like this produce a person like JP—so casual and laid-back. Hoodies for every outing? Like they come from two totally different planets.

Mrs. Abrigo looks JP up and down like she is studying him, trying to read or figure him out. JP on the other hand looks like he is trying his best to escape.

"Hi, hey. I didn't realize you'd been calling or texting . . ."

"Well, you would have if you didn't have that ridiculous phone," Mrs. Abrigo says, staring down as JP pulls out a small, old flip phone.

"I don't do smartphones," he says, as if he's reminding her for the millionth time, and there it is. A classic rich boy move. Pretend you don't have money. Use old-fashioned tech, dress grungy, all in an act to prove money doesn't matter to you, you could care less about it. No big deal at all. Yes, I was right about JP Abrigo.

"Of course you don't," I say, smiling.

"Well, if you had, you would know that you are late for our college conversation lunch, which you agreed on last night, and then we have booked you with one of the top tennis experts for the teen clinic that starts at exactly three p.m., so in order for us to not be late to that, we will need to hurry, and of course"—at this she looks at all the baggy clothes hanging loose from JP's body—"you will need to quickly go and change to be presentable."

"Resort wear," I say, teasing him.

"Exactly," Mrs. Abrigo says, smiling at me this time. "You know teenage boys. They never do what you want them to do." She shakes her head and so do I.

JP pulls the drawstrings on his sweatshirt, closing the hood over his face.

"I'm so sorry you won't be able to join us for arts and crafts, but we're doing kite making today and then flying them later tonight on the South Lawn. You are both welcome to join us," I say, figuring that I might as well get on the good side of the family.

"Very kind of you. My husband and I will be dining at the chef's table this evening. I have heard phenomenal things about the farm-to-table menu, and the sommelier who is doing the pairings has gotten rave reviews. But thank you for the invitation. I am sure that John Paul would be happy to bring Cass and Tiff for that experience. It is all about the experiences here, you know?"

I nod in agreement. "Then see you later tonight?" I say, looking right at John Paul or JP or whoever the hell it is I've been talking to. "Have a great tennis lesson," I add.

"Yeah. Thank you. Will do. Oh, wait! Do you think I could get your number?" he asks, holding his phone out to me. "Just so we can meet up later and whatever."

"Sure," I say, reading off my number slowly so he can type it into his phone from the early 2000s. "I'll text you." Got him. Easy. We're already in each other's lives.

"Hurry up, then," Mrs. Abrigo says, and grabs a hold of JP's arm.

"See you tonight!" I call out, and realize that I really hope I will.

JP

"Is Mia your girlfriend?" asks Tiffany. "And if she is, how is she going to stay your girlfriend when we leave on Sunday?" Tiff, Cass, and I have finished dinner in the dining hall and are walking to the South Lawn for the kite flying festivities.

"First of all, she's not my girlfriend." My heart sinks a little saying that out loud. I haven't even been on a date with Mia, but Tiff is killing me with the reminder that we're only here for a handful of days. "And who says I'm going back to New York? Maybe I'll turn into a kataw and live here in the lake."

"What's a kataw?" asks Cass.

"They're like mermaids, but without tails," Tiffany explains. "They have fish scales all over their bodies, big fins coming out of their arms, and sometimes they eat fishermen."

Cass looks uneasy, glancing over his shoulder at the boat docks behind us. "That sounds scary," he says.

"They're not real," I reassure him. "Kataw are just a myth. Something that someone made up in the Philippines a long time ago."

The dock and lake disappear behind us. On a winding path

through the back of the resort, we pass the always-pinging pickleball court and neighing horses at the stables. All sounds fade in the wind as we approach the South Lawn. The sweet smell of fresh-cut grass fills the air. A thicket of oak and pine trees opens to a massive sky filled with soaring kites in every color of the rainbow.

Tiffany and Cass run toward the Kids' Club table. Jasmine helps them find their kite creations and attach spools of nylon string. My eyes scan the field. Mia Malik is in the middle of it all. In the sea of resort-goers, she oscillates between the vintage nickel camera hanging on her left shoulder and the modern graphite one on her right. Her eye finds toddlers waving to the brightly painted monarchs and dragonflies in the sky up above. She aims a long lens west to catch a jellyfish and a lion dancing as the sun slowly fades into the horizon. Everything is photographs. Photos of newlyweds holding hands; photos of babies holding baby dolls; photos of every line on the face of every elder holding every story. Mia moves through the field with confidence and grace. Her cameras hold the entire night inside.

"Check out my kite, John Paul!" Cass shouts, nudging my arm. I look down at the pink and green swirls filling the triangle in his hands. A pair of asymmetric eyes with yellow lashes float over a circular scribble and toothy, cartoon mouth.

"I love this, Cass! Is it a crocodile?"

"No!" he huffs. "Guess again!"

"Is it an alligator?" The sour look on Cass's face shows his displeasure.

"It's obviously a piggy," Mia interjects. She gives Cass a double fist bump and brings an excited smile back to his eyes.

"How did you know that was a pig?" I ask her. Cass runs across the field holding the isosceles pig face high over his head.

"Didn't you see the nose?" Mia answers. "It's a perfect little pig snout."

"What? Where are you getting that?" I say.

"Soften your eyes a little bit, JP," she coaches me. "You'll start to see it." As Cass runs back to us, my eyes relax and begin to realize the perfect hog nose.

"Cass, your pig is amazing," I say. "I love the nose so much." We high-five and smile.

"Tiffany made an amazing kite too," Mia shares.

"Yes!" shouts Cass. "You have to see it, JP!"

Mia scans the field and spots Tiff—spool in hand—flying a massive green-and-gold kite. "Whoa! That's really high up there," exclaims Cass. I nod in agreement as Mia frames the kite up with a telephoto lens.

"It's a Filipino dragon," Mia starts. "She told me it ate moons and caused an eclipse."

"She made Bakunawa!" I exclaim. Mia shows me a photo of the kite from the screen on the back of her camera. Tiffany's creation is lush with detail and color. Using the entire diamond-shaped surface, she's coiled the powerful body of a snake with the head of a furious dragon. We all look up into the sky as Tiff flies the kite higher and higher.

"What is Bakunawa?" asks Mia.

"Bakunawa is old Filipino folklore. There used to be seven moons in the night sky. The dragon swallowed six of them and was cast far away when he tried to eat the seventh."

"Why did he eat the moons?" Cass asks. "Was he really hungry?"

"No," I answer. "He was in love with a human from one of the original tribes. A leader found out about them and burned their house down. Bakunawa lost control and tried to swallow all the moons before the humans and other gods kicked him out. If he couldn't have his true love, he wanted to punish people and make them live in total darkness."

Just then, the nylon string attached to Tiffany's kite snaps. Instead of falling to the ground, the Bakunawa flies upward toward the faint moon just starting to appear in the evening sky. "Is Bakunawa going to eat our moon?" Cass asks with concern in his voice.

"No," I answer. "When there's an eclipse, that's Bakunawa trying to find his way back to his long-lost love. He'll need the moon to find them." I glance over my shoulder looking for Mia, but she's gone. "Where did Mia go?"

"There she is!" Cass points. And, yes, there she is. Twenty yards away, past the folklore and the workers and guests young and old, Mia is comforting Tiffany, my eleven-year-old cousin who just lost the kite she worked all day on. Mia turns back to me in the delicate moonlight. In this moment, we are closer than we've ever been before—bonded by more than anything that can be put into words.

WEDNESDAY

MIA

"Ready to make a wish?" I ask as soon as I see JP on the shoreline of the lake.

"What's the legend again?"

"You make a wish before you jump in the lake, and then if you can make it all the way across to Big Rock before stopping, your wish will come true."

"Wow. And you've made wishes before?"

"Yup."

"And they've come true?"

"Well, I don't know about that exactly, but it's fun to think about it, right?"

"Definitely," he says, shading his eyes with his hand and squinting out across the water.

"Can you swim as good as you can skate?" I ask.

"Not quite as good, but I can try . . ."

I tell JP where he can put all the layers of clothes he is wearing. We both start to undress, and is that what JP looks like without his baggy clothes on? I make a sound like a whistle and am instantly embarrassed.

"What? Is this a weird bathing suit? I had to borrow it from my unc . . . I mean . . . my, uh . . . dad. It's weird. It's, like, Gucci or something." There it is again. The kind of rich kid who calls Gucci weird.

"It's cool," I say, trying to avoid the width of his shoulders and the muscles in his back. "Come on. Just put your feet in first. Get used to it. Acclimate," I suggest, standing up to my knees in the shallow part of the lake. I wave at Logan, the lead lifeguard. He raises his arm and gives me a thumbs-up.

"Good luck out there, Malik! I'm rooting for you!" he calls.

"Wait, why is he wishing you good luck?"

"Oh, that's just tradition," I lie, knowing Logan is in on the dare too. It's true he likely doesn't wanna part with his fifty dollars, but also true that he'd like to see one of the more pompous guests get burned just a little.

We're some of the first swimmers out, and most of the other people are in the roped-off area where the toddlers and babies swim. There are also guards across the lake on the other side. They know I'm out here with JP too. Everyone is in on this deception. On our days off, we're allowed to swim and grab meals at the Granary, but since I am with JP—a paying guest—I still need to be careful. The lake swim is the perfect diversion.

"You sure this is a good idea?" JP asks.

"Trust me. It is a type of magic unlike anything. It is game-changing, life-shifting, magnetic, heart-opening. It is the thing that I love most at the entire Majestic Mountain House," I say, and I know that once he does it, once he submerges and submits himself to the water, the unexpected yes of it all, he will understand me. Yes, that's it. He will get me, and in order for him to fall in love with me, he has to see all of me. He has to do this with me.

"Okay, I'm all in, then. Let's do this."

"Make a wish," I say, and grab his hand. He grips on to mine harder and looks over at me. We both wait a beat. I am wishing myself away from Monument. But I find myself wishing that JP won't get hurt at the same time.

"Done," he says, interrupting my thought.

"You wanna tell me what you wished for?"

"I wanna get in before I chicken out this time."

And so we both run as fast as we can until we're submerged under the lapping waves. The water shocks me immediately. The immense chill, the cold jolt of it, makes my skin come alive in goose bumps. I move quick from the shore to where the lake goes deeper and sink down fast, and as soon as I do, I kick my legs to skyrocket back to the surface, back to JP, whose face I already miss. I break open the water and feel the sunshine. "Oh my god, it feels sooo good!"

"Oh my god! It's sooo cold! You didn't tell me. Why didn't you tell me?" He shakes the water from his hair. Hot. That is a hot move. What the hell?! I just stare at him. Both of us farther from the shore and treading water now. "What?" he asks, while I am trying to keep my head above water, dumbfounded.

"Oh, nothing. I . . . I couldn't tell you how cold it was. You'd never have run in, so . . . surprise!"

"Come on. Let's do this thing. I can't lose my wish!"

"Oh, so this was a serious wish you had."

"Wouldn't you like to know."

"Yes! Yes, tell me," I say, and reach for his hand underwater. I brush up against his stomach and my breath goes faster.

He pulls me toward him a second longer and then his mouth is against mine and we sink quick below the water, so it's all arms and legs gripping and reaching for each other and my hair wild around my head. We stay this way until we both are breathless and reach up for more air. "We have to actually do the swim for the wish to come true," I say, laughing, splashing him with the water.

"That's what I've been saying. Come on! Stop playing. I know how bad you want me." We both start laughing at this, but what he doesn't know is that it's true. I do want him. More than I expected. Thank goodness it's still a game and he'll still leave in a couple of days.

"Oh, really? Do you know how bad I want to *beat* you?" I ask, and propel my body through the water, freestyling my way across the lake. My body carves through the small waves made by the canoes and kayaks already out this morning.

"Wait up!" he calls, and pulls his body through the water. Both of us out of breath and pushing into the cold, deep middle of the lake. We swim in silence for a long stretch, and right when we get to the middle, I flip over to backstroke, and he does the same. We move slow and steady together.

"I love this," he says, and I know exactly what he means. From the middle of Lake Majestic you can see what we saw from the cliff the other night, but from the base of it, so we see the Catskills in the distance and Majestic Mountain rising up above us. You can just faintly hear kids starting to yell and cheer from the shore and see people start to arrive on the massive porch, but here it feels like we're all alone, submerged in the basin of this resort. And the view is sick as hell.

"Now you know why it's my favorite thing to do."

"*Uhh*, yeah. What have I been waiting for?"

"Exactly what I was thinking. Race you to Big Rock?"

"You're on!" And so we both flip over and freestyle all the way to the opposite side, our bodies moving quick and double time. I touch the rock first and we reach up to climb out of the water—perching on the side of Big Rock together. We wait to catch our breath and look out at the resort from the opposite shore. Stunning. From every corner. Pristine. Perfect.

"And now we wait?" JP asks.

"For what?"

"Our wish to come true?"

"Oh, yeah. Yeah, now it's a waiting game. We'll see what happens. But we made it. We did."

"I can see why you come back to work here every summer. It's soo beautiful."

"Yeah. But I've always wondered what it would be like to visit here. You know, as a guest."

He nods.

"I always see these families come here . . ." I close my eyes and tilt my head back toward the sun moving higher in the sky. "And there are all these moments when they're laughing or paddling out on the lake or hitting balls at mini golf and I think about the kind of memories they're making. The kind they'll carry with them forever, you know? I love that. I want that."

"You and your family don't do vacation much?"

"Oh, we do," I lie. "But we're way more rustic. More camping, more out under the stars, more catch your own dinner and cook it over a fire. That kind of stuff." I have never, ever caught my own dinner. That idea nearly makes me nauseous.

"Well, this is the first time we're coming to a place like this," JP says.

"Wait. I thought you said you've been here for the last few years?" I ask.

"Oh, no! I meant . . . yeah. I got confused. I meant since this place feels like it's new every year. No, we've been here. I've definitely been here. All of us. My whole family. Sorry about that. Hey. We should get back, right? Make sure that wish is solid. Race you back?" And he's off, splashing back into the water and moving fast.

I shake my head to clear the thoughts. What's JP covering up? What's he hiding from me? But I push those thoughts away. I don't have time to figure it out. Stay focused. Get the job done. So I sail into the water right after him.

"JP!" I call to him before he gets to shore on the other side. "Let's wait on the dock here before we head in."

He pauses and turns around. Swims back to me. "Hey. Sorry, I got in my head. Started swimming without even thinking. Where did you wanna go?"

"The dock," I point, and we both swim over to the floating structure between the diving board and the shallow side where the kids are filling it up. I can see Jasmine with a group of our little ones. She waves as we climb up.

We pull up on the ladder and sprawl out like starfish beside each other, feeling the sun and the mountain air wash over us. "I have some questions," I start, realizing that there is still so much about JP Abrigo that I don't know at all.

"Questions? For me?"

"Uhh, yeah. You ready?"

"Oh, damn, questions . . . with an *s*. Okay, yes. I am ready." He sits up. "And I have some for you too."

I sit up too so we're facing one another. I don't know exactly where to start, so I try something more neutral. "I know you're from the city, but what neighborhood did you grow up in?"

"Jackson Heights, Queens," he says, and then pauses and shakes his head like he's trying to get something loose up there. "No, no, I mean Morningside Heights—Upper West Side. I just have a bunch of friends in Queens, so I spend a lotta time there."

"Cool," I say. "And I know you're headed to Brown in a couple of months. Congratulations, by the way. Did I mention that is amazing?"

"Yeah," he says, but doesn't seem amazed at all about it. "It's a weird place to be in, right?"

I nod, but don't say anything. Want him to keep talking. Trying to figure out exactly who I am sitting across from.

He keeps on. "Eighteen feels so real. Like you're supposed to know exactly what you want and what happens next, but what if you don't? And, yeah, Brown is amazing. Definitely. But I don't even know if I'd be going there if it wasn't my family's dream for me. Their idea of who I am supposed to be."

"But what about finance and the fintech or the 'markets' and all that?" He tilts his head and gives me a look. "Not as into that as you might have made it seem?"

He starts to laugh and shakes his head. "Nah. Not so much. If you wanna know the truth?"

"Yeah, of course," I say, though I know that I'm holding

back so much too. If I wanted the truth, I would not be sitting across from him right now.

"I wanna tell stories. Always have. I'm a pretty big comic book fan . . . Maybe Ellis mentioned that, but I love the way comic books hold all these images and these complex but simple stories. I want to do something like that. I don't totally know, but I'm pretty sure if I told my family I want to go into 'comic books' rather than 'finance,' they would be soo pissed."

"Yeah. I totally get that. My family does not love that I want to make photos for a living. They basically said that's not really a thing anymore, so . . ."

"So you're stuck?"

"Yeah. *Stuck* is the perfect word for what I am and where I am."

"Did you grow up here?" he asks. And maybe he wants to know a little something about me too, or cares enough to listen to what I say, who I am.

I go with it. Partly because I'm trying to win this bet and partly because I like the way he listens. "Yup. My whole life. Born and raised in Monument, New York. Also known as Upstate Hell . . . but I wouldn't share that with anyone but you."

"Wait a minute? I thought you loved it here. It was beautiful growing up and all that. What do you mean 'hell'?"

I look at him and wonder if he really wants to know and decide then that I might as well try. "It's a little more complicated, I guess. Some of it's the town, and maybe I painted it to be a little rosier than it actually is."

"But it is beautiful here. Just look around."

"Yeah, it's beautiful here on the resort side of the mountain. But on the other side, it's messy. It's a run-down community college town where the kids from the city and rich out-of-towners with their country homes run up the rent too high. It's all foreclosures, and copycat bars that smell like beer and piss, and dollar-slice pizza joints where half the town sobers up in the booths. Feels like it's been like this my whole life. Monument is frozen in time."

"I'm sorry, I didn't know."

"How could you? If you're coming to Monument just for the Majestic Mountain House, you'd never have any idea about the rest of the town. They do their best to keep that from the guests."

"Got it."

"So Monument is just a town full of hikers and mystics and healers and junkies. Sorry, not junkies. I know I should say people with substance use disorder. But it's also engineering students and student teachers whose parents pay rent and psychologists and social workers, and I don't even go to therapy because therapy is supposedly for rich White kids, and I . . ." I stop, realize I have already said too much, but there JP is again. Still listening, still studying. "I'm sorry. You just asked one question, and you got a lot of answers."

"No, don't apologize. I want to know. It's always complicated to talk about where you come from. I know that too."

"Yeah," I say. "Thanks. And I didn't mean anything by therapy. It's totally cool if you go and I definitely *should* be in therapy, but there's this whole narrative from one side of my family and I mean . . . I am White . . . I guess. Most of my family is, so that's how I show up in the world most of the time. But my dad is half Assyrian. Middle Eastern. And he definitely doesn't pass for White. But what does Middle Eastern look like, you know? What does Assyrian look like? I looked it up one time. They looked like me."

"So, he's Assyrian? Is that . . . ?"

"It's the land occupied by Iraq now. He used to say he was Middle Eastern and that was enough to make him different, to make him stand out. He looks ambiguous, you know? People would ask him all the time where he was from. He'd point to his nose, his deep-set eyes, tan skin, beard, and thick head of curls and he'd say: 'My people are from the desert and from the boot.' He's Italian too. Anyway, he always had this schtick he'd do like he was getting out ahead of their jokes or their comments, but it always made me feel uncomfortable. I think he felt that way in his skin too."

"Is that how you feel sometimes?"

"Not as much, no. But I feel for him every time someone tried to guess or second-guess who he was, like he had this hidden identity, some secret inside of him that people couldn't see, and I think it made him cagey or made him doubt himself. I feel that sometimes."

"I get that," JP says, and it feels like he really does.

"And because I'm not *that* Middle Eastern, I start to second-guess myself. How I look. How I show up. How much of me is all of me? That's a game I have been playing with myself lately. How much of me is enough?" I can't believe I am saying all this to him, but it feels freeing to talk to JP. Something about the way he pays attention, like he has nowhere else to go and nothing else to do with his time but get to know me.

"You're enough," JP says, and he is so serious that I pause for a minute. "We're all enough. It doesn't matter how much or what fucking percentage you are of something. You're enough.

When my family and I go anywhere, somebody says we're Chinese or Vietnamese or Mexican even. They tell us who we are. We correct them. We're Filipino. Me, I'm born here. I have mixed ancestry too, and I say I'm FilAm. That's what I am. Parts of my culture are from the islands and parts are from Roosevelt Avenue in New York. I get to claim who I am. No lie."

I smile at him. I have never heard it quite like that. "Thank you," I say, and mean it. "It's cool to hear someone else struggles with those kinds of things too, you know?" JP nods, and I feel like he really does.

Damn, I think. We got deep fast. Much faster than I expected. But a good deep, one that doesn't so much feel like sinking as it does propelling underneath the surface. Exactly where I would like to be.

We stay sitting in the sunshine. My skin so warm under the glow. Me delirious from all the talking. I catch a sideways glance at him and am embarrassed to see him looking back. We both smile. It feels like something blooming, like something opening up. *Don't get too close. This is all a game. Protect yourself at all costs. Nothing is what it seems. A dare is a dare.* But I don't actually say any of that. Instead I say: "So, what's next?"

JP

"You hungry?" Mia asks, squinting through the harsh light of the late-morning sun. Standing tall and confident at the edge of the float, she rolls her shoulders and stretches her neck to the left. Hands behind her back, she raises her head to the sky, breathing in a way that shows off every muscle in her body. Mia is strong. Powerful. Shifting her weight to the right, she looks at me quizzically. I've been staring too long.

"Yeah, yes. I could definitely eat."

"Then let's get food. It's a little bit of a hike, but we can grab box lunches up near the stables. Just follow me."

Mia dives off the float and cuts through the lake like captain of the swim team. I jump in and feel my body tense up in the cold water. "I'll follow you anywhere!" I call out. She looks at me over her shoulder in a way that puts me on blush mode. "I just meant . . . I'm right behind you." And that's where I stay.

We towel off on the sandy shore as green leaves form a canopy above our heads and envelop us. Despite the narrow path, the walk feels expansive. Maybe it's the sounds of the landscape—the calming breeze over the mountain, the call of birds down by the lake. The forest swells with natural life. Mia points to a deer and fawn wandering the thicket. We see a porcupine slowly making its way on the side of the trail.

"Let's give them some space," Mia advises. As the trail widens out, she reaches back and holds my hand. This feels less romantic and more *you can walk a little faster.*

"Don't porcupines shoot quills at people?" I ask.

"Only in comic books and movies," Mia answers. "Give them a little space and you've got nothing to worry about." We pick up the pace and I can feel my legs getting tight. Mia notices and asks if I need a break.

"I'd like to say the swim wore me out," I start. "But I think I'm just really bad at hiking. I have a list of things that I'm good at. Hiking is not on it," I tell her, and she turns to look at me again—a whole bunch of questions on her face.

"Wait a minute, you keep a list of things that you are *good* at?"

I pause, catching my breath. "Yeah, of course. Everyone has brag-worthy things . . . you know . . . things that you could show off if you needed to."

"A show-off list? What are you talking about? Is this a city thing? I definitely don't have a list like that."

"Stop lying," I say. "I know for a fact that there are things you know how to do that you're proud of. Let me give you two very clear examples. Swimming across the lake a million times without stopping. You know how to do it. You're good at it. And you would be totally cool doing it in front of other people. And hiking, of course. Unlike me, you know how to do it. You have the skills; you have know-how. Bonus—you make hiking look incredibly easy. It's like you don't even know what sweat is. You are never out of breath when we walk and talk. So, two plus two. Get it?"

"Okay, okay, okay, I understand what you are saying. I do think there might be a few things that I am good at that I would not be afraid to do in front of other people, but it doesn't mean I would just show them off or that the reason I am doing them is to show off."

"Yes, it does. One hundred percent it does. Even if you don't mean it, it's a way to prove something. Or, let me reframe that. It's one hundred percent true for me."

After a short rest, we're back on the trail. The smell of wet hay signals that we're getting close to the stables. Up ahead, we see Ellis with his back to us, sitting on a picnic blanket.

"Hey, Ellis!" I call out. He turns to look at me, revealing Jasmine sitting in front of him.

"Hey . . ." they say slowly in unison.

"Wait, what are you doing here?" Mia asks. "Who is running Kids' Club if we're both out here?"

Jasmine shakes her head, clearly embarrassed. "Don't worry. Staff has it covered and I was just taking a quick break for lunch and just happened to run into Ellis," she says. Ellis looks down at the two untouched box lunches of muffuletta sandwiches, Majestic Mountain potato chips, and apple crisp that sit beside them. I can tell by the way they are sitting so close together that this was no typical run-in.

"We don't want to interrupt," I say.

They invite us to join them, but Mia demurs. "Have a great lunch," she insists. "We'll see y'all around."

When we're almost to the grab-and-go tent and out of earshot, I tell Mia, "I think Ellis really likes Jasmine."

"I think she's really into him too," she responds. "They had little crushes on each other last summer, but neither one of them made a move." Mia passes me two boxes and heads over to the pump to fill her water bottle. We settle in at an empty picnic table and start scarfing down lunch.

"Okay," Mia starts. "You have to tell me the things on your list."

"What list?" I ask, still dialed in to the story of Jasmine and Ellis. "Oh! You mean my show-off list. I can dance. That's really number one. That is almost my only one. But . . ." I look up. Mia is staring wide-eyed at me, covering up a laugh with what's left of her sandwich. "What? You don't believe me?"

"No, no. It's not that I don't believe you, it's just that . . ."

"You totally don't believe me, do you?"

She shakes her head side to side.

"We should go dancing, then."

"How? When? No, don't worry about it. I totally trust you. I believe you can dance, and we can leave it at that," Mia says.

"Seriously, let's go dancing. We can even go tonight. There's dance and karaoke at the Mountain House. Let's go dancing! And we can karaoke too. That's not on my show-off list, but I love karaoke. C'mon! We've gotta do it!"

"There's just one tiny problem," Mia says. "The dancing and karaoke are for guests, not workers. Sorry, JP."

"What if everyone thought you were a guest?" I suggest.

"What are you talking about? Putting me in a disguise?" She laughs.

"Exactly! We put you in a disguise."

"What? No way. I have no clothes here except red polo shirts and khaki pants. What am I supposed to wear?" she protests.

"There's probably a ton of 'resort wear' in the lost and found," I say.

"Nope," Mia snaps back. "All of that fancy stuff gets thrifted, and staff divvies up the cash as tips. Can't mess with that system."

"What if . . ." I'm finding a new idea in the moment. "We go back to my suite, and you try on some of Dalisay Abrigo's clothes? Is that . . . weird?"

"Yes, it is totally and completely weird, but I am . . . I kind of love the idea, so how do we get me to your room without anyone noticing?"

I look down at myself and point at the outrageous amount of clothing on my body in this July heat. "Maybe you could wear some of this?" I suggest, and start to take off my sweatshirt and hat, embarrassed by the wild mop of hair flopping about.

Mia is swallowed whole by my hoodie.

"You look . . ." I track my eyes on Mia, then scan myself. "Exactly like me."

She ties her hair up into the hat. "Oh my god. People are going to think we are twins."

We're laughing so hard that we can barely breathe.

"Head up, shoulders back," I coach her. "You know what? Never mind. Actually, just head down and slump your shoulders. The game is not to call any attention to yourself."

"Yeah, why is that your game exactly?"

"No, I just meant . . ."

She gives me a look and then says, "Be serious. What's your real story?"

I want to tell Mia Malik everything, but I don't want this

feeling to end. I want to be cool, smooth JP. Not the kid with the dead dad who spends his days doing breathing exercises to keep the panic at bay. I want the ease of being someone with a functional, intact family. Someone who doesn't have to worry about what the future is going to cost. Maybe the real story is that I'm afraid to tell her the real story. Not because she can't handle it. But because maybe I'm not ready to accept what that means for me. I almost crack, staring deep into her dark eyes. But I keep my mouth shut. "Come on."

MIA

"You said you wanted to know what it feels like to be a guest, right? Well then, let's be guests!" JP says.

When we walk into the room, I feel like I might pass out. I've been in some of the guest spaces before, with the housekeeping crew, so I've definitely seen how some of them live, but this seriously takes it to a whole other level of wealth that I am not at all accustomed to. It's a suite with two huge bedrooms off the main living area, and a kitchen that looks fully stocked, even though there are three full meals a day that are offered here. *Oh, so this is how the real wealthy guests live at the resort.* I truly had not realized.

"Is this okay?" JP asks, even though he knows it's not. "Do you want a drink or a snack or something?"

"Do you have heat stroke right now? We can't just be hanging out in here. If we get caught, I am going to have to create a whole new identity for real. Let's move it."

"No, you're right, but I think we have time. The list of bizarre shit they rattled off to do today included some type of fifteen-bowl sound bath, axe throwing at the archery range, and the Hudson Valley history of the cocktail something or other," JP says, listing off all the things I am sure were written on the bulletin board. "You sure you're okay?" he asks again, noticing that I have not stopped gawking.

I shut my mouth and try to remain calm. *Snap out of it, you fool. Pull it all the way together and stop acting like you just arrived in the world.* "Yes, I'm totally good, I just don't want to get busted. That's all. Come on!" And so, we head to the bedroom in the back and open up the closet. That's when I really and truly understand that they are in another stratosphere. A place I could not even begin to imagine. There are racks and racks of gowns; a whole section of "resort wear" that includes slacks, sweaters, and light jackets; and then a whole additional section of athleisure that is so intricate and layered I have no idea how you even get into most of the items. And then, on the other side of the closet, there are accessories and hats, and then beyond that there's a massive safe.

JP sees me looking at it and confirms what's in it. "Jewelry. So. Much. Jewelry."

"And your dad has a whole other closet with his own wild amount of clothes?"

"You got it. They love to look the part. But I haven't shown you the best thing yet."

"There's more?"

"Yeah. It's what's gonna save us for sure," he says and takes my hand, leading me to the closet on the opposite side of the room. I think we are just going to look at his dad's clothes, but when he opens the door, there are five disembodied heads staring back at me and four very distinct wigs sitting on top of them. "She's wearing one of them today. The cropped pixie. That one's cool."

"Are you kidding me with this? They are *all* cool. Oh my

god! Talk about changing your whole identity." JP makes a face when I say this, so I take it that he thinks I'm joking, but I am totally not. "This is awesome, but I can't wear one of these, can I? She'll know, right?" I ask, leaning in and studying the way they look propped up on the head forms. They are all subtle in their differences. Two are jet black, one is honey brown, and the other is an array of chestnut and toffee or something in that family, and the styles range from chin length to long and layered.

"Tiffany tells me this one is closest to the wolf cut and this one is closest to the butterfly, which are her personal favorites. Dalisay loves to mix it up."

"Sooo . . . here I am thinking your mom is just this hard-ass, but she is obviously so much more."

"Yeah, she's definitely something."

"Tell me about her," I say, and he pauses and looks at me like he can't quite decide what to share, but then he starts.

"My mom is a lot of things. She's wildly loyal. Like, don't mess with her family. She works more than anyone I know. So much that it sometimes leaves the people she loves behind, but that's what she knows, who she is. She's just working like that to provide and to make sure everyone is taken care of, but somehow that means she's always taking care of everyone else."

"I get that. What did you say your mom did again?"

"Okay, Twenty Questions . . . Come on, no more talk about family, remember? Let's choose a wig for you," JP says, and starts to pull them down.

"Yes! But first, we need a playlist," and so I take out my phone and we turn up the volume just high enough not to call too much attention to us and start to move together in front of the bathroom mirror, trying on each wig, shaking our shoulders, moving in rhythm, and I can tell right away that JP has it and even though he's not spinning on his head, his hips are moving, and I'm smiling so wide I can't stop myself, so it looks like I'm out of body, both of us shaking and rotating around each other.

We keep exchanging wigs, so he's in the short chin length at first and I'm in the long layered one and the music is pumping and there's this freedom with him, this let go, this who gives a shit who's watching, just move and be loose and don't worry about the future or what happens next. There's an energy, an intensity that feels like I'm flying just above myself, just watching what could happen.

And I want him. I look right at him, pull him toward me, and steady his hips against mine. His mouth is hungry, finding mine right away. We kiss and it's that same exact heat from Monday night and this morning in the lake, but now I know what I crave. Cannot get enough, and I push him against the counter, his mouth suddenly on my neck, and this feeling is so fast, so intense. I wasn't even supposed to feel *anything*, but I tell my mind to turn off and keep kissing him back. I am floating, feeling my whole body come alive, when suddenly we hear the key in the lock.

"What the hell?" JP whispers at me. "They were supposed to be at the barn tour all morning. Why are they here?"

"Come with me," I whisper back, and pull him into the gigantic bathtub covered by a silk curtain. I push him to the bottom and lay flat on top of him. My heart pounds pressed against him, the panic rising up in both of us. "Shhh."

"I told you we needed to have reservations," we hear as his mom and dad rush into the main room.

"Well, we don't have to let it ruin our whole day," his dad replies. "Come on."

"I am done. This trip has been way more trouble than it's worth. Let me just take a nap and forget about the disaster of this vacation."

I look down and JP has his hand covering his face like he can't stand another second. I put my head against his chest and keep my fingers crossed that no one leaves that main room. My entire existence at the Majestic Mountain House is threatened. *Please, please, please . . .*

"Let me make it up to you," his dad says, and then I swear we can hear kissing, loud smacking coming from the open door, and JP starts to shake his head. I feel mortified for him. "Let's go down to the shops before dinner and see what we can add to your closet."

"Really?" his mom says.

"A little shopping spree?" his dad replies, and after looking through her closet I have no idea what more she could buy.

"Okay, I think that might help. Just let me grab my jacket. I think I left it in the bathroom." Our bodies tense. We can hear his mom's footsteps approach the bathroom and then she's standing right there in front of the mirror just outside the bathtub. "You know, I just did not think it would be this complicated with John Paul," she says, and I push up and see his hand still covering his face.

"Let's not think about that today," his dad calls back.

"I know, but we have to be there for him. We are responsible for him," she calls back. *Of course they are, because they're his parents*, I think.

"Can we not think about John Paul for the rest of the day, please? Just focus on us," his dad says, getting closer to the bathroom.

"But I can't find my jacket," she says, opening and closing the closet door near the sink.

"Let's buy a new one," his dad says. More kissing, more smacking. And then we hear their footsteps leave, the door opens, shuts closed, and we're alone again.

"You know, this would be super sexy if you weren't wearing a wig that makes you look like Lady Gaga," I say, and JP's body convulses with laughter. "I gotta get out of here. You gotta get outta here, especially since their worry for you nearly wrecked their whole day."

"Yeah, I guess they think I'm a mess."

"Are you?"

He shakes his head but does not answer. "Yeah. I think let's just go," JP says. We climb out of the deep tub. "What wig are you gonna wear?"

"Forget the wig. I'm going with a baseball hat and maybe . . . a scarf?"

JP smiles. "See you tonight," and then gives me one more kiss.

We meet up at seven. *A real date*, he keeps saying, and I do not know what fifties housewife he has been talking to, but it tickles me every time he says it. How old-fashioned he is while still seeming right in the moment. His style, the way he dresses. I cannot place him in my head—don't know what I assumed he would wear or how he would act, but this is not it, and somehow, I kind of like it. Am kind of into it.

I wear the hat. I wear the scarf pulled over me like I'm some wealthy celebrity guest who is trying to go unnoticed. So much so that I almost fool Jasmine and Ellis, who are working the arcade tonight. We hug when they see it's me. I grin when "Love on Top" by Beyoncé comes on and start to shake my head a little, thinking that even though JP swore it was number one on his show-off list, I'll have to lead the way on the dance floor, can already see how embarrassed I'll be and how much I'll be made fun of in the bunks tonight. But when I start to see him really move beside me, it is not in that slightly stunted or hiccupping kind of way—he can really get down. Like hip-hop B-boy style, like hips shaking, shoulders matching, oh and there go his hips again. Rotating. Grooving. Sudden and so smooth it makes me catch up with my breath that's already out of my lungs. Is *this* what an out-of-body experience really feels like, because that is what I am feeling right about now. Completely and totally out of my whole damn body. And it seems like maybe he is too.

"I told you I could dance," JP says, and moves right in time with me. His smile feels like a heat wave washing over me. I twirl and roll my shoulders beside him while I study his skills and want to know everything I can about this boy I just met.

When the music switches to a slow song, I press my body closer to his and hold on to his shoulders. Rest my head against his chest and can feel his rapid heartbeat matched to mine.

"You were totally and absolutely right," I whisper into his ear. He rests his cheek against the top of my head, and we sway there. Steady and slow. The dance floor starts to get crowded with other couples and we find ourselves in the middle of the room.

"I don't ever wanna leave," JP admits, and I look up at him. Shake my head because I feel the exact same way. I don't have to say a word. Just keep holding on and hoping this feeling lasts.

JP

"Hey, what's your karaoke song?" I ask Mia, when the music switches again to an upbeat song. She shakes her head and turns her back to me doing the cabbage patch. I slide low across the dance floor and snap up to face her boy band style. "I'm serious! What's your karaoke song?"

"You couldn't handle it," she quips.

"Olivia Rodrigo? Mariah Carey? Am I getting warm?" Mia laughs and breaks out a wild eight-count from this year's *Just Dance*. She's got some moves.

"You want to do a few songs?" she asks.

"Oh, it is on!" I shout.

Mia, in full-on running man, beckons me off the dance floor. She pulls her hat down to hide her face as we pass a floor manager at the exit. In the hall, guests mingle while hospitality staff serve champagne and cocktails. Mia's feet are suddenly frozen to the floor. Her head swivels left, then right, then left again. Workers are everywhere. Mia's heartbeat is a drum solo of anxiety and fear. On the dance floor, I'd forgotten about the clear divide between staff and guests. If we get caught here, nothing's going to happen to rich boy JP. But for Mia Malik? The stakes are much higher.

We need to make a move. Mia breaks right through a knot of society ladies in sequined dresses. She freezes again. Twenty feet down the hall, she's locked eyes with Bee playing her cello. Mia spins one-eighty. I'm leading us through a sea of skinny ties and bejeweled designer bags. We start to pick up the pace, following closely behind a rolling bar cart. I look over my shoulder to check on Mia. We share a reassuring smile then BANG. The bar cart has stopped, and I've run right into it. Tall glasses, wine and whiskey bottles fall to the floor. The room goes silent.

I drop to my knees and start picking up the mess I've made. The good? Not a single glass shattered. Not a broken bottle in sight. The bad? All eyes in the place are now on us. I've managed to get almost everything back on the cart when a pair of polished dress shoes appears in front of me. Is this it? The moment it all comes apart?

"JP," says a steady voice. I look up to see the shiny leather wing tips belong to Caloy. They point to a hallway off to the east.

I mouth the word *thank-you* as Mia grabs my hand and we make a run for it. "That was bananas!" she shouts, pulling me by the hand and running like Joanie Swift, the best Flash of all time. As we tear down the hall, we laugh with relief. We slow to a walking pace, and I notice the walls are plastered with signed headshots of famous entertainers, past and present. I recognize the faces of TV actors, movie stars, singers, and comedians.

"All of these people stayed here?" I ask.

"A lot of them even performed here. I'll show you the speakeasy sometime. It's hidden below the karaoke lounge."

I'll never get used to the expanse of this place. Halfway into vacation and the Majestic Mountain House keeps revealing new things. We head down a half flight of stairs and Mia slowly opens the heavy door labeled FL 1½. Her eyes sweep left and right.

"C'mon, we're almost there," she whispers excitedly. At the end of the long hall is another metal door with a gigantic American flag propped on a stand to the right. The stars and stripes are massive. The New York state flag sits on a stand to the left. *Excelsior.* Meaning onward and upward; toward progress; forward in the most amazing way. *Great word.*

We can hear distant voices on the other side of the flag-framed door. Mia peeks through a thin crack in the doorway. Her face winces as she slowly retreats.

"Ugh," she exhales. "Layla—my boss—is at the other end of the hall. If we get busted—"

"I've got an idea," I say. Without hesitation, I push through the door solo. Far down the hall, Layla pauses her conversation and turns around to see me. I wave an awkward raised hand. "Good evening. Is this the karaoke lounge?" I ask.

"Good evening. Yes, all of the rooms are open" Layla says to me before turning back to *Ellis*? What is Ellis doing here?

"I'll finish stocking the snacks," he tells the boss. "Then I'll call it a night."

"Layla's finishing her rounds down here, JP," Mia whispers through a crack in the door. "She's going to walk over here, come through this door and see me. We've got to run."

"We can't run," I whisper back. "Follow my lead."

Ellis, happy to see me but very much on the job, has the best seat in the house as I pull the New York State flag into the hallway, hiding Mia behind the block of dark blue and the sunlit scene of the Hudson River.

Layla calls out to Jasmine, who appears from a karaoke room holding a box of red, white, and blue decorations. She sees me and smiles. Then Layla turns back to me again. Another awkward raised hand. Ellis's eyes nearly burst before Layla turns back to him and Jasmine. Mia pokes her head out from behind the flag and waves to her friends. Jasmine and Ellis explode in sweat and smile the awkward smiles of guilty schoolchildren.

Finishing the conversation, Layla turns and walks right at me like it's business time. *Oh, shit.* We're busted. What gave us away? Jasmine's stroke of panic? The heavy sweat patches on Ellis's shirt? Me not knowing how to wave? Maybe it's the comically large New York State flag that suddenly appeared out of nowhere, with a pair of feet belonging to Mia Malik poking out from underneath.

"Enjoy your journey with us," Layla says to me as she walks out the door. *OMG—IT WORKED.*

Jasmine runs forward whisper yelling so as not to alert the boss. "What in the hell are you two doing here?"

Mia pushes the flag aside and asks, "Karaoke double date?"

"Yes!" Jasmine says. "I am officially off the clock, and after Ellis stocks the snacks, so is he."

We head down the hall to one of the karaoke rooms, fire up the system, and plug microphones into a metal box. Mia turns dials and adjusts sliders to get the perfect mix of sound.

"Check one, check, check," she says into the mic. "Who's up first?"

"Kick it off, Mia! We've got next," shouts Jasmine. She and Ellis are scanning the heavy binder of songs.

Mia types numbers and letters into the machine and takes the stage. Electronic chimes and sitar slowly build. The beat drops and Mia Malik is transformed into M.I.A.—my favorite rapper of all time. Mia—M.I.A. of Majestic—struts like she's headlining Citi Field. Mia Malik's karaoke song is "Paper Planes." She shakes her hips and marches all over the bridge before an epic mic drop on the last chorus. All smiles and incredibly pleased with her performance, she sits down next to me on a brown leather sofa.

"That was awesome!" I exclaim. "You killed it. And what was that remix? I don't think I've heard it before."

Mia smiles. Knows she's got me. The night glows up in a harmony of pop songs, rib-cracking laughter, and movie box candy. I can barely carry a tune, but I love singing out loud. It just feels good. Jasmine and Ellis close the night out with a dramatic duet from Silk Sonic. My mind wanders back to the winter.

"Turn that up, John Paul!" my dad says. He's dancing and folding our towels, fresh from the dryer, at Bubbles-Bubbles Laundromat. I turn up Bruno Mars on his smartphone and get back on T-shirt duty. A neighborhood lolo bops his head and beats on the folding table like it's a dabakan. Little kids start clapping. My dad three-sixty spins and belts out the chorus at the top of his lungs. He points past a row of out-of-order front loaders and has the card players in the back joining in on the fun. Babies giggle, aunties wave their hands in the air. In an instant, everyone in the laundry becomes the Tagalog Tabernacle Choir. We sing the praises of Free Soap Tuesdays. We play songs of rejected singles at the change machine, the kundiman of quarters falling on the tile floor. Over the hum of fluorescent tube lights and buzzing neon, we harmonize, sort, wash, and

fold. Sign reads: Last load 11 p.m. We dance our clothes into drawstring bags and head home down the block.

Mia and I whistle and applaud our friends. It's after midnight. We clean up and say our goodbyes to Jasmine and Ellis. "I don't want this day to end," I tell Mia.

She smiles and takes me by the hand. "C'mon." We slip into the lobby of the speakeasy down below. A handful of guests follow the round sounds of live jazz into the main room. Mia and I vibe with the lobby's dark-paneled walls decorated with large black-and-white photographs in ornate frames. Kites, water, all the subjects in the pictures are kinetic. They are alive with vivacity and movement.

"These are all yours," I declare, and Mia nods. "Are these from this week?"

There are photos of Caloy and the bellhops, elder guests on roller skates, Tiffany flying Bakunawa, and *me*? Me smiling like a little kid, eating s'mores. Everyone in each frame is held with so much care. Gardeners planting flowers; cousins laughing; young people tasting something magical for the first time. The details, the circumstances—no element is wasted or out of place. Individually, the prints are meditations. Together, they are the rhythm of the human heart.

I'm speechless at the brilliance on display. I move around the little jewel box of a lobby, entranced by every treasure. "I've never seen pictures like this," I tell her. "These are magnificent."

I turn to face Mia. "The way you see me, people, the world . . ." I swallow hard. "Mia, I think I'm falling . . ." Before I can finish, she pulls me forward, kissing me deeply. All breath has left my body.

"Tell me another time," she says.

MIA

My body and mind are buzzing, vibrating, full of electricity. I don't want to go right back to the bunkhouse since I'm afraid I won't be able to fall asleep. It's possible I will never sleep again, so I move slow and methodical back through the dark. Don't pull my phone out because I know this landscape by heart now and don't want to ruin it with some artificial light. *The way you see me, people, the world.* I keep replaying JP's words in my head. A revolving message, and all I can think about is feeling like that's the way he is seeing me too. Clear and constant. Even though I've been trying to prove myself all week and pretend I'm more unafraid than I really am, he has still somehow seen something in me that is real. Maybe I am more than who I thought I was a few days ago. Expanding, far-reaching. Someone brave and honest, even if I've clouded it all in a lie.

I collect and calm my breath and try to slow my heart down. Steady. I maneuver through the tall grass and blooming mountain laurel along the path. Halfway home, I stop at one of the tree houses and lean against the wooden frame. The sky looks otherworldly tonight, full of massive stars shining and glowing around me. I want to stay here with this feeling for as long as possible. Forever, if I can hold on to this bliss. And it's not about the heat of JP's eyes on me, my body moving, his hands on my hips, though that feels real too. But it's about him seeing and paying attention to me. Everything I want for myself. He sees me doing it. Now. Making photographs. Witnessing people for who they really are. Honoring them. He's been watching that happen all week. He doesn't just see me for who I want to be in the future. He sees me for who I am right now. And that feels . . . game-changing.

"Mia? You okay?" I jump when I hear their voices and look over to see Jasmine and Ellis, who are making their way back to the bunkhouse together.

"Ahh, yes! I'm totally fine, even though you just scared the hell out of me!" I add, shaking my head at the two of them.

"Where's JP?" Jasmine asks.

"You mean Loverboy?" Ellis wants to know, and even in the darkness, I can see his grin.

"I told my new *friend*, JP, that he should get back to his room and that I wanted to head home on my own."

"No good night kiss?" Jasmine asks.

"Oh, there was definitely a good night kiss."

"Ohhhhh! Damn!" Ellis says, both of them laughing now. "Putting yourself out there, huh?"

I nod and laugh along with them. "Yup! Taking all the risks. You know me."

"Uhhh, no. This is not like the old Mia I know. This Mia is different," Jasmine says, taking me in. I give her a shoulder like I'm posing for a photograph and think about what JP said.

Again. How I see him, how I see everyone around me, how I'm always so busy watching the world, that maybe I haven't spent enough time seeing myself. My own reflection.

"But this Mia can still rock the karaoke mic," Ellis says.

"Thank you very much. At least Ellis knows the real me."

"Come on. I know you too!" Jasmine adds, pulling me in for a hug. "And did we all check JP's moves? I mean?"

Ellis and I both start to giggle and mimic the smooth style JP had. His body so comfortable and at ease on the dance floor.

"I totally did not see that coming," I say. "He surprises me. There's something about him . . . Like I think I know who he is and then he does something totally unexpected and then I'm upside down again. None of it makes sense."

"That's the truth. I never thought you'd take Wolf up on a dare like this one," Ellis says, looking at me hard now under the moonlight.

"I know. I feel like a jerk half of the time, but . . ."

"I get it," Jasmine interrupts. "I know you need this. And we got your back," she adds, bumping shoulders with Ellis. "Don't we?" He nods.

"Thank you. I promise to make it as painless as possible. I won't hurt him," I say, even though I know that's probably another lie I'm telling.

"Besides, you're unstoppable Mia Malik!" Jasmine whisper shouts.

"That's right! Fearless, confident, courageous . . ."

"Reckless," Ellis butts in again, but smiles. "Gutsy."

"Bold. Resolute," I finish. Even if those are just the things I keep telling myself. We all go quiet, staring up at the sky. I lean my whole body back and look into the expanse surrounding me. *Yes*, I think. I can be all those things and more. Can show up unshakable. The Mia Malik I always knew I could be. Maybe even the one I've been all along.

THURSDAY

JP

I'm awake before the sun is even up. Cass and Tiff are still out cold as I move stealthily across our room to the door. In the fog of it all, I pat my pockets to make sure I have everything I need. Phone, room key, wallet, ChapStick—everything in its right place. I put my shoes on in the hall. Grandfather clock by the stairs reads 4:58. *Ugh.* They say the early bird gets the worm. I say the early bird gets to avoid twelve rounds with his aunt who wants to talk college and career and future and next steps. I just need some time alone before the day starts.

Mia Malik and I are in orbit—breaking it down on the dance floor, singing cheesy hits from back in the day, and kissing. The kissing—sweeter than buko pie. Want her mouth on mine all the time. Seriously, thinking about her lips has every inch of me—

Gong! The clock in the hall rings out five. It's going to be at least an hour before I can grab coffee or breakfast. I make my way down four flights of stairs to the ground floor. Front desk is empty. No attendants, no bellhops, no guests. Not a soul in sight. A chalkboard in the lobby says today's low is sixty-eight and the high will be seventy-nine. Sunrise 5:26 a.m. and sunset at 8:34 p.m. I step out the main doors expecting to see darkness and stars, but I'm awed by the deep blue of the morning sky. I've seen this color once before—in a landscape painting from Visakhapatnam. Aniya, my barber in Queens, has a postcard of it taped to the mirror at her station.

The blue color is full and rich and holds the whole of the morning sky. I learned in my art class that photographers and painters love it because it's natural and surreal at the same time. An hour before sunrise and for the hour after sunset, when the sun is far enough below the horizon, blue wavelengths of light are adsorbed by the ozone, creating what's called the Blue Hour. It looks good in art, but that's nothing compared to this. I pause, wanting to hold the brilliance and wonder of this moment for as long as I can.

I walk around the massive Lake Majestic until there's only a few minutes of Blue Hour left. I don't want to be here when it ends. Don't want to be anywhere when something so beautiful ends. I walk past the little tree houses and boat docks, past a putting green and the koi pond, through the stone entrance of the east porch. Standing at the door to the Mountain House, I turn back for one more look. The Blue Hour is done. There are only a few days left of vacation. I need to talk to Mia. Tell her how I feel. Tell her *everything.*

My stomach is making wild sounds by the time I get to the soda fountain.

Ellis is making something called a Hive Latte for a very particular customer who argues with a friend over FaceTime about honey being vegan or not. Ellis mouths to me, *It is not.*

After the morning rush of runners and trail riders, we recap the evening that was. "Dude, you cannot sing worth a damn, but you were on fire last night. Floor rocks and freezes? Where did you learn to dance like that?" he asks.

"I dunno." I smile. "My dad was a pretty good dancer. He and his high school buddies were hip-hop old heads. They had some moves back in the day. You should have seen what those guys could do on cardboard." Ellis laughs as I do a half wave with my right arm then push my head—robot style—to the left and right hand to chest and pull everything back to center.

GRAAAAAAWWWW! my stomach screams.

"JP, order something. That beast in your belly is scaring people away."

I'm so hungry now that I have no idea what I want. I stare at the specials on the chalkboard above the counter. Too many options and not enough brain power to choose.

Ellis solves the problem for me. "You want the Halloumi eggs. They're Mia's favorite." He catches me full smile and blushing at the sound of her name. "You really like her, don't you?" he asks.

My hands grip the coffee mug in front of me tightly as I feel a rush of warmth through my body. "She's brilliant, Ellis. I've never met anyone like Mia." I exhale a great weight from my chest. "I don't think I've ever felt like this before." A pause. And then another. It's one thing to feel something; it's entirely something else when I finally say it out loud.

"You should tell her," Ellis counsels. I place the coffee down in front of me and press my palms full to the table. He's right. I need to tell Mia how I feel. But before that, I have to tell her everything else.

MIA

"Mia, let's go."

I hear Jasmine's voice before I see her and know it's time to get up. We run together every Thursday. She jumps from the top bunk and I'm awake as soon as I hear her.

"Got it. Gimme five minutes and meet you outside." I go through my routine. Wash my face, throw my sweats on—careful not to wake anyone else up. We are stealth, quiet, stretching in the fresh and cool air of the silent morning.

I still feel disoriented from last night. From the ridiculously sexy dance moves that JP was absolutely not lying about, from singing ballads to each other in front of Ellis and Jasmine, and especially from the kissing that felt like it lasted forever and neither of us wanted to stop, but it was late, and we had to, and I feel dizzy still from it. Couldn't sleep because I was all in a haze smelling his skin still on mine. Kept waking up remembering the taste of his mouth and the way it felt on my neck, and I did not expect to feel this way about JP Abrigo. His name. I say it again and again. I see it in my head, along with the rhythm of his hips and his voice vibrating through me. Yeah, that was it, a whole vibration of language and an unexpected electric slide that had us all laughing and high-fiving and I was basically like *what in the hell is even happening?* Last night felt like a trick, like a mirage, and I was just trying to make it through at first and then I never ever wanted it to end.

And now it's Thursday and I have to keep my head in check. Keep it clear and calm. I have one goal this week: Get him to say *I love you.* Record it, share it with my coworkers, and move the hell on. He almost said it last night, but I had no way of recording it. In a few days I will not be thinking about JP Abrigo at all. He will be the furthest thing from my mind. Dammit. If that's true, then why can't I stop thinking about him now?

"You good over there?" Jasmine asks, pulling me away from my daydreaming.

"Yeah, totally fine. I just got a lot on my mind."

"Same," Jasmine says, and I start to *oohh* and *ahh.*

"You like Ellis, am I right?"

She smiles to herself. "Was it that obvious?"

"Oh, only if this is obvious," and I start singing right at Jasmine, looking deep into her eyes in exactly the way Ellis was doing last night.

"Shut up! It wasn't as bad as you and JP dancing up on each other, I mean, hips and shoulders and it was basically smoking hot in that karaoke room. You might need to check to see if you're falling in love yourself," she adds. "Come on. Let's start on the path behind the mountain."

I shake my head and follow behind her. "I am just doing what I said I would do this week. Just making it happen."

“So, you mean to tell me you’re not feeling anything at all for this kid?”

“Nope,” I lie. I can’t even admit it to myself, so why should I tell Jasmine? “I mean, he’s nice, sure. He’s a cool guy, but I did not get into this thing to fall for someone. That is not in the game plan and besides, he’s a guest. He’s got his own thing and he’s leaving here on Sunday. That’s not . . . I’m not . . .”

“Well, you don’t have to convince me. I know how bad you want to get out of here and you know I got your back. So, what is the plan?”

“That’s what I’m trying to figure out. We have to get through today, of course,” I say, thinking about the big hike that we do with the Kids’ Club at the end of every week. “And then we have the Turkey Kick tomorrow afternoon and that’s perfect for hiding out since you know none of the managers come to that. It’s just all of us, so if I can get him to hike up with me, then maybe we can hang out there and I just need to get him alone long enough to talk, to have a serious conversation. I think if I can get him on his own, I can . . . trap him.” When I say this my whole body feels a wash of shame.

The trapping part, the trick that I am trying to pull here—I feel like a complete jerk. We spent the entire day together yesterday, from the time we met up until nearly one in the morning, and I didn’t want to stop hearing his voice and I didn’t want it to end, but I also knew that the closer we got and the more we laughed and the deeper we got, the easier it would be to get to this moment. And I know I have to do it, but I feel sick to my stomach about it just the same.

Just then, my phone buzzes. It’s Ellis.

Damn Mia. What'd you do to this kid? He just left the soda shoppe and he is HOOKED! You got him good. All systems go.

"What'd he say?" Jasmine asks.

"It's about JP. He says I've got him hooked."

"Then tomorrow's the night, huh?"

"Yeah. I think that works best. But I have to spend some time with him today too. Somehow."

"Definitely. We'll figure something out."

"Okay, here's the plan," I start. I was up half the night thinking about all this too. "Once we get to the Turkey Kick tomorrow afternoon, let's all hang and chill just like we did last night. You be on the lookout just to make sure that no management sneaks in, and we all just play it cool. Natural. Chill," I repeat again. "And then at the end of the night, I text you that it's time and walk with JP to the lookout spot. You gotta give me some time because I gotta get it right. There's some things I have to say to get him first, but you'll follow us after and get behind that big Majestic sign so you can record us. And whatever you do, you cannot laugh or be silly or . . . Just film it and go. That good?"

"I got you," Jasmine repeats.

"And I don't want to hurt him. Whatever we do. I don't want him to know." I pull my phone out of the pack around my waist. Text JP.

Staff is having a big party tomorrow. It's called the Turkey Kick. Wanna join us?

~~I wanna see you.~~

I need to see you.

And despite the fact that JP has a seriously dated phone, he writes back immediately.

Yes! I am in. See you at Kids' Club drop off.

As soon as Jasmine and I get to the Kids' Club, we start to get the morning prepped. Snacks ready, maps out, first aid kit. The scramble is one of the biggest, most serious parts of the week. We don't take any chances.

"Mia! Mia! Hiiiiiii," Cass calls. I can hear him all the way down the sloping hill. He is running. Bounds in the door and throws his arms around me.

"Hiiii," I say back, and look at JP. "Hey." Chills. Goose bumps. My skin feels like it goes warm all over again just seeing his face, his lips. The ones I want to be kissing right now.

"Good to see you again," JP says.

"Ohhhh, good to see you toooo," Tiffany teases, looking at me now. "JP, get it together." We both laugh and I open the door and usher them all in.

"You two are in for such an awesome day," I say, and pull out the map of the scramble, which is almost four miles top to bottom. "This is one of our best days ever! We get to go to the Majestic Waterfall and it is so beautiful! You will truly love it, and we bring special snacks and sing special songs, and play games along the way. It is amazing. And it's only for campers ten and up, so you get to be with all the big kids today. It is the best, trust me."

Instantly Cass starts to cry. Big, fat tears rolling quick down his face.

"What? What is it?" I ask, alarmed now.

"I am only nine," he reminds me, and I feel the look on all our faces. JP, disappointing his brother, me disappointing all of them. I can't be the one to ruin this day, and besides, Cass is athletic enough and no one checks any actual birth dates here. We one hundred percent work on the honor system. Who is going to tell anyway? Did I say this is the day we don't take any chances? There is a first for everything. This is new territory. Anything goes.

"You know what? I think just this one time we can make an exception," I say, and the way JP is smiling, it's clear I am coming out the winner. I look down at Cass and tell him this will just be our secret, and no one has to know. "Besides, you look like you can handle it, right?" Cass nods his head and wipes his tears away. All good from here on out.

Our hike starts easy. It always does. We go over the rules with the campers—tell them to keep their fingers off three-leaf plants. We tell them to be sure to pick their feet up off the ground and watch where they step, because this is nature and there are rocks and tree limbs and brambles and leaves and sticks to get through. Nothing is ever as it seems out in the wilderness like this. Tell them to watch out for snakes and what to do if they see a bear.

"But that won't really happen, will it?" Liam asks. He just turned twelve and does not understand the world does not bend and dip to his every desire, that there are in fact bears, snakes, and cliffs, animals and danger lurking around every corner.

"I just want to remind everyone that we are headed to the

cliffs, so we have to listen close and pay attention. The waterfalls are magical and views over the cliffs are magical, but what won't be magical is what can happen if you all don't listen and pay close attention to us. Understood?"

"Understood," they say in unison. We have been practicing this routine and we are ready to roll out. I count heads. Twelve kids plus Jasmine plus Penelope, one of our new assistants. She looks more terrified than the campers when I start talking about snakes and bears, but I try not to think too hard about it. Push it out of my mind.

"Okay, so we need you all to focus up, put your thinking caps on, and follow Jasmine. She is your lead, and I am your anchor. Penelope is your middle guide and we're all here if you need any assistance at all. Now let's get out there and chase the magic," I shout, overcome with my own excitement.

We start steady and slow, all of us, singing camp songs along the way, our voices melting, shaping, the sky opening up, the leaves drifting overhead. The clouds above us are thick and puffed out. A whole ocean of silver and white in the sky. Cass is walking close to me and moves to hold my hand.

Chase the magic. We've been saying that same corny line for three years. It's not magic. It's make-believe. When I started at Majestic, I was running away from everything and everyone I knew. Trying to hide from my own family, from the past, up here in this near-perfect place. Just down the mountain, the town felt like it was dying, like I was dying inside it, wasting away.

Despite the ideal family image I have been trying to present to JP, the truth is mine has all but disappeared. Addiction can ravage and rage on a place, on a family. I spent so much of my time as a kid searching for answers about where my parents had gone, or when they were coming back.

Answers to questions about why they ended up in the emergency room, or at the shelter at the edge of town? Why they could not remember where they lived or my name or Aunt June's name? Why they couldn't leave each other. They couldn't leave because that's where the sickness started. And they were in the ER because overdosing is real and scary as hell. I remember being called in to get them and them not even remembering who I was, and they have no idea who I am now.

Do I even know who I am? Am I supposed to tell JP Abrigo that my parents both have substance use disorder, active addictions, and that I haven't seen either one of them consistently for years? He doesn't want someone with a broken family history. Who does?

Staying here on the mountain every summer almost makes me forget about them. I have no idea where they are and sometimes, I like it that way. They are shooting stars, comets, imaginary creatures who had me and then promptly disappeared. I see them in my dreams though. Sometimes as themselves, and sometimes as maple trees, or goldenrod, sometimes as river trout or eel, and I hold them, or try to, even if they slip through my fingers. They are fast and splintered, and have splintered all our lives, but in my dreams, I am still trying to hold on to them, and still searching for who I am with them, and still trying to remind them who I am, why I love them, and most of all why they are supposed to love me.

Here I found a home with a bunch of other misfit kids, ones who have been thrown out of their homes, and ones who left on their own free will. Sure, some are locals and happy, but I found my people and the ones that really matter. Jasmine and Ellis, and even Wolf for a while. But I always had rules too. Never get too close to anyone. Always keep a proper amount of distance, don't fall too far into the deep end, keep your bearings. Trust only yourself. That one is important. Say it again. I live those rules, and if I don't leave town, I will sink deeper and deeper here. A pit of myself, a lost cause.

"Mia, can we go ahead?" I hear.

"Yes," I shout back. "Are you sure you want to stay here with me?" I ask Cass, and he smiles shyly.

"Thanks for letting me come out here. My mom doesn't let me do anything," he says.

"Oh my gosh, nothing? I'm sorry to hear that. I like to live on the edge sometimes."

"Really?" Cass asks. "So does JP."

I stop and look at Cass. "Are you serious?"

"No," he says, and starts to laugh at his own joke.

"He kind of plays it safe, doesn't he?"

Cass nods at this again, still laughing. "But he's super fun. And he knows a whole lot about a whole lot of things. Superheroes, spicy ramen, pancit, Queens, comic books . . ."

"Roller-skating, singing karaoke, dancing," I add.

"Yeah. He can do all sorts of stuff. He can even do the splits and spin on his head!"

"Wow. With all those skills, I bet he has all kinds of people who like him, huh?" I ask, realizing that I am now prodding a child with questions about JP and his love life.

"You mean like a girlfriend or something?"

"Yeah. I was just . . . curious. That's all."

"I don't think he has a girlfriend. He had a crush on some

girl last year and he was all stuck in his room with his music on and probably crying too, but that's also 'cause . . ." Then Cass stops.

"Because of what?" I ask, now seriously curious. If it wasn't just a girl, then what was it?

"I can't remember. But why are you asking anyway? Do you like him? 'Cause I think he really likes you," Cass continues. "And maybe some girl named Bee who keeps talking to him. Her name is super weird, but she keeps showing up, so . . ."

"Oh really?" I ask. *Freaking Bee.* "And to answer your question, yes, I do like your brother."

"My brother?" Cass says, seeming confused.

"Yeah. JP! The person we've been talking about."

"Ohhh, oh yeah! Yeah, no, I know. Right. Can I, uhh . . . walk up ahead with my sister now?"

"Sure. Go for it." I watch him run off toward the rest of the group, a whole slew of questions crowded in my mind.

As soon as we get close to the waterfall, the kids can hear the rushing water. We have been promising unmatched views, so they start to pick up energy. It has been a long, sweaty walk, the temperature creeping up. The back of my neck is drenched and I'm glad that I made all the crew stop fifteen minutes ago for a water and snack break. Salt is always good for sweaty little campers.

I'm also glad Cass spent the first thirty minutes of the hike confirming that JP Abrigo doesn't have a girlfriend, likes comic books, and, despite not being a risk-taker, can actually spin on his freaking head and also do the splits!? Some of these facts seemed so fantastical before, but now that I have seen JP Abrigo in action, I know he is the truth. And Cass is the sweetest kid, and even though he's been sweating like wild, he's doing an awesome job at keeping up with everyone.

The kids are running to see the waterfall now, hustling and moving, spinning around each other. I see Cass and Tiffany speeding up together and I'm proud of myself for making this happen, for not always playing by the rules, and I think, this is new for me, breaking some of those same rules I always feel like I have to follow. *Yes,* I think. *I did this. I turned a tearful, sad morning into a beautiful afternoon.* I hear all the kids laughing and hollering, whooping and calling out to one another, and just when I am starting to really congratulate myself, I hear it. A sound you never, ever want to hear when you are with a group of kids in the woods. A skull-splitting scream. *Oh, shit.*

My heart goes rapid speed. I look up ahead of me and see Cass flat on the ground, not moving. Tiffany is the one screaming, her voice piercing through the woods, echoing and breaking open. I sprint toward them.

"Mia! Mia!" Tiffany is shouting, her voice hoarse. She is standing right in front of Cass, who still has not moved. My pulse goes faster and faster. I work at keeping my own breath steady, even.

"What happened?" I ask, kneeling down to check Cass's pulse and see if he has one. *Please let him have one. Do not panic. Do not overreact.*

"He ran headfirst into this branch," Tiffany shouts. "He was running so fast, and it just punched him back and he landed here," she cries, pointing at the rock behind him, where a small stream of blood trails from the back of his head. "He's bleeding, oh my god, please help!" Tiffany is panicking, and a couple of the campers who were running with them are huddled in around us now too.

Jasmine has run back from the front of the line, and her face goes flat just as Penelope starts to scream. Loud, piercing cries, which then set the other kids off even more because she's one of the people who are supposed to be in charge, and she is shouting her head off. All of this happens in less than sixty seconds, and I take it all in like a robot—computing, analyzing, reacting, not short-circuiting at all—because no one can hear us out here in the woods, and so the screaming and crying is worthless, and I am the one in charge, and I am the one who said Cass was old enough.

I am also most likely the only one who has ever seen someone unconscious and bleeding. I think of my mom when she was so drunk and high she fell off the front porch of our house. I was nine, the same age Cass is now, and I remember that night like it was this moment, and if I let it, that fear will all come rushing back to me, but this is not that moment. I am eighteen now, and I've spent the last nine years working my ass off to never ever be that scared, or that out of control, or that lost, ever again.

"Tiffany, Cass is going to be okay," I say, calm as humanly possible. "Jasmine, I will stay here with Cass. You run down as fast and safe as you can. As soon as you get signal, call 911 and tell them our location. Be safe, but hurry," I whisper. She locks eyes with me, nods, and takes off.

"Penelope, please calm yourself down. Take deep breaths. And then calm everyone else down and bring them off the mountain. Remind them that Cass will be okay. He will be okay," I say again, looking at Penelope hard now. She will have to be the one in charge of this. I say all this while confirming that Cass does in fact have a pulse, is still breathing. Alive, but not alert, and still bleeding.

Penelope pulls herself together and hustles the kids down the other side.

Tiffany asks if she can stay with me, and even though I know I shouldn't let her, I say yes. I owe her this. I owe JP this. I nod.

"You have to stay calm too. Do you understand?" She agrees and sits close beside me. I do not move Cass's head or body. Do not know if he has broken his neck or has internal bleeding or a severe concussion. I check behind his neck without moving his body, without jeopardizing anything. Steady, slow.

"Is he dead?" Tiffany asks. And I remember she is only eleven and scared. I remember being scared too, thinking my mom was dead, and the fear I felt, the way my hands shook calling 911.

What is your emergency? they asked, and I could barely get the words out. *My mother. My mother is passed out. She hurt herself. Please hurry.* I did not know how to save her then. I still don't know. But I hold on to Cass's hand, just like I did with my mom. And I keep track of his pulse and track of his breathing and it's steady.

"He's not dead. Jasmine is going as fast as she can. In ten minutes, she will get a signal. It won't take long. Cass is breathing, he has a pulse. The bleeding looks like it's from a small cut on the back of his head," I say after looking beneath him. I am hopeful that is all there is. Without moving him I secure a small bandage from my first aid kit. "Cass, can you hear us?" I ask.

"Cass! Cass, please listen to us. We love you. I love you," Tiffany says. "And I'm sorry if I'm sometimes a dick to you," she says, and looks at me apologetically. "If you wake up, I swear I'll be nicer. I promise!"

"Cass," I say again, louder this time. "Cass, are you with us?"

"Can we pray?" Tiffany asks, opening her eyes wide. "I think we should pray."

I nod in agreement, even though I absolutely do not believe in the God I am assuming Tiffany and Cass believe in.

"Dear God. Please let my brother Cass live. He's not meant to die right now. He is only nine years old, and he has his whole life ahead of him. He's just a kid. We're just kids and it was just an accident. Please let him survive. I will never forgive myself if he doesn't live," she finishes, and I squeeze her hand.

"It's not your fault," I tell her. "And he will be okay." We sit this way, holding hands, breathing in, breathing out, praying, holding on, staying steady, until we hear the EMTs racing up the side of the mountain. They reach us and immediately take charge.

"Name's Gloria. Update us," she says, and I do. They move into our places and, once they check that Cass has no broken bones, begin to place him onto a stretcher to take down the mountain, and just when they do, he opens his eyes. Thank God. Maybe there is a God, or gods, or . . .

"Where am I?" Cass asks, and looks at me and then Tiffany. "Who are you?"

JP

I'm so HYPED. So GASSED UP for tomorrow. I'm invited to the Turkey Kick—whatever that is. I'm in. Mia is pure adventure. I need more of that in my life.

Adventure seems to be the theme today as I make my way down the southern trail past the Mountain House and into the Hemlock Forest. I'm meeting Tita Dali and Tito Alvin at the stables. We're taking a horseback riding tour of historic Majestic Mountain today. I'm wearing the recommended jeans and hat—baseball because I don't own or have the confidence to pull off a cowboy lid. I don't have boots, but my newly rescued Jordans should get me through the ride.

The stables look like classic illustrations from the back side of Belmont Park, but a little more posh, a little more polished. There's a refreshment station with crystal drink dispensers filled with fruit-infused water, loose-leaf iced tea, and spicy tomato juice. I drink cold cucumber water from a half-size Ball jar and let out a long *ahhhhh*.

Following the step-by-step instructions of our guides, Dali, Alvin, and I check the placement of the skirt and stirrups on our western saddles. A team of three barrel-chested men help Alvin onto his horse while I stand beside my ride, Mr. Pickles. This horse is hilarious. Every few seconds he turns his head to me and makes the biggest circus-clown smile. I pull out my phone and snap a pic, text it to Mia.

Ha, she replies. *Mr. Pickles is the BEST. Also, what's up with your camera? Pic is all fuzzy.*

I don't know how to describe VGA resolution other than to say it's painful to look at in a world with one hundred megapixel photos and 8K video. It's awkward doing modern things on a vintage phone. There's no high-res camera, no touch screen, no emoji, no swipe keyboard, and no apps. Since January, I've been a teenager with a dumb phone.

For me, it's a way of avoiding the pitfalls of modern communication. In the winter when everything went to shit, I got a bazillion messages over IG, WhatsApp, WeChat, and all the socials. People posted pictures of my dad and me on their stories, timelines, etc. I'd silence notifications, but I couldn't escape the red badges in double, sometimes triple digits on my home screen. Read the messages? Have a panic attack. Don't read the messages? Have a panic attack.

So, I pulled an old phone out of Tita Dali's drawer of dead tech. Refurbed battery and charger from the wireless shop on the corner—$15. I get unlimited calls and texts from my wireless company for $9/month and no more public trembling, tingling hands, cold sweats, and nausea.

Tito Alvin, sporting the goofiest country western costume I've ever seen, is doing his very best not to freak out on top of his ex–Hollywood stunt horse, Cujo. Affecting his best cowboy voice, Alvin says things like "Good boy" and "Whoa" while

Cujo holds perfectly still. His show-off first-time nerves entertain the stable workers immensely.

Dali shows much more confidence. Before she was a rich lady on the Upper West Side, Dali worked a ton of different jobs. For a while she was a horse groomer at a private stable out in Elmont. She's worked in hospitality, healthcare, cosmetology, and customer service. The crazy thing? She was freaking great at all of it. She's just one of those people who excelled at whatever was put in front of her. She sits atop her horse, Mrs. Patrick Swayze, with power and poise.

As the barn managers help the rest of our group onto their mares and geldings my pocket dings with a text from Mia.

Hey—thanks again for last night. You really surprised me:)

Before I can even respond, the booming voice of Duke, our trail guide, fills the air. "Okay, riders! Welcome to the Majestic Mountain Trail Tour. This ride is of medium difficulty and lasts approximately ninety minutes. There is a ten-minute break built in at Overlook—one of the best vistas in the area. We're gonna have a wonderful time today, but first a few simple rules. One, always pay attention to your horse and your trail leader. Two, no devices while riding. That means no phones, no cameras, no radios, or other distractions while you're on a horse."

I flip my phone closed and put it in my pocket. I'll try and ping Mia back when we take a break.

A half hour into the ride and I'm already sore. Duke shows me how to use my legs to communicate with my horse. "Give him more calf contact," I'm advised. "It's like there's a spring between your legs and Mr. Pickles. You don't want to squeeze the spring too much, but you don't want it bouncing all around either." Basically, I'm supposed to find a balance in holding on to an impossibly powerful, two-thousand-pound animal. This feels like an allegory for my life. Hold on, JP, but not too tight. Not too loose either. Don't fall. Don't fall. DON'T FALL.

When we take our break at the Overlook, my legs are twitching involuntarily. Some of that is from how damn physical this ride is, some of it is because I can't stop thinking about my dad. He would have loved this. When the family decided to go to Majestic, he was most excited about swimming in the lake and horseback riding—two things he'd never done in his whole life. I've never done them either, and it feels so strange trying them without him. I am panicky and nervous. Gotta change it up, and quick.

Alvin and Dali pose for selfies with Cujo and Mrs. Patrick Swayze. They're probably sending them out to the fam on the West Coast and all their friends on the socials. I breathe in the lilac scent of the mountains and Mia jumps right into my head. I realize I haven't messaged her back. I flip open my phone and see a missed text.

JP there's been an accident.

"Hello? Hi, Mia? Mia? Can you hear me?"

The phone goes dead. Two rings and then silence. *JP there's been an accident.* I read the text over and over. *What kind of accident? With who?* I try again.

I call again and listen to her voicemail greeting.

Hi, this is Mia Malik. I can't answer your call right now but leave a message and I'll get back to you as soon as possible. Have a great day.

"Mia, it's JP. I've been trying to reach you and . . ." Beep. *No, wait!* The phone cuts me off and goes dead again. I have no idea what's going on, and that's the problem.

"Alright, folks. Break time is over! Let's saddle up again. We got more trail to see and more of this good open air," Duke calls out, but he's looking at me.

"Yeah, I'll be right there," I answer, and dial Mia's number one more time. *Please pick up, please pick up.*

Your call cannot be completed at this time.

"Shit," I whisper to myself. I've tried calling Mia at least a half dozen times. My imagination is working overtime as the group saddles up again for the remainder of the trail tour. Going back alone or getting out ahead of everyone isn't an option. I have no idea where the hell I am and have less than an hour of real-world riding experience.

We pass a carriage ride driven by a team of draft mules, and dry grit and dust kicks up into my face. I can taste earth and salt and get suffocated in tiny chips of trail rock and horsehair. I wheeze and cough until our trail leader passes me his canteen of water. I wash my mouth out and wet my palms to clear my eyes. I manage to get a *thank you* out between thick coughs.

A call over Duke's radio breaks through my sputter. "Duke Seven-Four, Duke Seven-Four, what's your position? Over."

"This is Duke Seven-Four, we're approaching mile three, over."

"Duke Seven-Four, we have a jay-nine-oh-one with members of your trail party. Requested back at the main are the Abrigo family."

Everything that happens next is like a movie in fast-forward. Duke instructs the other trail leaders to take the group forward except for Dali, Alvin, and me.

"There's been an accident with your son, Casper. I'm sorry that I don't have more information right now. I'm gonna get y'all back to the stables as fast as I can. We'll know more when we get there," Duke assures everyone.

In an instant we are on another trail—a shortcut back, as Duke puts it. Tito Alvin's eyes are full of worry the entire ride. Tita Dali is trying not to boil over. She's focused on getting back to the resort, but she's going to rain hellfire when she gets there. I'm nauseous and dizzy and feel like I might just pass out. Holding the reins with my left hand, I tap my thumb to each of my fingers on the right. *1-2-3-4, 1-2-3-4,* over and over. *Hold on, Cass. Stay sharp, JP.*

When we arrive at the stables, Layla, the resort manager, explains the situation. "Cass was injured on a trail hike. Staff immediately aided him. Emergency services were immediately called. Cass was immediately transported to the hospital in town."

"Immediately-immediately-IMMEDIATELY?! Is this the only word you know?! I need to see my son. Take me to my son, now! IMMEDIATELY!" Dali fires off.

"I have an employee here with a vehicle to get you to the hospital," Layla says, and waves at the stable door, where a familiar figure enters.

"I can get you guys to the hospital. My truck is right here." Wolf, of all people, is here to save the day.

"Yes, thank you, Wolf. Mr. and Mrs. Abrigo, Wolf is our acting assistant manager and can get you quickly to the hospital," Layla says.

Dali and Alvin slide into the cab of his pickup truck—an old-school compact with a bench seat. There's just one problem. The truck only has room for three. I'm the freaking fourth wheel.

"What about me?" I ask.

Wolf, commanding the universe from the driver's seat, responds, "We'll let you know updates as soon as we get them." He flashes a grin at me.

"Who is with my son and who is with Tiffany?" Dali asks.

"They're with Mia Malik," Layla says. "Please don't worry. They are in good hands."

"I'll have you there in no time." With that, Wolf's truck spins its tires and rockets down the mountain road.

I'm left standing there without a damn clue about what to do. Cass is in the hospital and Mia is with him. I try calling Mia's cell again. Straight to voicemail. *Shit—what now?*

Things working against me: I don't have keys to my uncle's SUV. Even if I did have keys, I don't know how to drive. *Why didn't I learn how to drive?* I'm about to throw up.

"The shuttle that brought you to the stables is off-site with another group," reports Layla. "It will return in time for the rest of the trail ride group's return to the Mountain House."

Sweat is coming out of me everywhere. My jaw aches; I feel a roller coaster plunge in the pit of my stomach. Layla starts to say something more when, all of sudden, I double over and vomit. Layla and the stable workers are all looking at me with faces of shock and pity. I rise to my feet, eyes locked on the road. Before anyone can say anything, I'm fully recovered and in an omega-level sprint down the mountain.

I've never moved like this in my life. My lungs, my legs, and my feet are in perfect rhythm. The hemlock, pine, and cherry trees along the road narrow into a vanishing point. *Cass, I'm on my way. Love you, Cousin.* I am all kinetic. I am lightning. I am Filipino Wally West. *And fuck you, Wolf. I could have fucking fit in that fucking cab.* I rocket down the mountain fueled by urgency and anger; insistence and inertia. The adrenaline in my system is jet fuel for my heart and my legs. Every electric stride is throttling me faster and faster.

Then, a fork in the road. I stand still. Muscles and thick veins I never knew I had carve sharp angles through my clothes. I can feel the pulse in my throat. Which way? Damnit, which way? I close my eyes and relive the whirling of sirens; the crackle of radios and street life under the seven train. I smell the staleness of old cardboard boxes propped sideways to hold my comic books and Hong Kong DVDs. I see the shimmer of broken glass on the floor of my basement apartment. I see the EMTs performing CPR. I hear them counting their compressions. I see my father's lifeless body on the floor. My eyes explode open; my hands wrench themselves into claws; my voice roars over the mountain with the thunder and fury.

Just then, an all-black hardtop pulls up. "Need a ride somewhere?" The alto voice is unmistakable. "Get in," Bee insists.

MIA

"We need some info," the receptionist says to me after they take Cass back.

I scan the room and take it all in. Even though it is a Thursday afternoon, it is crowded already. "Yes, of course," I say, trying to stay focused.

"I need the child's name and age, please."

"Casper Abrigo. Nine years old," I reply, and watch how they move quickly. Anyone coming from the Majestic Mountain House gets first-class service. Because they have good insurance, or can pay out of pocket because they're rich like that, because the healthcare system is corrupt.

"Are you his guardian this afternoon?" she asks, and I feel like I have seen her before. I used to know the receptionists by name after coming for my parents so much. I have been here before, know the constant beeps and bells, the smell, the antiseptic-sick scent that you get covered in.

"I am," I reply. "I work at the Majestic Mountain House. Mia Malik," I tell her, and when she looks up, I know she recognizes my last name.

"Please have a seat and we'll call you when we have any news or updates."

I nod my head. "Thank you." I look for a place to sit. I try and ignore the faces in the waiting room, the moans and calls for help from people in pain, who are struggling.

It used to be, in Monument people would be sick on the streets downtown or over near the shelter, but over the last few years, the protocol is to call 911 on anyone who you suspect to be overdosing. This is what the town does now, everyone on alert, watching. The waiting room is full of near disasters.

"Can I stay with you?" Tiffany asks. "Please."

"Of course. I'll be with you until your mom and dad get here."

"They're gonna be soooo mad at me!"

"At you? No way. They will be so happy to see you," I tell her, moving us to a set of benches in the corner. *Me, not so much*, I think, and then realize I am covered in sweat—head to toe. "I'll be right back," I tell Tiffany. "Just running to the restroom."

Once I'm alone, I grab paper towels and wipe off my forehead. Look in the mirror and keep trying to hold back tears. I have already informed management, and they are sending the family and someone to pick me up too. I know for sure I am in trouble. I could lose everything. But I try not to predict a future that does not exist. Try and stay in the moment. I know this feeling.

"Can we breathe together?" Tiffany asks as soon as I get back to her. She is taking in the scene at the ER, and I imagine she's also trying not to panic.

"Yes. Definitely," I say, and she takes hold of my hand.

"Let's close our eyes. Breathe in for a count of four." We do. "And hold it for four. Now let it go." We do this a dozen times, and I can feel my own pulse start to slow. "You want a snack?" I ask. "Think you can eat?"

"I'm starving," Tiffany admits. "Can I get a soda and maybe some chips?"

"And how about some cookies too?" I would get this kid anything to make this day stop. She smiles weakly up at me, her face clouded over, brow furrowed.

As I head toward the hallway for snacks, I see a figure huddled on a gurney in the corner, his body doubled over, and I am not totally sure at first, but it's his beard, his tanned skin, and the hook of his nose that I recognize. I would know him anywhere. That is my dad. Mike Malik, asleep or unconscious or on his way to dead in a corner of the emergency room.

I didn't even know he was in town. *How did he get here? Where is my mom? Where is Aunt June?* My heart starts to pound again. I do not want him to see me, but I need to know if he is okay. I text Aunt June.

> Hey—This is random but something happened at work and I'm at the ER. I'm ok! But I think I see my dad here. Is he in town? Is mom? Are you okay?

She writes back instantly.

> He's there. Yeah. So sorry you had to see that. Said they're gonna keep him there a couple days.
> That's good!
> Your mom is okay. Staying at the shelter for now. Keep me posted. We all love you. Take care of yourself.

I stare down at the texts. How has this all been normalized? My parents are both sick. Have been for so long. I remember all over again what I am trying to get away from and how much it will cost me. I have to get to California. Have to get off this mountain and out of this town and away from this life.

I pull a notebook out of my backpack, rip a sheet of paper out of it, and write, *You are loved. Always.* I slip it onto Dad's lap. He does not notice, and won't have any idea who it is from, but that doesn't matter. What matters is that I do still love him, and leaving is still the best option for everyone.

Walking back from the vending machine, I find Tiffany asleep in the waiting room. She doesn't see her mom and dad come running into the ER with Wolf, who gives me a smirk.

"Where is my baby? Where is my son?" Mrs. Abrigo says, rushing over to the reception desk. They talk quietly in the corner while I wake Tiffany, who races to her mom's side and holds her around the waist.

"Hi, Mr. and Mrs. Abrigo," I start. "I am so sorry for what happened, but please know we acted as quickly as possible and have done everything we can . . ."

"I just want to know that my baby is okay," his mom says, her eyes full of tears. "When can I see my baby?" she asks the receptionist again. "Do you know anything? Do you?" she asks, looking at me again.

"Yes, I can tell you that he hit his head on a tree branch and was unconscious for a short period of time, but we called 911 as soon as we were able to get service, and the EMS arrived very shortly after, and he was transported to the hospital immediately. Tiffany and I both rode in the ambulance with him here."

"Is he awake? When can I see him?"

“He woke up, but he didn’t recognize me,” Tiffany wails now.

“Excuse me, ma’am,” the receptionist starts. “The doctor will be out shortly to let you know how your son is doing. If you could please take a seat.”

“No, I will not take a seat. My son. My only son was taken to the emergency room after getting lost on a cliff at the Majestic Mountain House. I want an update and to speak to a doctor as soon as possible. This is unacceptable,” Mrs. Abrigo says as Mr. Abrigo puts his arms around her shoulders.

Her only son? Is she that pissed at JP about his future that she has disowned him?

“This is unacceptable,” she says again. “And when I asked your manager about this trip,” she says, gesturing to Wolf, “he informed me that this is a trip for the older kids, and so I am confused how my Cass, who is only nine years old, was allowed to go on this four-mile-long hike up a mountain? There are rules, you understand? And they are meant to be followed so that something like this doesn’t happen.”

“Mr. and Mrs. Abrigo? I’m Dr. Rogers,” the doctor says as she approaches. “I am happy to let you know that Cass has woken up and is doing great. He has a mild concussion and a few scrapes and bruises, but he will be just fine. Let me lead the way.”

“Yes, thank you so much. Please take us to our son,” Mr. Abrigo says. Tiffany mouths, *Sorry*.

They walk back into the ER and Wolf stares straight at me. “Hey, Malik. Way to go back there! I think you might not actually get your man,” Wolf says, sneering at me. “What will I do with my winnings?”

I sneer right back. My life is over. And just when I think it can't get any worse, the door to the ER opens again, and it's JP and Bee walking in together, holding hands. *What the hell is happening?*

Bee and JP run right up to me and Wolf.

"Is he okay?" JP asks. His voice shakes. His hands are knotted up.

I do my best to sound reassuring. "He's awake."

JP releases a breath he's been holding, unlocks his fists, and wipes away tears from his eyes.

I reach a hand to his shoulder and guide him to a seat in the waiting area. "Your parents are in with him now."

Before I can sit next to him, Wolf interrupts. "Mia, we need to get back to the Mountain House."

We are still standing over JP in awkward silence until a confident stride of cowboy boots pierces the matrix. Mrs. Abrigo walks up, her eyes squarely on me.

I know it's time to go. We leave without a word.

"Never gonna happen," Wolf says as we load into his truck. "Just accept you lost the bet."

"Shut up, Wolf. Just stay out of it. Could you do that?"

"Well, of course I *could*, but do I really want to? Nope. And come on. You made it easy. His brother's in the ER right now."

"Yes, I am aware of that."

"Then you know you totally messed up."

"Yes, I know that too. Can you just drive!"

"Digging your own grave, Malik," he says, before he turns up the radio and does just drive.

I look out the window and watch Monument float by. My

dad still on my mind. The way his body was curled up. Seeing him makes me want to stay and leave all at the same time. I look down at my phone.

From Layla: **Come see me in my office as soon as Wolf brings you back to Majestic.**

From Aunt June: **Hey honey—you okay? I know seeing your dad like that is awful. We love you. Thinking about you. Call us when you can.**

Nothing from JP. Not that I thought there would be, but I wished. As we climb up the mountain, I do not keep my eyes open to see all the damage I have done.

Wolf walks me to the main office and smirks at me the whole time.

"Are you serious right now? I know the way to Layla's."

"But I want to accompany you," he says. *Jerk.*

When we get there, Layla opens the door and thanks Wolf. "You saved us this afternoon. Thank you so much for getting the Abrigo family to the ER, for moving so swiftly. Excellent work."

"Anytime. You know me. I'm always here to help," Wolf says, and looks at me one last time.

"Of course, and thank you again. Mia, please close the door and take a seat."

I slump down in the chair opposite Layla's desk. My throat hurts from trying not to cry. An ache I can't seem to get rid of. "I'm so, so sorry," I start, and when I say it, the tears come rushing out. I'm thinking about Cass lying in the woods unconscious and the medics rushing up the mountain and my panic in the ambulance but trying not to let Tiffany see me fall apart.

"What happened out there, Mia? You are one of my most responsible and capable employees. This is a hike you've done every week since you started. You know this hike. You run the entire Kids' Club. You play by the rules, and suddenly this week you let an underage kid join you all on the most intense activity we have? Do you understand that you put someone's life in danger? And for what?"

"I don't know," I say. I weigh my odds. How can I tell her that it all hinges on a stupid dare I took four days ago to get me out of this sinkhole of a town and it would in fact change my whole life? I don't even know if I believe that anymore, but that's what I think I'll have to say.

"Well, that's not good enough, kid. You have to come up with something better than that because the resort does not look kindly on an incident with a nine-year-old kid who was on a guided hike for kids who are ten and up. It looks unprofessional and sloppy. Looks like we're not doing our job, you understand?"

I nod, still wiping tears from my eyes. It's nearly four. I have been in the woods and the hospital all day long, haven't eaten anything since this morning, nearly lost a kid on my watch, and saw my dad passed out in the ER. My life is unraveling.

"Do you understand that this is grounds for firing you? That the Abrigo family has asked us what actions will be taken?"

"They what? Come on, Layla. I took care of Cass. I got him out of danger right away. I did everything right."

"But you lied, correct?" And there it is. The truth. I did lie. If only he had stayed back at the camp with the other under-ten crowd, then we would never be in this situation.

"Yes, I lied," I admit.

"Thank you for admitting that. I do not want to fire you, Mia, but I am struggling with why you did it. It was a mistake. A big one. And that's the one point Mr. and Mrs. Abrigo seem to be pretty furious about. One that could get us sued. Or Cass could have been seriously hurt and then what? I do not want to end your summer here, because you are one of my best workers, but I can't do *nothing*. My hands are tied, so here's the deal. You are suspended, without pay, for the remainder of the days that the Abrigo family is here."

"What? No, no, please, I can't . . . You can't do that!"

"I *can* do that, and I *have* to do it to show that there are repercussions for your actions. You can still stay in the bunks and your meals are still covered. But you may not be seen around the resort, and whatever you do, stay away from the Abrigo family. Is that clear?"

This has to be a joke. The one person I am supposed to stay away from is my only way out, and now without pay for . . ."Wait a minute, when do they leave?"

"Sunday morning. As soon as they are in their car down the mountain, you are back on schedule. That's just two days of work you will miss."

I do the math in my head. Twenty dollars an hour times eight hours times two days, that is three hundred twenty dollars—a quarter of what I will owe all of my coworkers if I don't win this bet, which means that I *one hundred percent* have to win this bet. If I don't, I will be way more broke than when I started. Broke and stuck. *Shit.*

"I'm really sorry this happened. You're a great kid, Mia. I really do see you going places and making things happen, but you can't be reckless, and you definitely can't be reckless when dealing with children, so we will talk about another placement for the rest of the summer when the suspension is over. Maybe the breakfast bar and catering?"

My eyes glaze over. My life and my job are done. "I get it. I do. I'll lay low," I lie, knowing that the only way out of this is to get way deeper into it. "I am so sorry to disappoint you. It won't happen again," I say.

"Thank you. I appreciate you, Mia. Now, you go and spend some time by yourself please—away from the guests and especially the Abrigo family."

"Yes, definitely," I say, panic plaguing me. As I walk out of the office, I feel my heart pounding. Tell myself to just suck it up and figure it out. Work my own magic. Forget today. Forget Tiffany's screams. Forget seeing my father. Forget the past. Focus on the future. Look toward California. The West. Expansion. Look toward an exit plan. Do not get stuck in this town—whatever you do.

I pull my phone out of my pocket.

Hey- I need to see you. Can we meet up? Granary—
soon as you're back from town.

JP

Cass and I are laughing and rhyming words together. *Troop, soup, hoop, poop.* Nurses come by every hour or so to check on him. They hold up a chart of colorful animals to test his vision and recall. Cass literally runs circles around the balance assessment, standing on one leg for thirty seconds then spinning around before doing the same on the other side. By the third check-in, Dr. Rogers is giving Cass the all-clear.

"Casper may have experienced a very mild concussion," she says. "We're not seeing any symptoms to cause concern. I think he's ready to get back to vacation."

"We don't need to go back to the city?" Dali asks.

"No, he should be fine at Majestic. The fresh air will be good for him."

We're given a list of things to look out for—dizziness, confusion, nausea. Alvin and Dali sign the discharge papers, and we're on our way back to the Mountain House.

The resort has arranged a driver and massive, four-row SUV to take us. My phone buzzes as I settle into the back with Tiffany. Tita and Cass are in the row in front of us. Alvin, still dressed like pinoy Hank Williams, slumps with relief in a captain's chair.

Hey- I need to see you. Can we meet up? Granary—
soon as you're back from town.

Mia sounds serious. Where the hell is Granary? Also, what the hell is Granary?

"A granary is a raised storage barn for grain or animal feed. They were invented to protect crops from floods and rodents," Tiffany answers.

"Are you reading my texts and my brain?" I ask.

"Your brain doesn't know enough words, JP. You should really read more than just comic books. Also, your phone sucks." Good to know that Tiffany's disposition has not been altered by this near tragedy.

Dali runs her fingers through Cass's hair. She calls him Boi-Boi, his baby nickname. She is tender with him. She is another thing entirely with Tito Alvin. In a torrent of Tagalog and English, she vents and charges and threatens. I can't follow all of it, but when she says *Majestic* and *putang ina mo* everyone in the vehicle is terrified.

Tiffany whispers to me, "Do you think Mia's going to get fired?"

"What? Why would she get fired?" I respond.

"Well," she starts, "my mom thinks she almost killed Cass."

"That's crazy," I spark. "Mia helped Cass. She got him to the hospital. She's the reason he's better right now."

Tita Dali glares back at me tiger-mom style. "That girl is the reason Cass got hurt in the first place!"

"It was an accident," I say softly. "She was just doing her job."

Dali, almost foaming at the mouth, shuts me down. "Her job is to protect children. Not to take them out in the woods and give them a concussion!"

A beat of silence. "Mild concussion," I interject. Dali spins back toward me. She doesn't say a thing this time. Her eyes narrow and heat vision burns right through me.

Tiffany gives me some free legal advice. "Shut up, John Paul." Check.

When we arrive back at the Mountain House, everyone on the staff welcomes Cass back by name. *Welcome back, Casper. Good to have you, Casper. Casper, Casper, Casper.* Why did my aunt and uncle name a Brown boy after a white ghost?

We head up to the suite and change out of our sweat-filled hospital and riding clothes. We're ten minutes late for dinner. No one says a word about it. Things are tense, but nothing is boiling over.

I text Mia. Headed to dining. See u in an hour.

Mia texts back. Thumbs up. My old-ass phone doesn't get emojis.

We move to the dining hall. Dali doesn't talk, so I don't talk. Tiffany's eyes oscillate between us, monitoring for any friction or edge that she knows can be defused with precocious eleven-year-old humor. Before we are seated, Dali heads straight for the string quartet. What in the world is she doing? Is she going to talk to . . .

"Bee?" Tita Dali reads off the vampire cellist's name tag.

"Thank you for taking John Paul to town today. That was very kind of you."

Bee smiles and touches my right forearm. "JP is such a strong and sensitive young person. I couldn't bear the thought of him not being with his mother and brother at such a time." Dali's face tilts in confusion. *Oh noooooooo!* This is it. This is the moment a stupid-ass lie wrecks—

"Oh, John Paul is not my—" Tita Dali starts.

"Bee, you are such a talented musician," Tiff interjects, grabbing Dali's arm and pulling her across the room. "You play everything so well while living with acute episodes of delirium."

Dali, now out of Bee's earshot, asks, "Did that girl think I was John Paul's mother?

"Yes," Tiffany replies. "She has a lot of problems identifying family relationships. Yesterday she thought I was his sister."

"Poor girl," Dali says softly. "She must know I'm much too young to be John Paul's mother."

Bee furrows her brow at me from across the room. She mouths, *What-the-hell?* before starting into an instrumental version of Joy Division's "She's Lost Control." I'm not exactly sure how Bee chooses the songs she plays here at Majestic, but somehow the arrangements work for the resort-goers.

Cass and Alvin are queued up at the children's buffet. I join Tiff and Tita Dalisay at the table. My aunt imposes the evening itinerary. "After dinner, we will go to a blacksmith demonstration. They are making horseshoes tonight. Then, to relax, either a cursive workshop or a healing sound bath—"

"Tita Dali," I interrupt. "I think I'd rather do my own thing."

Dali's enthusiasm hits pause. "I didn't realize you had plans tonight."

"I do . . . I don't. I just kinda wanna see some of my friends."

Tiffany's eyes go wide with horror.

"John Paul, after the day we've all had, I would very much like the family to stay together," Dali replies firmly.

"I've met a lot of cool people here. And there are only a few more nights left," I push back.

"Who are these *friends*?" Tita Dali asks.

Tiffany shakes her head and waves her arms, trying to get me to drop it. My mouth keeps running as my inability to read the room buries me. "There's Ellis and Jasmine and Mia—"

"Mia?!" Dali cuts me off. "Where is your head, Boy Reyes? That girl from the hike? The one who almost killed Cass?"

I point to the dessert bar, where Cass is doing the tootsie roll and holding a boat of soft serve above his head. "Cass is fine, Tita Dali." Dragon fire is about to blow from her nose. "He bumped his head. He's over there doing TikTok dances."

A group of guests applaud as Cass takes a bow. Tiff face-palms. She knows the cardinal rule of generational FilAm communication—a rule I always seem to forget at inopportune moments: never contradict an elder.

Dali takes a deep breath, then says, "That girl is the *help*. Worse, she is the kind of help that doesn't even do her job right. Stay on the clean side of the street, John Paul."

I am, in a word, disgusted. Her money and power let her do and say whatever she wants. Righteously looking down her nose at other people, she can place blame like a pin or a wild-fire, precise or reckless and anywhere on the map. She has totally forgotten who she used to be: Dalisay Corazon—the hardworking girl from Baguio who, along with her sister, could do anything. Dali to her family, Cori to her friends, now Mrs. Abrigo to the doorman, delivery woman, manicurist, concierge, priest, Manhattan Borough president, Majestic Mountain Kids' Club worker. She gets to say who belongs on the other side of the street now. This is so ugly. I should just leave.

"I'm seeing my friends tonight, Tita Dalisay," I snap.

Her back straightens, her tone sharpens, her eyes command all the armies of shame. "Do as I say, Boy."

"You're not my mother."

"When Alvin comes back here . . ."

I cut her off. "He's not my father." I turn and walk off. Walk off the ignorant way she's talking about Mia; walk off that Upper West Side classist cut in her tongue; walk off, walk off, walk it off. Before I'm out the door tasting fresh air, I pass the stealthy eyes of Bee. No flirtation or innuendo this time. Just judgment. And then I realize I've broken the other cardinal FilAm rule—never, ever fight in front of strangers.

Mia needs to see me.

Need. That word. Floating in my head. I need to see her too. It's nearly eight now. Dusk.

After the tense ride home with the family, the fight with Tita Dali, I need time to reset, recenter. Away from everyone.

I'm going to meet her at the Granary.

"Mia?" I ask. She's got her hair pulled back and a baseball cap on. "Are you . . . are you okay?"

"Yeah, it's me," she says, lifting the lid away from her face for a second and looking around. "I just . . . we can't really let anyone see us."

"Why not?"

"I'm suspended."

"What? No . . . come on."

"Yep. Suspended and forbidden to be around the Abrigo family as a whole."

"Oh, that's fine, 'cause I'm not . . ." I stop. Nearly forgetting my lie just to make it so she can be around me. "I just mean . . . I don't consider myself a part of them right now either. We had a big fight about the whole drama and I basically walked out just now, so I'm pretty sure that I am also forbidden from being around the Abrigo family. Can we just stop talking about family? Is that okay?"

"Definitely," Mia replies. "But first—is Cass doing alright?"

"Just a mild concussion. As soon as we saw him, he asked for a new video game, three in-app purchases, and then he wanted a Happy Meal plus a McFlurry on the way home. He's doing just fine. Don't worry about him."

"But I really messed up. I should definitely not have let him come on the hike. That's on me."

"That's on all of us. Come on. The way he started crying? The way I looked at you . . . We were all in on it, okay? It's not all on you."

"Thanks for saying that."

"But you got suspended?"

"The rest of the week. As long as the Abrigo family is here, I have to stay away."

"That's so messed up."

"There's a lot that was messed up today. Did I see you holding hands with Bee at the hospital?"

"She gave me a ride. When we got to the hospital, she grabbed my hand and pulled me through the door."

"Bee gave you a ride to town? Are you into her?"

"What? No. In fact, she makes me pretty uncomfortable. But I needed a ride, since there wasn't room in Wolf's truck. Also, I didn't really wanna ride with Wolf. Turns out, he makes me pretty uncomfortable too."

"Those two make everyone uncomfortable. You know Bee gave herself that name, right? The whole Bee-sting thing. So weird."

"Did Wolf name himself too?" I ask.

"No, that's from birth. Short for Wolfgang. You know, like Mozart?"

I shake my head. *What is wrong with people*?

"Can we stop talking about them now?"

"I'm really sorry, Mia. I don't want you to be in trouble. I feel like this was all my mom's fault. She doesn't get it. Actually . . . she should. She used to be a worker. She did all the jobs here, every one of them. She was in it and then she married Alvin and became this alternate version of herself. Instead of the money making her better, it just made her the opposite, thinking people like you and everyone on staff are beneath her. It's gross."

"You call your dad Alvin?"

"Oh, only when I'm pissed at him. So, what do we do now?" I ask.

"Hide the best we can. I still want to see you," Mia says, grabbing my hand in hers. Electric.

"I want to see you too. As much as I can for the next two days."

"Well, then let's make it happen. Turkey Kick is still on."

"Could you just . . . I feel like I have heard those two words together a bunch and I still have no idea what that actually is."

"Oh, sorry. It's a staff cookout at the start of July—right before the Fourth—before things get totally wild and busy at the resort. It's a tradition that goes all the way back to the fifties."

"Got it," I say.

"It's a big potluck up on the mountain. People show off with their cooking and there are drinks and music. It's awesome. I promise you. Guests generally aren't allowed, so it's pretty big that you get to come with me."

"Will that be weird though?"

"Not at all. You'll be with me."

"Mia Malik. Queen of all good things."

She smiles at me, and I feel like I would do and say anything to see that smile as often and as much as possible. "It starts after lunch and goes until late night so people can rotate coming up before or after their shifts. I'm going to lay low in the bunkhouse tonight, since management has their eye on me, but tomorrow let's meet at one. Partington Trail entrance. Cool?"

"Are you sure?" I ask, not wanting Mia to get into any more trouble, but wanting to see her so bad at the same time.

"See you there," she says. She looks around to see if anyone is watching and then reaches up and kisses me. Just like that. Her mouth soft and warm.

I never want to let this feeling go.

FRIDAY

MIA

"So let me get this straight," Jasmine says. "You're suspended."

"That's right."

"And you are not to be anywhere near the Abrigo family."

"Uh-huh."

"And . . . you're still trying to win the bet?"

"Yes. For sure. I am losing two days of pay here, and if I lose the bet, I'll be more in the hole than I was before. I will be totally screwed and also . . . I'll still be stuck right here."

"That can't happen. So, what's the game plan now, then?" Jasmine asks, smoothing out her hair in the mirror and adjusting her name tag on her polo. Jasmine is in charge of the Kids' Club all morning, with me out.

"I already saw JP at the Granary last night."

"You already broke the rules?"

"I know. I can't stop myself. It's like I'm a whole other person. I texted him while I was sitting in Layla's office."

"What?!"

"I know. I'm in too deep. And Jasmine . . . I saw my dad yesterday in the ER."

"What? Oh no . . . I'm so sorry. Was he . . . okay?"

"What do you think?"

Jasmine shakes her head. She knows the history of my family, understands how much it hurts to see them fall apart. "Did you tell JP?"

"About my mom and dad? Are you kidding me? No way. He doesn't need all that baggage. Especially when he's from this wealthy, loving, amazing family where their only issue is that he doesn't wanna study the same things they want him to. Such a joke. We don't fit together. At all."

Jasmine doesn't say anything for a moment, just pulls her thick hair into a knot at the top of her head and puts her hoops on. Then she speaks again. "Look, I know you wanna win this bet. And I know you think it's all about getting out of town and saving your ass and leaving your family, but is it possible that JP is already more than just a bet to you?"

"That's why I feel like such an asshole about it all. I like him. A lot."

"So then you have to tell him who you are. Don't think about the bet for the next twenty-four hours. Just think about getting to know him more, and maybe even taking a risk and sharing who you are with him. Have you thought about that?"

I shake my head.

"And maybe . . . and I'm not saying this is a reason to, but maybe in sharing some of what makes you actually real, he will show you some things that he hasn't before. You know? And just maybe . . . not that it's about the bet . . . but maybe it will make him feel closer to you. Like you're sharing this secret with him, and that will bring the two of you even closer together, and then . . ."

"He'll say he loves me."

Jasmine opens her eyes wide, shakes her head, checks herself in the mirror one more time, dabs on her lip gloss, and gives me a quick kiss on the cheek. "You got it. Try a new technique. See how far it gets you."

JP

Pretending to be asleep is every teenager's superpower. I lie motionless under the heavy weight of hotel bedding while the suite buzzes with action. Tita Dali's hair dryer is on full blast in the other room. Cass, fully recovered, dances next to my bed. Tiffany moves like a freight train through the living room, bathrooms, and bedrooms asking if anyone has seen her favorite hair clips. After the dinner that wasn't, I don't want to see anybody. Want them to leave me alone. Leave me in peace. I'm going to be here a while.

Just then, I feel a hand on my shoulder. "Wake up, John Paul," Tito Alvin says. "I want to talk to you. Let's take a walk."

We step out into the hallway. Alvin sports pastel resort wear. I'm in pajama pants with lightning bolts all over them. I pull my black hoodie over the tidal wave on top of my head.

"I don't want to fight with you, JP," he starts. "You're not going to be with us for much longer."

"Tito Alvin," I say softly, "I don't want to fight with anyone. We have a little bit of vacation left. Then a little more summer . . ."

"Then you'll be gone," he says. "You've had a very difficult year. I don't want that to define you or define your relationship with the family."

As he talks, I realize this is the longest conversation I've ever had with my uncle. We grab coffee from the lobby and step out onto the grand porch. The rocking chairs are surprisingly empty. It's Friday. Folks are staying in bed later, taking a vacation from their vacation.

"In America, everything is a choice," Alvin says. "If you want something, you must choose it for yourself."

"I don't know," I say back. "I don't think we get to choose everything. Sometimes things just happen to people."

Tito Alvin nods. "Yes, but choice is critical in the way we carry those things. College, work, the future—these are choices just as much as they are experiences."

"What about love?" I ask. "Is that a choice too?"

"Yes," he answers. "Love is the hardest choice of all."

"Why's that?"

"Because, when you choose love—real love—you have to be honest."

"Honest?" I ask.

"Honest with yourself. Honest with the people you want to share that love with. Honest about everything," he says.

We watch the water move slowly and peacefully over the lake. The sun is warm and welcoming and promises a day of possibilities. "Make some choices for yourself today, JP," Alvin says.

The afternoon is coming soon.

By mile three of Partington Trail, I know I'm in over my head. Mia Malik, who I've managed to keep pace with at karaoke, dancing, and night kissing, is smoking me on this hike. To call the trail *rustic* would be a gross understatement. We've been hiking for over an hour and Mia can't say for sure how much longer to the site. The terrain is rough and rocky in some stretches, then forested and green in others. Uphill, downhill, anything-but-chill, it's almost impossible for me to even recognize this as a trail.

"It's not on any of the maps we give out to guests," Mia says, "but there's not a better hike to see just how thick the mountain is with chestnut, oak, and birch."

I don't know if it's because I stayed up so late or got up so early, but I have to keep taking little breaks.

"I thought you city kids were used to walking everywhere," Mia quips, flashing me a smile. We pause in the shade of a red cedar. She passes me her water bottle.

I'm so out of breath, I can barely sip the water. "We definitely walk everywhere," I get out through an embarrassed smile, "but it's nothing like *this*." My black T-shirt, drenched in sweat, is pulled tight to my chest. My normal baggy fashion has become extremely formfitting. I catch Mia checking me out. I'm blushing and she's blushing and the whole thing is all at once silly and sexy.

"You look good when you're exhausted."

Flirty banter colors the next hour of our journey until we can hear the chorus of voices chanting. *Turkey Kick! Turkey Kick! Turkey Kick!*

Mia rips down the hill, fist pumping in the air, to join her work family in celebration. I pause and take in how much she's loved here. Everyone knows Mia and Mia knows everyone. Hugs and high fives go round-robin as folks spread out in the field. Dining room staff and the bellhops square off in a game of soccer. The front desk team are cracking jokes with the garden crew on the sidelines. The valets drink home brew and ginger beer cocktails from red plastic cups while the lifeguards see who can do the most cartwheels in a straight line.

To the west I see Jasmine and Ellis playing cornhole with the folks from the gift shop. They're smiling and laughing and looking so good together. To the east are two makeshift grills—large metal drums cut in half—blazing with hot rock charcoal. Beef, pork, and chicken sizzle on one while thick cuts of portobello mushroom, whole-ear corn, and skewers of spiced onions, peppers, and zucchini make the mountain air deliciously fragrant. Back in the city we have our share of block parties, but I've never been to anything like this.

"Hey!" a voice behind me calls. I turn around, startled. It's Bee, but something is different about her. "Look, I don't know what your deal is, JP," she says with a bracingly serious tone. "I don't know what weird thing you're doing with your family or what game you're trying to pull on staff, but you can just knock it off."

"I don't know what—"

"Cut the crap. Whatever you rich kids do to real-people workers in the city ain't gonna fly here. Got it?" she snaps.

"What are you talking about?"

"You're not talking right now. This isn't the Majestic Mountain House. This isn't the Upper Yup-side. You're in the wilderness. I know that you're not who you say you are."

Shook, I nod. I don't know what Bee knows about me, but

she's right that I haven't been honest with Mia about who I really am. As Bee walks off, I say, "I want to tell her. I'm going to tell her."

Without turning back to me she finishes, "Make sure that you do."

I slowly make my way down the hill. I nod at Jasmine and Ellis as I walk up to Mia by the picnic tables. Casserole dishes, pastel Tupperware, and woven baskets sit atop a pale gingham tablecloth. Little handwritten cards introduce a smorgasbord of Catskills specialties—radish raita lamb stew, mixed green salad with balsamic maple dressing, salted cornbread with pork belly and garden jalapeño.

Mia opens her well-worn daypack and pulls out four glass jars. She arranges them neatly in a little line with heavy spoons for serving. Cards in her old-time cursive read, *Dilly Beans*, *Mango Chutney*, *Dandelion Jelly*, and *Mike's Hot Mustard*.

"What's dandelion jelly?" I ask. Mia smiles as she loosens the shiny gold top. She runs a finger along the edge of the metal threads, picking up the flaky crystals of sweetness.

"Taste it," she says. Her finger is in my mouth for just a second, but my lips are swollen wanting more.

"That's delicious," I say, flushed with red.

"Dandelions are a really special flower. Assyrian people and now people in Iran, Iraq, Syria, Turkey, and Kuwait—use them as medicine. I think they're also beautiful to look at. Unfortunately, most of the people here think of them as weeds, so the gardeners pull them up and either compost or toss them. I pick up what I can to make the jelly."

I look at Mia and melt. Mia Malik, Countess of Condiments. Mia Malik, Mystic of Mount Majestic. Mia Malik, Mia

Malik. Mia Malik, how did I let it get to this point? How did I let you and me start with a lie?

"You feeling okay?" she asks. I'm anything but okay. Covered in cold sweat, my head is just spinning. I let Mia think that my cousins were my siblings, let her believe that my aunt and uncle were my parents, believe that I'm a rich boy going to Brown. It's so weird and so bad, I barely believe I'm here. I've been living this lie selfishly. Avoiding the truth to not feel all the things I feel when I think about my real family. Mia is under the impression I have a good family and that we've got it all together and that I'm actually fun to be around. But my real family is either chaotically absent from my life or dead, I've got nothing together, and—because of all this—I am not a good time.

"Mia," I start, my voice cracking.

"JP, you look terrible," she says.

"I need to tell you something . . ."

"No, dude, seriously," she stops me. "You look like death. I think you need to eat something."

Before I can even blink, we're sitting at a packed-out picnic table splitting a steaming hot bowl of spicy, sour soup. Everyone from the stables is joined up with us in a sound bath of chewing, slurping, and satisfied swallows. The earthy flavor of ginger, lemongrass, and chilies reactivates me. *I'm going to tell Mia everything and I'm going to do it now.*

"Mia, there's something I've been wanting to say to you," I start slowly.

"Oh, no. Wait . . . just . . . hold on one second. Hold that thought. I just have to . . . I'll be right back. Promise," Mia says, and then abruptly races up and away from the table and off toward the cornhole game. Was I about to spill my guts in front of Duke and the equine staff? I think I was. When Mia gets back, maybe we talk somewhere a little more private. I just need to set things straight. Get this lie off my back or go live on the moon or both. My anxiety is about to swallow me whole. Hands shaking, I take another sip of the soup. I've had this before.

"This is amazing. What is this?" I ask the table.

"It's Caloy's cansi. They make it every year," Duke replies. OMG. Cansi! I've only had this dish a handful of times. Last time was over two years ago at Mira and Elvi's. Dad and I had tried to make it at home, but we could never get the sour flavor quite right.

Speaking of the chef, I see Caloy over at the potluck table stirring the soup in a tall stock pot. I slurp the broth down loudly and head over. In front of Caloy's propane burner reads, *Cansi with NY sour fruit.*

"Kaibigan, this is the best cansi I've ever tasted," I start. Caloy, in true pinX fashion, shakes their head and deflects any and all compliments. "What is NY sour fruit?" I ask. Getting the sourness just right drove my dad crazy. He added grapefruit. *Too bitter.* Lemon and lime. *Too citrusy and sweet.*

"In the Philippines," Caloy explains, "you would use batwan fruit. Very cheap, very easy to find. In New York, there's no way to grow batwan. There's also no place to buy it, so I use sour cherries and a little vinegar."

Bee steps up to the potluck table and Caloy fills a bowl for her. She smiles at them then glares right at me. I feel sick all over again.

"Are you okay, JP?" Caloy asks.

"I started something wrong," I admit flatly.

"That happens sometimes," Caloy assures me. "I didn't start out making good cansi. Getting one thing wrong made me think that everything was wrong. But truthfully, there wasn't much I needed to change."

We talk for a long time, going over different cansi recipes. Caloy has successfully adapted versions for both vegetarian and vegan diets. They revel in getting the perfect red-orange color from fresh ground annatto seed.

"I always had these wrong turns and false starts making it, but I could hear my Lolo telling me the most important thing is to not give up when things are bad and especially not to give up when things are good."

I nod and try to remember advice my dad used to give me about resilience and staying with something even if it was hard. I think about Mia and me. I think about how things are so great. I shouldn't be afraid of fixing things. Correcting what's wrong; mending, fixing, strengthening are acts of resilience. They are acts of love.

Caught up in the moment, I say, "Caloy, you have to start your own restaurant. This cansi is seriously one of the best FilAm dishes I've ever eaten, *and I'm from freaking Jackson Heights!*"

Caloy pauses for a moment. "I learned how to cook from my Tito José. He worked in hospitality at a hotel in Brooklyn. When I was a kid, we always dreamed about starting a kainan together."

"That's awesome!" I exclaim. "What did you want to call it?"

Caloy smiles. "Tito Boomboom. That's Tito José's nickname."

"There's a place called Tito Boomboom in Jackson Heights. It does big business after church on Saturday and Sunday."

A pause from Caloy. "I know. Tito José owns it. I've never been."

Another pause. I don't want to assume anything about expansive identities or Caloy or normative identities and Tito Boomboom. Don't want to assume anything about the way church shows up in any of this. After another long beat of silence, Caloy waves their hand and shakes their head. They want to move on. An excited voice pierces the moment.

"JP!" yells Jasmine, iPhone pointed at me. "Say what you were going to say to Mia!"

"What?"

"Say what you were going to say to Mia," she repeats.

"Are you recording me?" I ask.

"Of course I'm recording you."

Mia grabs the phone from Jasmine and scowls. They mouth something back and forth, but I don't think either of them can understand what the other one is trying to say. I'm entering peak confusion when Caloy interjects, "Mia, isn't it time to take the group picture?"

MIA

This is the part I love the most. The group shot, the summer family portrait—the moment when we all get to stand up next to each other or lie down on the ground, make funny faces, scowl, or hold up the peace sign, bunny ears, or tickle someone just as the camera clicks. It's the one that happens during every single Turkey Kick since the 1950s, and the photos line all the halls in the back of the original building.

Sometimes I take my time going through those corridors and pick out the people I would have been friends with—the outsiders, the ones who are making silly faces or cocking their heads to the side. The ones dressed in costume or carrying props, wearing funny hats or sunglasses. I have my favorites and have been studying the way these photos have been done over the decades. It's what inspired me to do all the family portraits at the Mountain House. I started studying all the different ways people showed up together—the grandparents, cousins, the aunts and uncles, the siblings, the stepsiblings, the people who brought their animals and best friends—and I wanted to document that.

It's what made me start to document my own family too, even in their complicated moments. I wanted to find ways to hold them, to make them feel seen and loved. I saved up my entire first year of work at Majestic to buy my first SLR. It's the kind of camera where you can change lenses to make different types of special photographs, ones unlike any I had ever made before. Mx. Diaz, my art teacher, showed me how to use it and let me be the staff photographer for the yearbook. I started doing family portraits downtown in Monument on the weekends and people would come in all sorts of formations. It was donation-based, and we started calling it Family Monument.

I've been the staff photographer ever since, and it's my favorite moment because it really does feel like we're all connected, like we belong together, like we're family. That word. Something I never really felt a part of and something I am still searching for. There's energy here, and love.

"Come on, can everyone please get together? Over here—on the steps. Just line up by height or by spacial relationships. You know your windows. Find your spots and angles!"

"What is this?" JP asks. He is standing beside me now. "You want me to take it? You could get in it this year?"

"Yes!" Ellis shouts. "Show him how it's done and stand up here with us. You gotta be in it this year." I don't tell them that standing outside of the family portraits is one of my favorite things to do—so I can take it all in, so I can see it from afar. Part of it, but apart at the same time. But maybe this year, things are different.

"You sure?" I ask JP, and he holds his hands out.

"Just show me what to do." And so, I set the exposure, dialing in the aperture and shutter speed, and frame everything up exactly right. Then, I show him how to trip the shutter.

"Before you make the picture, make sure you got your breathing right."

"My breathing? What does breathing have to do with taking a picture?"

"You're not taking anything. You're *making* a photograph. Remember, slow breath, then squeeze the shutter." I hand off my most prized possession. I must really trust JP Abrigo. I run up to the steps to stand right next to Jasmine and Ellis, who have made space for me between them.

"Could you all . . . get a little closer together please?" JP shouts. I've placed him pretty far out in the field so that he can get everyone into the picture.

"Awww, you got Loverboy to take our photo. That's so sweet," Wolf whispers, and everyone that can hear him starts to giggle around me. A sea of snarky voices. "Has he said 'I love you' yet?" More laughs. "It's getting pretty late in the week, you know. Tomorrow's already Saturday, so you better get up on it, Malik."

"Shut up," I whisper shout behind me.

"I'm just trying to help you out—make sure you get that cash money."

"Never gonna happen," I hear someone else say, but I can't place who it is. I know there are at least a few other people who are betting against me.

"Can we stop talking about this, please?" I beg, hoping JP doesn't suspect anything.

"Everyone okay up there? I think I'm just gonna count down from three—is that cool?" JP yells at us.

"All good," I holler back.

"Yeah, it'll be all good once you give it up," Wolf says, starting to push it now.

"Shut the hell up," Jasmine says, full-on turning behind her.

"Come on. Stop being so sensitive. I'm just playing around."

"Well, it's not funny," I add, turning around now too.

"Uh . . . should I wait to, uh . . ." JP asks.

"Yeah, hold up, man," Ellis calls back. "Pull it together, y'all. Come on now."

The sea of bodies settles. JP counts to three. Click.

My mind sees things in pictures, photographs. Evidence. Click. Click. Roll film. Roll phone. Point. Shoot. Collect memories. Hold them close to me. That's the way it has always been. My whole life caught up in photographs or moving images. Could always see the way I wanted it to go. Holding the whole world in front of me.

The afternoon sun feels whole and warm. It's not perfect because I'm a total liar and don't know how I am supposed to get around this, but it is delicious and energetic and full of so much laughter and excitement. I feel it in my bones, so even when I can sense that JP is about to tell me something and that something seems like it could be *I love you,* I find myself stopping Jasmine from recording it. I can't do it. I don't want to. I can't face it. There is something about the way JP looks at me, all steady and close. The way he studies all the different changes that my face makes. We used to do close reads in my AP English Lit class. It was where we all read as slow and steady as possible. To really find the meaning and peel everything apart—unveil all that we needed to know. That's how I feel like JP is reading me. So close I almost can't breathe, but I want more. I want to stay longer and steadier, walk beside him to feel his breath near mine. I have not felt this kind of fire before, and it makes me unsteady and unbalanced. I'm all akimbo when he's around, so when it looks like it's almost going to happen, I cut Jasmine off. Wave my hand to say no. I don't want to do this right now and am not even sure how to get out from under it or away from it. Shook. That's exactly how I feel. I move to tell JP it's time for us to leave but see Wolf wobbling toward me.

"Baby, baby, baby," he calls out into the wild. His voice echoing throughout the mountains. He is reckless and loose tonight. He is also drunk, and I know this as soon as he weaves in my direction. I turn around and try to ignore him. His bravado. His excess. His know-it-all ways. Wolf gets close enough that I can smell the bourbon on his breath, and he leans over and pulls me toward him. "Look, come on, baby. Just gimme a second." He yanks harder now so that I have to take a few steps toward him. "You still wanna win this bet, huh?"

I look around me when he asks this and shake my head yes, since it's true. I do still want to walk away with enough money to get me across the country. I take note of the camera slung over my shoulder and think of the group shot we just made. The movement and pulse of all those smiles and all that friendship. We made a photograph to memorialize that. That's the work I want to do forever and so, in a way, this has nothing at all to do with JP. It has everything to do with leaving town and studying photography with people I have admired for so long. Yes, it is true I need to leave, but truer that I have to hurt someone who I am falling for just to get out of Monument.

"Can you please play it cool?" I ask Wolf, trying to untangle myself from his grip.

"But, baby. I can help you win the bet. You just gotta trust me."

"Get off me," I protest, trying not to make a scene, but starting to get pissed now. I can see JP and Ellis from the corner of my eye and they're on their way over.

"You wanna make your new man jealous, don't you? You wanna make him wonder what we've been up to or what we might be up to in the future. Don't you? Just give me a little . . ." And then he leans down and starts to move his mouth toward mine and I jerk away from him.

"Leave me alone, Wolf!" I shout it loud this time and instead of JP and Ellis running up to Wolf, they do something different. Something unexpected. They stand right beside me. Both of them looking dead at Wolf, who is sweating now. They do not threaten him with violence or act like they're about to fight. It's just like some unwritten code that they've agreed on. Wolf does not deserve their sweat or their energy or their riot. They stay calm.

"Leave me alone," I say again, steadier this time. I know what I want, and I have a crew behind me to help me get it.

"Such a bitch," Wolf says.

This sets Jasmine, who has been standing just behind Ellis, totally off. She pushes JP and me to the side, pulls her right arm back, and socks Wolf right in the eye, his body hiccupping back and tripping into the grass. He holds his palm to his face and a few people around us *ohhh* and *ahhh* at him.

"Keep your mouth to yourself," Jasmine says. "You got that?"

I look at Jasmine and grab her hand beside me. The two of us standing in front of JP and Ellis. Our bodies monumental, grand, in front of him.

"You know I do not condone violence," Jasmine says, looking at Ellis now. "But he needed to get his ass kicked."

I smile at Jasmine and mouth, *Thank you*. Then look at JP. "Let's get out of here for real."

JP

We move fast. Fast past the picnic tables with all the tasty potluck offerings. Fast through the field of milkweed and poppies. Mia names other flowers that I've never heard of—purple hollyhock, hummingbird mint, and coneflower. We pass the employee shuttle van on the side of what is barely a road. *Is that how Caloy got all their chef stuff up here?* Our bodies are synchronized. Left foot, right foot, hike, run, run, hike. We've probably gone a mile and a half before the adrenaline dip shows up and slows us down.

"That was *a lot*," Mia punctuates. "Field parties are usually more party, less Jasmine in fight-song mode."

"Jasmine is a good friend," I say. "And a *total badass*."

Mia laughs and keeps pushing ahead. All of a sudden, we're on a never-ending incline. The terrain is rocky and dry with less green to shield us from the sun. An arrow-shaped sign, barely a foot off the ground, points forward reading *Garlic Press—1.5 miles*.

"What is the Garlic Press?" I ask, somewhat afraid of the answer.

"Well," Mia starts gently, "it's the way up to Bald Creek Ridge. The Ridge has the most magical view of everything."

"Yeah, but *what is the Garlic Press?*" I ask again, this time my voice with a slight, barely detectable quiver.

"Don't be a punk, JP," Mia simplifies. "The Garlic Press is *fun*. You want fun, right? Not some as-the-crow-flies basic hike, right?" I start to nod as Mia lays into a description that activates my acrophobia. "It's awesome, JP. Like nosebleed, head in the sky, eating clouds, ears popping, nerves shooting, heart bumping, breakneck adventure."

"Oh, so like a *real* adventure?" I ask.

"Like a real *breakneck* adventure," she answers.

"Yeah, yeah. That sounds really great. My ears are already popping. I've never broken my neck before. Sounds like a really good time."

We hike another steep mile. Hot and gravelly in the scorching sun, loose and muddy in the mountain shade. Mia knows the path like she knows the name of every flower on this trail. "Trout lily, yarrow," she adds to the list. "Oh wow!" she exclaims. "Look at the orchids!"

Mia takes us off the path into a sun-drenched bounty of surreal pinks, greens, and yellows. Time stops as I feel the pleasure of her pleasure. She glides her hands gently over the petals of a large flesh-colored flower. I touch the smooth stem of a similar-looking yellow bloom. "That's a large yellow lady's slipper," she tells me.

"Is that one a large pink lady's slipper?" I ask.

"Actually, it's just called a pink lady's slipper. These are high-altitude orchids. In a week or two this will all look different. We found them in peak bloom. I think orchids are my favorite type of flowers. You ever notice how they look like . . ." Just then, Mia hits pause.

"Vaginas?" I ask without thinking. Then another pause. "Did my saying 'vagina' make things weird? I'm not trying to make anything weird."

"I don't think I've ever talked to a guy who used the word 'vagina' so earnestly," Mia responds. "Most guys I know and even some of the girls can't even say the word. They say 'pussy' and they're almost always saying it to call something or someone weak. That's some bullshit."

"Total bullshit," I agree.

"Pussies . . . er . . . vaginas are strong as hell!" Mia fires off. "They can tighten and stretch to push babies into the world, if they want to."

"Yes to all of that," I say.

"I appreciate your love and support for vaginas," Mia says, laughing now.

"There's a nurse in the family. She gives me sex-ed talks every time she sees me."

"Ohh, that's cool," Mia says with a raised eyebrow. "So you know a lot about sex, huh? Did you know that the clitoris has only one single purpose?"

"Pleasure," I say.

Mia's face lights up in a smile that spreads across her face. "That's right. Tell me more about that," Mia asks.

"Well, there's the outer labia, inner labia, the clitoris and its hood—stimulation works differently for everyone, but the clitoris is so awesome because of its sole purpose, and . . ."

Am I ~~explaining~~ mansplaining sexual stimulation right now? Shut up, JP. Shut up.

I pause. "I'm sorry for talking so much."

Mia stares at me, head cocked to the side. She is enjoying every moment of my incessant awkwardness. My face flushed, lips purple, I'm drowning in discomfort. Mia smiles wide. "I like that you know so much about what can make someone feel good. That's powerful. That's . . ."

"Sexy?" I ask, trying to get a lifeline. Trying to make it all sound like I know what I am doing.

"Yes. Definitely and completely sexy. Come on. I have more to show you," she says.

The next leg of the trail is tricky, so we stay focused. As the pathway narrows, things start to quiet down and get more serious. I find myself increasingly losing my footing and tipping off-balance. Mia pulls herself over the top of a huge boulder and offers me a hand up. The stakes are definitely rising. We move into the isolated shade of tight rocks and high mountain walls.

"It's all scrambling from here," she says at the first narrow passage. "Use your hands, JP."

What the heck does that mean?

A cool breeze tightens my skin as Mia looks my body up and down, finishing her gaze on my eyes. Slow and hesitating, I bring my hands to her hips. I can feel the warmth of her body on my palms. She puts the weight of her hands over mine, pulling me forward. Her chest pressed up against mine, our lips so close to touching, Mia whispers, "I mean use your hands to help you on the trail, smart guy. You don't want to lose your balance up here."

She slides my left hand from her right hip to the rock wall. "Do what I do, and don't fall," she punctuates. For the next quarter mile, I learn scrambling from the best. Where Mia puts her feet, I put my feet. Where Mia takes a handhold, I take a handhold. Somewhere between trail hiking and mountain climbing, this stretch of the journey is as much mental as it is physical.

I understand now why this path is called the Garlic Press. The trail thins and narrows. Mia bends and contorts and dances high-level ballet through small windows in the rock. My body, less sure, less confident, struggles just to squeeze through. I can hear the sound of falling water as we belly crawl under a choke of earth. The sound grows full and abundant as we rise to our feet. Mia dusts off her hands as we emerge onto a natural terrace adjoining a waterfall.

"You're going to have to trust me on this next part," Mia shouts over the boom of fast-moving water. "We're going to jump through that waterfall!"

"This feels super dangerous! Are you sure there's not another path we can take?" I yell out.

Mia laughs and wrenches me into a deep kiss. As the sound of the water thunders, she takes my left hand in her right. "On three," she says into my ear.

"Mia, I can't see anything past the water—"

"One . . ."

"What if—"

"Two . . ."

I erupt in sweat.

Then everything is slow motion. Our lungs heaving, our hearts pounding like mad, we leap. The excitement of our voices is swallowed in a wash of round sounds. Together, our bodies pierce the cascade of white and royal blue. In this moment, we are flying. We are everything.

Hands clasped tightly, muscles taut and strong, we land on a gentle slope of bedrock. Inertia tumbles us apart. Mia is laughing and howling pure joy as she jumps up and down. I am collapsed with my back on the ground. Yells of excitement and sighs of relief bounce off the walls of the narrow split in the mountain. The weight of the water pulls every inch of our clothing into a heaving silhouette of collarbones, chests, waists, and thighs. I spread my arms wide, gripping the rock on either side of me. I'm trembling. My relief is gone as quickly as it came. Mia's roar simmers to slow exhales, her deep breath in conversation with mine. Everything is heightened. Built up with no path, no way to release.

I sit up, my hands still holding the walls for dear life. "Mia," her name is all I can say. I feel the hot and cold of myself rising from the pit of my stomach. The whole of her comes forward. Toward. Somehow, I feel the hot and cold of her too. She lowers herself over my body. Body. My body. Her body.

Sitting over me, her hands take mine from the wall to her hips. I am under the weight of her now, her hands holding my face, mouths passing want and breath and guidance. We are closer than ever before. And again, we leap.

SATURDAY

MIA

"JP! JP, wake up!"

"What? What happened?" he asks, his eyes still closed, both of us curled over one another. His chest pressed against my back, holding me.

"We fell asleep," I say, sitting up and stretching my arms above my head. I look at my watch. 5:47 a.m. The sun is just starting to peek out—all gold and orange.

"What?" He moves fast, sitting up now. "Nooo. Ahhh, nooo. I am dead."

"But your parents knew you were out last night, right?" JP had texted that he was in a heated tennis match with some other future Ivy Leaguers that he met up with after dinner. "And you told Tiffany where you really were, right?"

"Oh, right! Okay." He checks his phone and reads the messages out loud: *"JP—we got you covered. Say hi to Mia for us! Mom and dad got back from dinner, and we said you were asleep. All good! Have fun! Get back before they wake up!* My cousin's use of exclamation marks is out of control."

"Maybe she's just really excited for you!" I say, standing up.

My face goes pink thinking about last night. JP's body close to mine.

"Because of you," he says, stretching his body. "We gotta hurry, right? How long will it take to get back down?"

"Under an hour if we move fast."

"I can do it."

"Then follow me," I say, and we start to make our way past the bloodroot and wild geranium. I point to things as we go, and when we've been out for a stretch, I remember Jasmine saying I should tell JP the truth about my family. Maybe revealing that part of me will ease some of my guilt for going ahead with the bet. Or maybe it will get me closer to winning it. Either way, I feel anxiety climb its way inside my chest.

"JP," I start, "I wanted to tell you something."

He pauses. "You okay? Do you need anything?" And I think about the ways JP has paid attention to me this week. How attentive he has been. How sincere. Checking in with me, asking how I'm doing. I've never been with anyone like that.

"No, I'm good . . . I just . . . I wanted to let you know something that I, um . . . something about me that I didn't totally share with you before."

"Oookkkaaayy," he says. "Should we pause? We can sit."

"No, no. Let's keep moving. You don't need to have any more fights with your mom and dad. It's just . . . when you were telling me about your family and I saw you all together this week, it was so . . . cool to see how much they love you and how amazing you are with Tiff and Cass and I . . . I guess I wanted you to think my family was the same way too, so I kind of made up a perfect family to match yours . . ."

"Oh my god . . . I have to tell you something too . . ."

"Wait, let me finish. I feel like what I'm about to say . . . is a lot. Ummm . . . when I was in the ER on Thursday . . . I saw my dad."

JP stops walking. "Wait, is he . . . ?"

"And it's not the first time I have seen him there. I . . . my dad . . . and my mom too, actually, are both suffering from substance use disorder. They have been in and out of rehab facilities since I was a kid, but over the last few years, they have been living in shelters and on the streets. Sometimes here, sometimes a few towns over. But that perfect family I tried to pretend I was a part of . . . it doesn't exist."

"I'm so sorry," he says.

"You don't have to be sorry. Just be thankful that yours is real. That you have them in your life, because not everyone does."

"No, I know. I agree, and they're not perfect—"

"Look, even if they're not perfect, they love you. I spent a lot of time trying to pretend my parents were somewhere else." I grab JP's arm and start walking again, knowing we are on the clock and I have to get him back to the room before his family wakes up.

"So you pretended to be someone else, that your family was someone else. I get that, because—"

"Exactly. It was a game of how to pass the time when they were away and I wasn't sure if they were coming back. They were always in and out of town. And it felt too heavy to tell the truth."

"I know that feeling. Exactly."

"It just took me apart. The sadness felt like a blanket, all heavy and suffocating, so I just never said it. It became a lie I told again and again. *Mom and Dad are traveling for work. They're out of town for business. They're busy with family in another state, down South.* When all the time they were just taking care of themselves, of their own addictions. They weren't taking care of me or our life together. So, my aunt June, my mom's sister, took me in. And that felt good, but I couldn't shake the feeling that no one wanted me." I pause then and guide JP through a thicket of overgrown grass and weeds on the path. "I'm sorry. Is this too much?"

"No. Not at all. It's your life. How could it be too much? I'm listening," he says.

"Thank you," I say, and keep on. It feels good to finally tell JP the truth, and I can't stop the words from spilling out of me. "So, I was there in body with my aunt, but I did everything I possibly could to figure a way out for me, for her too. I am blood, but not her daughter, and I know she has another life she wants to live without me in it. And that's not to sound harsh or anything like that. It's just the truth. It's just the way it is."

JP keeps nodding his head like he understands something he is not telling me, and I don't want to stop talking. I don't want us to end, because there is something about the way he listens and the way he stays paying the closest of attention. He makes me feel so alive. His eyes on me, and steady.

"Can I ask you what they are addicted to?"

"Name it. So I don't drink or do any drugs or . . . Not any of it. No way am I going down that path. So, that's why I've always been like this—followed the rules, staying in line, not doing anything that could hurt myself or someone else. And as soon as I could, I got a job. Started babysitting when I was twelve and got this job at sixteen. Somehow, them being sick made me resilient as hell."

"I can see that. I see that every time I'm with you," JP says. "So it's just you and your aunt?"

"And my cousin, Chelsea. Chelsea's dad's not in the picture, so I was like her little auntie. Feeding and bathing and changing diapers, helping her with homework, getting her ready for school. Aunt June is always busting her ass to try and hustle for us, but it's never enough. It's like you're chasing this forever moving ship and every morning when you wake up, the ship has moved farther and farther away and you can't keep up with it and you can't catch it, so you're just out there on the lake and it feels like you are drowning. Like you can't catch enough air. That's what my life feels like . . . so much of the time."

We walk in silence for the next section of the trail. Can start to hear the resort wake up under the perfectly clear sky. It is Saturday and the Fourth of July. It is the day I have to win the bet. And I've gone and done the one thing I said I wouldn't. I've told JP the truth about who I am, and instead of being a jerk, he's just listening. He's just real.

"I want people to feel like they're being seen. Like they are wanted. I grew up feeling like it didn't matter if I was here or not. That kinda thing can mess with your head. It has messed with mine for sure. I never know where I belong or who I belong to. Why any of it even matters in the long run. I want to belong. I want to be with people who love and want me. That's all."

"I want you," JP says, "and not in that superficial kind of way that people say to each other. I want to know you. The easy and the complicated. I want to know everything about you. I really, really do."

JP

I barely make it to the room in time to catch a shower and change clothes before meeting up with Tiffany and Cass outside the dining room. It's Fourth of July and there's no Kids' Club today. Tita Dali is waiting there, arms crossed, tapping her foot like a rich villain from some SoCal drama. I'm prepared to get grilled about my absence from last night.

"Make sure that everyone is changed and on the main lawn before seven p.m.," she reminds me without any discernible malice. "You don't want to miss the fireworks tonight, Boy." A quick turn, and she is gone.

Today I'm just expected to be the help. I get it. I stayed out by myself all night. Before that, I spoke my mind when nobody asked me anything. Before that, I was the pain-in-the-ass teenage kid who crashed the guest room. Today I'm just a babysitter, and that's fine by me.

"Did you say hi to Mia for us?" Tiffany asks.

I freeze up as my mind wanders its way back to last night. It started with a day hike. There was spicy cansi with sour cherries instead of batwan fruit. There was Bee putting me in my place. There was me trying to explain everything to Mia in front of the entire staff. There was Jasmine's first-round knock-out of Wolf. There was the neck-break adventure of the Garlic Press. And there was Mia and me . . . Mia and me, and all the stars in the sky . . .

"Wake up, JP," Tiff snaps. "We've got a lot to do today."

"Yes. I'm awake now," I affirm. "What's on the list?"

"It's our last full day here and we want to go in the lake!"

Tiff and Cass ping-pong a million water activities back and forth. Swimming, diving, canoe rides, water volleyball—the sound of their voices fades into the background as it sets in for me that today *is the last full day that I'm here.* I have to talk to Mia again. All this time at Majestic Mountain House started with a lie. It's time to close things out with the truth.

MIA

After saying goodbye to JP, I can't get my heart rate to calm down. I don't want to go back to the bunkhouse. I want to get rid of all this energy and fire. Last night made me feel unstoppable. Like I could be myself with JP, but to feel that way, I had to trick someone . . . someone I'm falling in love with. How do I say that this is a game I cannot play any longer?

I walk out to Lake Majestic and stare across the iciness, quiet, and calm. The lake is so cold it shocks me. My bones feel like they could break in the chill, but I like it. I need it. The weightlessness, the energy below. It's the lack of fear, near drowning beneath all the clear, glassy surface. I am no longer the rule follower. I am trying to be my own self. Drift, drifting. I swim away from shore, thinking, rummaging, feeling, tumbling in my mind. Try to turn my brain off so I can stop judging and questioning. I don't want to see myself as lacking. I'm not the girl without parents, the orphan who is so damn sad, who people say is broken. I'm not broken or broke down. I don't want that to define me anymore. Lap after lap. When I get out, I see Ellis standing above me.

"You scared the crap out of me," Ellis says.

"I'm fine. Don't worry about me. What are you doing up so early?"

"I was coming to find you is what I'm doing. You can't be out here swimming alone. You know that's not safe. You know the rules."

"What rules? I don't know anything. I haven't been playing by the rules all summer. We both know that."

"It happened, huh?"

"What?" I ask.

"You fell for him, didn't you?"

I shake my head yes and wipe the tears away from my eyes.

"I knew it. I could see it last night. You know what, I could actually see it on the dance floor during karaoke, but I wasn't positive until I saw you hand your camera over to him at the picnic. That was proof right there."

"I'm so clouded right now. My mind is not in the right place. And I have completely rocked my entire life. Something I did as a dare is about to come back and completely ruin me and him and . . ."

"So just tell him the truth. What if you just admitted what's happening and that you lied? Just be honest with him and tell him how you really feel. I think he might actually understand."

"Who would understand?" Wolf asks, loud as hell, showing up at the edge of the lake in sunglasses covering his black eye, all hungover and sloppy. "Who are we talking about over here? Sweet Loverboy JP Abrigo?"

"What are you doing here? Just stay out of it," I say, so frustrated that I ever fell for this stupid bet.

"Damn, harsh. Already you're trying to get me gone, huh? As if you never wanted me."

"You know I didn't want you," I say back, knowing he's trying to get under my skin, and not falling for it this time.

"That's not what it seemed like when you were—" And before he can say anything else, I push him into the lake, the muddy beach part that we're standing beside. I don't have time for his bullshit or his ego or his reminiscing about the past. I do not belong to him or anywhere near him. He stumbles and falls right over, the mud caking his skin. He stands back up and he's pissed.

"All you do is bring trouble around you, you know that, Malik? You wreck everything in your path. You mess it all the way up. Just like your good old mom and dad," he says, smiling at me.

"Screw you. The fact you're even bringing them up just shows what a baby you are. Crybaby. You're afraid to even be in the water," I say, watching the way he's brushing himself off and moving away from the lake.

"Oh, so you think you're all that, Malik?"

"Yeah, I do. I think I got you beat at everything."

"You're serious?"

"Yeah, I could beat you. I could out-hike you, I could out-hospitality your ass, and I could absolutely, definitely whoop you going across the lake."

"Oh, you're on. Let's do this," he says, peeling his shirt off and throwing it to the side. "Clothes on or off?" he asks, and starts to laugh at his own joke.

"Hey," Ellis says, "I kind of don't think we should be racing this early in the morning before everyone is up and the guards are out. Let's not be stupid."

But that's exactly what I want to do right now. Not listen to logic, not care about what other people think we should do or how we should act. Wolf messed with the one good thing in my life last night, almost ruined all my chances with JP before I even got a shot at telling him the truth. If this is gonna end, I'm gonna be the one to do it. Wolf doesn't get to be the one to screw it up.

"No, we're racing," I say. "And if I win . . . when I win, you leave JP alone and you don't sabotage it and you don't mess with his head, and you *definitely* don't share any other details about me or us. You keep your mouth shut."

"I mean, that feels so harsh to me," he laughs. "Last night was a joke. I was just messing with him, and you went and got all sensitive. You know I was playing around."

"Yeah, well, it wasn't funny. So, when I beat you, you leave him alone. Got it?"

"Yeah, yeah, but you're not gonna beat me, so what do we do then? What if I win?"

"If you win, I will cover your early morning shifts for the next three weeks."

"Mia, that's messed up," Ellis says, clearly still not getting behind our plan. "STOP MAKING BETS! You'll ruin the whole rest of your summer if you do that."

"I am not gonna lose," I say. I know I can win. I have to.

"Fine. But let the record show that the two of you are complete fools to be doing this and I don't like it at all."

"Ellis, you call the time. Whoever makes it across the lake and back first wins. No stopping. No playing around."

"Call it, baby," Wolf says, and I can see his smile light up. A wolf for sure. Or snake. Or something that can easily hurt its prey.

Wolf and I stand together in the same muddy beach that Wolf fell into. The still morning sun is just starting to heat up. We both get into starting positions and Ellis calls it. "Three, two, one, go!" And we both shoot off into the water. There's no use opening your eyes because the lake is completely dark underneath. I do not think about the fish or the snakes inside. I just swim as hard and as fast as I possibly can. My arms and legs pushing and weaving inside the water. Lifting and jutting. My breath going faster and more ragged.

I can see Wolf is pushing with all of his energy, the water splashing and crashing around us. I sip air when I can, push harder, swim faster, catch breath, push, swim, breath, push, swim, breath, until I can't see or hear anything and the cold slips in all around me and it feels like I could be soaring over the water or could become some fish or animal, accustomed to moving fierce and impossible underwater. I am fearless. I do not think about the finish line yet or cheering or navigating anything except stretching my whole body beneath the surface until I hit the opposite shore.

Once my hand touches, I turn around and speed back past Wolf, do not wait or slow down. If I am going to win this race, it will take some type of ungodly energy, and so I tag it and reverse, heading back to the other side of the lake, where I can see Ellis waving his arms at us to return. I push again, harder, faster, my legs starting to go numb underneath the cold, my arms aching, heart jumping, racing. I feel Wolf coming up beside me, but kick away. I do not have time for this anymore. I don't wanna be the girl who gets caught up in some guy who cares more about himself and his ego, who only loves the sound of his own voice and cares more about what everyone else thinks than what she thinks. No, I am not that girl anymore at all. The finish line is close, closer than I thought possible.

Then I hear Ellis screaming for me to stop, his voice ragged and piercing. "Mia, Mia! Stop. Oh my god, stop!"

I pull out of the water, head up, legs treading below, and see Ellis pacing and waving his arms, shouting and yelling at me. "It's Wolf! He's caught on something. You gotta help him!" And the shouting scares me. We are at the edge of Lake Majestic, all of it ink black. I try not to panic looking at Wolf, who is gulping water as if he's getting pulled down over and over by something underneath.

Ellis is still pacing the shore. He knows not to jump in after us. One of the first rules is that if someone is drowning you do not go in without a flotation device, without something that could save you in case the drowning person tries to take you down too. That is Lifeguarding 101, but there is no one out here. We are in this all alone. I swim over to Wolf, who is struggling now, going up and under, his arms flailing about the surface, his mouth and face up to the sky struggling to catch breath.

I swim as fast as I can to where Wolf can hear me. "Wolf, Wolf, you have to calm down. I think you are stuck on the vines."

"Help me!" he screams, and my heart rate starts to rip and shatter in my chest.

"I have to run for help," Ellis calls out to me.

"Not yet," I say. "Just let me try this!" I know my words are falling short, and that my decision could shape everything, but I am worried we don't even have enough time for Ellis to leave and get help. We are stuck. We are fools for even trying this, but I push on. "Keep treading, Wolf. Keep your head above water!" I am shouting and kicking my own legs below, trying to stay afloat and feeling like I am failing somehow.

I use my hands to push Wolf away from me so that he can't grab on and take me down under with him. I swim below to find what is holding him. Try to open my eyes in the murky water. It is thick and dark below, but I can see vines twisted around his ankle. I rush up again to take a big gulp of air. Ellis and Wolf are both shouting now. Gulp, gulp, go back underneath and hold my breath just long enough to untangle his ankle and push him up into the air. He struggles for another minute, shocked that he is free.

"Swim to shore," I yell, pushing him on.

He is coughing and spitting, his voice cracking and hoarse. He grabs onto the branch that Ellis is holding out and pulls himself to the beach. By the time I get there he is slouched over and sobbing.

I look around and realize we could have lost him. I would have been responsible for his death, and when I think about that, I start to cry too, thinking about my decisions. Ellis and I both move over to sit beside him and that's when he starts to rage. "I hate you for this, Malik!" he yells.

"I saved you," I say. "Are you kidding me? You're the one that wanted to race me in the first place. It wasn't me; it was you," I remind him, and he scoffs, starts to laugh while still spitting up loads of water. "You're welcome," I say.

"I'm ruining this for you, Malik. Watch out. Because it's over!"

I walk into the bunkhouse and see Jasmine still there, standing at the mirror and adjusting her uniform for the long day ahead.

"You okay?" she asks as soon as she sees me.

I choke up again. Can't help myself. Like I have been holding in this hurricane of emotions and tears. All of me feels wrecked and helpless.

"Oh no, come here." And I walk over to Jasmine's arms, and we make our way to the bunkhouse floor, and she holds me steady and close. I do not tell her that I needed this, that I wanted to be held and comforted. Try and ignore the panic that has been setting in ever since I said goodbye to JP a few hours ago. The way the morning shimmered around me. Soft and glittering, like we were both blanketed in it. I did not want to leave him. Not for a second. And so now I am here and feeling sick to my stomach but trying so hard to stay steady, stay calm.

"I think I'm in love with him," I say, betraying all the tranquility I was searching for. "What am I supposed to do now? I'm not supposed to be falling in love with *him*. It's the other way around," I say. Of course, she knows, but I need to hear it all out loud. "It was supposed to be easy. Simple. He was supposed to be full of himself and just like every other goat on permanent vacation . . ."

"But he's not."

"I know. How am I gonna do this? I don't wanna hurt anyone. I couldn't even hurt Wolf, and he is the absolute worst."

"Wait, what? What are you talking about?"

"Ugh. We were just at the lake, and we decided to race because I am basically full of very bad decisions, and then his leg got caught on a bunch of vines underwater and I pulled him out."

"You what? You buried the lead here. Did you not want to start with the near-death experience out there on the water?" Jasmine asks, pulling away from me now and looking me over, realizing that my hair is still damp.

"Ellis was there. He helped me. We're fine now. It's just . . . I don't wanna hurt anyone anymore. Not now. Not ever."

"Ellis was there?" Jasmine asks, and it is clear where her mind is lately.

"Or should I have said your boyfriend, Ellis?" I tease. "At least one of us should have an actual love-filled summer. You better tell him how you really feel."

"Okay, Ms. Bossy. And what exactly are you going to do?"

Just then the bunk door comes flying open and Layla rushes in, clipboard in her hand and pen on paper like she is ready to make things happen. "Oh my god! Jasmine and Mia, I am so glad to see the two of you. Is everything good?" she asks, eyeing us and seeing that we are still sitting on the floor and I'm wiping away tears.

"No, no, we're all good. We were just catching up," Jasmine says, standing up and helping me to my feet at the same time. "What do you need?"

"Oh, just about everything you can imagine. We are slammed for this afternoon. A few people called out sick and there were a ton of new last-minute reservations for the Fourth of July cookout, so I am deeply understaffed." She looks right at me. "I know I put you on suspension and I know you are pissed about losing the days and especially the money, but I am hoping that you will do me a huge favor and clock in to help today?"

I look at Jasmine, who nods her head at me. I want to shout, *Hell yes I can help out today* and confess I was going to be there anyway, but I was going to have to sneak around so, um . . . yes, I will be there, especially since I have to figure out what I am supposed to be doing with the rest of my life. Instead, I just say, "Oh yeah. Yes, I can do that."

"Good. That's good. That's what I was hoping to hear. So, can you two get finished up and meet me down at the main lawn in fifteen minutes? We have a ton to do this morning before the party gets started. And Mia, please remember that you are still to keep a very low profile, and whatever you do, please avoid the entire Abrigo family as much as you possibly can. Got it?"

"Yes, absolutely. I will not go anywhere near them," I lie, and as soon as Layla is out the door, I look over at Jasmine. "What?"

"Nothing, I just . . . what are you gonna do now?"

"I can't do it," I say finally. "It's over. Now I just have to figure out how to end it."

JP

I'm standing on the shore of the bay beach while my cousins splash and play in the shallow water. Cass throws an oversize beach ball into the air. Tiff launches herself out of the water to head it between two beach chairs set up as a soccer goal. They cheer and shout and carry on and on.

As the temperature rises, I pull off my shoes and wade ankle-deep into the cooling waters of Lake Majestic. *Lake Majestic, Mount Majestic.* Tomorrow we're set to leave and there's no telling when I'll find my way back. I don't think I've ever been to a more beautiful place. This has been the most unexpected year, and the most unexpected summer of my life.

"Hey! JP!" calls Ellis from the trail behind. The oversize box in his arms has little flags taped all over the sides. "How's your Fourth of July?"

I shake my head. "You know, July Fourth is also Filipino Independence Day."

"Who did the islands claim independence from?" he asks.

"The United States."

He nods and smiles his knowing smile. Then Ellis quotes

Frederick Douglass: "The rich inheritance of justice, liberty, prosperity, and independence, bequeathed by your fathers, is shared by you, not by me. This Fourth of July is *yours* . . ."

Then in unison, we say, "Not *mine*."

"It's a complicated world, JP."

I nod and smile my less knowing smile. "I'm waiting on it not to be."

"Well, it's a big day here. Glad I caught you," he says, turning back to the Mountain House. "I've gotta get these flags up to the gift shop, but we should figure out a time to hang in the city."

"Trip to Midtown Comics?" I offer.

"One hundred!"

With that, Ellis is off to work and I'm back to living my best beach life. The kids and I make "chocolate" mud pies, doughnuts, and cupcakes. Cass writes his favorite words in the sand with a stick. *Bayanihan, Mango, Jupiter, Butt.* He laughs his head off crossing the double *t* in the latter.

Morning is about to turn into afternoon. We'll all need lunch soon. For one last lake activity I recommend making wishes on the dock and then heading to the dining hall. Tiff raises the stakes.

"We should go to Big Rock," she says. "We can swim across the lake and make a wish from there."

"C'mon, JP. Let's do this!" Cass shouts.

I check with the lifeguards to make sure that our timing works. Then, somewhat nervously, I agree to attempt the swim again. I'd feel so much better if Mia was here. Cass and Tiffany are expert swimmers with years of private lessons under their belts, so I'm not worried about them. But I am worried about my wish and if it will ever come true.

I start to make the wish in my head. *I want Mia to forgive—*

"That's not a good wish, JP," Tiff advises. My eyes open wide. My head turns to my cousins both looking at me disapprovingly. *How are they reading my mind right now?*

"Make a better one," Cass counsels.

I do.

We stand side by side at the edge of the deepwater dock. Before I can count off or figure some other way for us to start, Cass and Tiff dive in and start cutting through the water. I jump feetfirst and feel the coolness of the lake take me in. Maybe I'm not the best swimmer. Maybe I'm a bit out of my depth. But I really need a wish right now.

I bring myself up to the surface, take a deep breath, and start making my way across the lake. Slow and steady, I'm feeling good. I don't think about the way the water keeps itching my nose. I'm more concerned that I can't see more than a few inches into a murky future. Can't see my feet. Can't see my hands. Can't see Mia leading me through to the other side. By the time I make it to Big Rock, Tiff and Cass are already standing in the sunshine waiting. "You're halfway there, JP!" Tiff cheers. "C'mon!"

I pull myself out of the water and onto the mossy rock. I don't need a wish. Don't need to lie. It's time to step into the light.

MIA

"Hey, team," Layla calls out. "Can we all gather together before we get this party started, please?"

We start to bunch around the picnic tables, and I notice how close Ellis and Jasmine are standing. I think what they have is real love, the kind that can't be tricked or faked. It didn't take a dare or a bet to get them there.

"I want to first thank you all for the immense amount of work that you have put in already this summer. I know many of you have been nonstop on the weekends since Memorial Day and those of you who are full time have been in summer mode since May, so I want you to know how much I appreciate you. Please remember this is a big day for the Lake Majestic community. Not only is it a celebration of our country . . ." A few groans are heard in the crowd.

"I just don't understand why people love red, white, and blue so much," Ellis whispers.

"It's the stars and stripes for me," Jasmine says. "Just straight up tacky for a super problematic holiday. Let's focus on Juneteenth instead," she says, and Ellis gives her a fist bump.

"We did a whole unit senior year studying the Declaration of Independence and our teacher kept asking us who they were talking about when they wrote that 'all men are created equal' and had a right to 'Life, Liberty, and the pursuit of Happiness.' She kept asking who that vision was for."

"Definitely not Black or Native Americans or Asian Americans," Ellis says.

"And not women either," Jasmine adds. "And who the hell were they hoping would be happy and able to pursue the life they wanted?"

"White freaking men," I say.

"You guessed it," Ellis says.

"And because of that, I really don't want to be decorating tables with star-filled balloons or streamers or patriotic top hats and stickers," I say. What kind of party am I supposed to be throwing right now anyway? I try and steady myself. *Get focused. Sharpen up. Figure my life out and get out of town.*

"Could we please focus up here?" Layla says after all of us have had time for our side conversations. "I know, I know. Fourth of July is very complicated and believe me, I get it. But we work at the Majestic Mountain House, and we will put on a good face for our guests . . ."

"Goats," Jasmine whispers to me, and *bahhh*s quietly in my ear.

"We will make everyone feel welcome and we will celebrate with the best of the best tonight!" She gestures at the massive television sets that have been stationed around the main lawn. "We have a camera here and across the lawn"—she motions to each corner—"and they are placed to get footage of the grounds, of all the fun and wonder that you all have set up. I have pinpointed a few of our staff who will help to run the cameras, and the large TVs are just another way to add excitement and fun to the evening. You can enjoy yourself and watch your fellow guests along the lawn, and then of course once the fireworks start, these screens will have footage of other fireworks shown across the East Coast. We are trying very hard to get into the technology frontier," she finishes, laughing. "Any questions?"

"This is gonna be a long night," I say to Jasmine, who shrugs her shoulders at me.

"When are you gonna tell him?"

"As soon as I see him, or as soon as the time is right. But it will be tricky to pull him away—Layla is gonna have her eyes on me all night."

"Don't worry about Layla. I got you covered. Just find JP and figure the rest of this out."

Jasmine is right and so that's what I do. I work and keep my eyes open and try not to think about JP and the mountains and the way his body felt against mine as we scrambled to the top. I try not to think about the way his face looks when he's listening to me and I feel caught up and wrecked and alive and loved all at the same time. Will I ever feel this way again?

I do all this while catering to everyone at the party, which is now full of people cheers-ing and laughing, asking for more drinks and more hot dogs and more scoops of ice cream. Kids are running through the grounds with sparklers flying from their hands and asking about the fireworks, what time they'll start and for how long they'll go. It's a nonstop celebration.

Finally, I see the Abrigo family walking toward the crowd. Just seeing JP sends goose bumps all over my body. There is so much I want to tell him. So much more time I want to spend. But I brace myself.

As soon as he sees me, he starts my way, quickly leaving his family behind, and we meet in the middle of children hollering, people dancing, lights dimming and the night setting in. Both of us standing in the middle of all that chaos. He moves like he's about to kiss me, leans his body in toward mine, and I pull away.

"You can't kiss me here," I say, shocked at his boldness.

"I want to kiss you everywhere," he says, and moves even closer to me.

I full-on blush, my whole body a deep shade of pink. I want to lean in, to feel him up against me, and I hate that I have sabotaged the one good thing that has happened to me in so long. I hate myself for thinking I could do something so shitty to someone so good, so kind. I have to make it right. I have to fix this.

"Listen, I just . . . Can we talk . . . somewhere away from the crowd?" I ask, and he nods and moves to hold my hand. "We can't do that here," I say, surprised at how much he doesn't seem to care who is watching us or what we are doing.

"I'll follow you anywhere," he says, and I look at him steady for a minute. Just hold his gaze across from mine.

The crowd is big now, with more and more people streaming in. The televisions are up and running, filming other pockets of people, and as kids see themselves up on the screen, we hear cheers and people even kissing when they find the camera. It's kind of a schtick, but people seem to love it, and I smile thinking of all the joy this night brings to families. Maybe if I just think of it as a field party, as the family version of the

Turkey Kick, then all is right in the world. Maybe if I just think of JP like some great love, then I won't feel so devastated when I have to end it. Maybe I don't have to end it at all. I could just pretend I am not falling.

We walk to the back of the party, and I take in the whole scene again. The way the sun is just about to set in the sky, the way the mountains rise and rise all around us, hulking and massive against the backdrop of the resort. There is nowhere else this beautiful, this rich, this serene.

"You wanted to talk, I know, but is it okay if I start?" JP asks, and studies my face with a steadiness that shocks me.

"Oh, yeah. Sure," I say, studying his right back.

"I just. I wanted to say. I wanted you to know this has been the best week of my life," he starts, and I go all unsteady on my feet. Nervous and not ready for anything he is about to say, but I listen. "I don't know . . . I have never met anyone like you. Never anyone who takes so many risks or says whatever is on your mind or just . . . You make me see things in a different way. You make me better or more myself or . . . Last night . . . on the mountain . . . I felt alive in a way that shook me. My whole body . . . everything feels electrified or shocked or something and I just . . ."

And that's when I hear it, a slight echo coming from JP, and slow-motion-like, I pull around and see his face up on both jumbotrons. *Oh my god.* "No, no, JP . . ."

"I want you to know that I love you. I love you in a way I . . . Wait . . . Is that an echo?" JP asks, and he can hear himself reverberated back to him. *I love you. I love you. I love you. I love you* on a loop, a twisting and winding lilt all through the crowd, and everyone is suddenly watching and seeing the two of us, our faces massive on the big screen. *I love you. I love you.* An echo.

The guests think it is a sweet moment being captured and shared, and so they start to clap and cheer, and all my coworkers think it is the bet being won and so they start to whoop and holler with the crowd. JP looks at me, shocked and concerned.

"What is happening?" he says, still up on the big screen.

"JP? Is that you?" I hear from behind us. "What are you doing on that camera?"

"Mom?" JP says.

When I look, I expect to see Mrs. Abrigo, but it's a completely other woman standing in front of me.

JP

Holy shit. The moment I tell Mia how I really feel is playing on jumbotrons like they have at Mets games. What was supposed to be private is now a full-on public display. Everyone around us is howling and cheering like we're at Citi Field. This is the moment I was supposed to reveal everything—tell Mia that I love her, explain the stupid lie I let her believe—how my family isn't really the family she thinks it is. Instead of an explanation, we're caught in a storm of confusion.

And then there's the business of my mother. The real one. Standing right in front of me. And Mia. And what feels like thousands of our closest friends.

"Boy Reyes, why are you on the TV?" she shouts.

My eyes scan the crowd, looking for whatever camera is aimed at me. I'm in a dizzying panic. Then, I see Wolf's pointy smile. He's smirking at me from behind a huge remote camera, clearly having the time of his life.

Dali, Alvin, and my cousins have stepped into the circle. I can see myself dead center on the screen above their heads. Fireworks burst in the night sky.

"Hi, Mom," I sputter.

"I thought she was your mom," Mia says, pointing at Tita Dali.

"That's my aunt."

The brightness of red, white, and blue bursts in the sky. Cass and Tiff are on either side of Dali holding hands tightly. "Hi, Mia!" they say, waving.

"Are Tiff and Cass your brother and sister?" Mia asks. Her eyes are undone. More patriotic shapes go off above. This is a holiday-themed nightmare.

"We're his cousins!" Tiffany shouts.

Mia, tears welling in her eyes, her voice cracking, points toward Alvin. "Is that your dad?"

"That's my uncle. My dad—"

BOOM. BOOM. Overhead a cluster of rockets and candles light up the night. The shapes swell and drip memories of the year gone by. *Back-to-school shopping with Dad in September, Fresh Jordans; going into Manhattan for comics over fall break, Batman is a domestic terrorist; trying to make halo-halo with oat milk. Could we get used to this?*

Me and Dad, ang aking ama; Shaw Brothers movies on DVD, superhero movies on the big screen in Times Square. Small talk. Big Talk. Thanksgiving dinner at Krystal's Diner—cheeseburgers and pastrami sandwiches better than any turkey, sweet potato pie with tube whipped cream; and then, the cold of December.

We're ten days from Christmas. The apartment smells of radiator heat and fish sauce. On the kitchen counter—blanched bok choy, reheated pork, homemade chili oil, and lime wedges. I've seen pieces of the day for months, but never all together like this. Never in the order that it happened.

I hear Pilita's first Christmas album playing in mono. I see the rolling boil of water in our heavy stockpot. I smell the sweetness of green onion from the butcher block. I'm about to cook the egg noodles when Dad stands up from his seat at our little table.

I turn and see him staring right at me. He blinks twice. Looks at me confused and starts to tighten his right hand. I hear the table legs splinter under the weight of his falling body. I rush across the room asking every question there ever was. I ask loud. I ask soft. He does not answer. I feel the cold glass of the phone dialing 911. I hear the all-business voice of the operator on the other end.

There is no breath in his lungs, no beating heart in his chest. There is nothing remaining behind my father's eyes. The medics are there in minutes. I hear the cracking of his ribs and sternum as they give CPR. I see little reflections of our little apartment in the chrome frame of the stretcher. I smell bleach and pine air freshener in the back of the ambulance. I hear the sticking and poking and clicking sounds as my father's body is hooked up to all the monitors. I feel all three jolts of the defibrillator. I hear it, smell it, see it, and feel it all at once.

The defocused lights inside the ambulance sharpen into the fireworks of Fourth of July. "My dad is dead."

Mia looks at me in complete disbelief.

Appearing from nowhere, Bee puts an arm around her, whispers something in her ear, then takes her hand, opens it, and presses a $50 bill into her palm. Penelope, Logan, and a line of other workers queue up to give Mia a mix of 5s, 10s, 20s, and well-worn singles.

I have no idea what's happening as a blanket of stars and stripes bang and crackle above. Ellis and Jasmine step up to

Mia's side looking melancholy, but protective. Ellis shakes his head left and right, peering through me. Jasmine finds my eyes and mouths, *Go*, pointing with her face toward the Mountain House.

I can't breathe, can't get grounded, can't think straight. If everything is out in the open, why do I feel completely empty, and why are Mia's palms full of hot bundles of cash?

Wolf stacks a brick of bills in Mia's hands. Her eyes are on me like she wants to say something. But she can't.

"Congratulations, Mia!" he bellows. Then to me, "You played a good game, goat."

"What? What game? What's going on?" I ask, starting to get a new rise of panic and dizziness.

"Malik said she could get any goat to fall in love with her. She was right. Big Money Malik is goin' out to Cali, y'all!" With that Wolf hollers and shouts his way through the crowd of workers and guests, throwing high fives and chest bumps.

Mia looks at me like there's some way to explain all this. My eyes must look the same. Neither of us have the words to match the weight of our hearts. A final crescendo of fireworks fades to black. Everything else follows.

MIA

"Malik! Are you kidding me?" I hear. Layla is behind me fast. She hears everything. "A bet? To trick one of our guests? Follow me. Now." I look back at JP one last time. The hurt and confusion covering his face. I shake my thoughts loose in my head. I have ruined everything.

Layla walks at a clip ahead of me, but when I think we're headed to her office, she makes a turn and goes to the bunkhouse.

"What are we doing here?" I ask, trying to figure out a way to get back to the party, to explain myself to JP.

"It's time for you to start packing," she says, turning the light on in the room.

"No, Layla, please . . . can I just explain?" Layla pauses, looks at me. I clear my throat. "I know what I did was wrong. I know that. And I know it was foolish and ignorant. That is all true. But I also know that people make mistakes." At this, Layla rolls her eyes and moves to cut me off, but I keep on. "Eighteen-year-old kids make mistakes. Especially ones who have been dreaming about leaving town since they were twelve and finally found the only way they could do it, or the only way they thought they could do it," I say.

"That's not enough, Mia. I'm done. You're done. Start packing. Now."

So I do, but I can't stop trying to make it all make sense. "It's just. I got caught up. Without my mom and dad, it's not . . . I'm eighteen now and I am on my own, and I'm stuck, and I'm sinking, or at least I can feel myself sinking and I don't want to go down. I want to get out. And I know it was wrong. I have to make it right."

"And how do you expect to do that?"

"Maybe I could . . ." I rack my brain to think of a solution. "Could I stay on at the resort through the fall and winter? I am open to any job or anywhere you think I would fit. But I am gonna make the money on my own, not on some stupid bet. I'm gonna stay and make the money the right way. I have to."

"Mia, are you seriously asking me for a bigger job? You landed a child in the ER a few days ago and tonight was total chaos. I can't let you keep this job. It's over. And the sooner you realize life is not a game, the better."

I don't mean to start sobbing, but that's what I do. Big, heaping tears running down my face. "I can't believe I hurt him," I say.

"Is this really about the kid? JP?"

"I think I'm in love with him," I say, and start to toss my clothes in my duffel bag.

"Then you'll figure out how to make it right," Layla says. "You just won't do it at the Majestic Mountain House. Now finish packing and head to the front desk. I'll get someone to run you down off the resort."

An hour later, I am sitting in the main lobby alone. The walls are covered with pictures of families, the ones I have been photographing over the last couple of years. I see the ways they are holding on to each other and smiling, the mountains rising up behind them. Their joy as they celebrate their vacation or getaway. I made all of these families feel safe and confident and now I made one of them feel ashamed and embarrassed.

Then I see Bee walking toward me with keys and carrying an envelope in her hand. I shake my head. "You're my ride, huh?"

"Yup. Your ticket off the mountain."

"Got it. Is, uh . . . is JP okay?"

"Oh, come on, are you seriously worried about that goat? That fool made up an entire family to mess with you all week and you're still wanting to know if he's okay?!"

I don't tell Bee that I did the same thing. "I just didn't want to hurt anyone. That's all."

"He didn't seem to mind. And I kinda had the feeling he was messing with you, so . . ."

"What? You did?"

"I just didn't think he was being honest with you, that's all. You deserve to get out of here. I know we haven't always gotten along, but when you work at a resort like this, you gotta band together. Here. I collected the rest of the money. Maybe this will make you feel better. You earned it," she says. "Congratulations."

I shake my head. "Thanks for this, but . . . I'm not gonna go. I, *uh* . . . I can't do it."

"You have to," Bee says. " 'For all of us who can't get out just yet." She tosses the envelope toward me, and I drop it in the bag. "Come on. Let's get outta here."

I am completely weighed down by my mistake and carrying it around with me. I am not leaving, but I have absolutely everything if I change my mind and decide to go.

We wind so slow down the curving roads. The trees billow and shake around me as we snake from the main resort house all the way to town. Monument looks so small from way up here, but the closer we get to the bottom, the more I remember my past, the way my mom's and dad's faces seem to show up in the hillsides and inside all those rolling fields. I see them everywhere. Make photographs in my mind. Snap. Click. There's the trees we climbed atop, and the sloping ranges we caught fireflies on, and the rambling downtown with its crystal shops and tarot card readers, its used bookstores with pride flags and sidewalk sales, its outdoorsy shops with kayaks and paddleboards and CBD stores that promise to get you relaxed and calm and chill. I see the college students still here for the summer and people who look to be struggling in the back alleys as we drive through the maze of streets. Everyone's hurt is worn. I bow my head and make a wish because somehow it feels like I need it, like I need something to be granted to me this time. I direct Bee to Locust Road and thank her when she drops me off.

"I know I was messing with you, and I'm sorry," Bee says as I grab my stuff from the back seat. "But don't forget what I said. You gotta make it out. Somehow."

"Thanks for the ride," I tell her, and walk up to the front porch. It's covered in toys and looks scattered and wild. The yard is overgrown and almost looks abandoned, but I hear voices inside the house. "Hey!" I holler. "Anyone home?" Chelsea comes running down the hallway. I can hear the quick pounding of her feet. She knows my voice. "Aunt June? Y'all in there?"

"Hey, girl. What are you doing back here? And on the Fourth?! I figured they'd be working you to the bone," I hear from the back of the house.

"I messed up," I admit, walking inside and sitting my butt right down on my favorite chair, the one that looks toward the mountains in the back. Chelsea piles on top of me and gives me hugs and kisses nonstop.

"You see she has kinda been missing you, huh?" Aunt June laughs and pulls Chelsea off to give me some space. "How'd you get down here anyway? You hitchhike?"

"Nah, nobody woulda picked me up even if I had. I got a ride with a friend."

"But aren't you on the clock? What happened?" At this, Aunt June and Chelsea start listening for real. Aunt June pours me a glass of iced tea mixed with lemonade and we open the back door so the mountains look like they're sitting in on our conversation this time around. I tell them everything, and between Chelsea playing in her kitchen and serving me fake food, she gives me quick hugs around my neck.

I don't want to leave either one of them. How can I love something so much but still know I have to leave it to keep me whole?

"So that's how I found myself packing my bags. I'm fired."

"Oh no! Mia, what are you gonna do, honey?" Aunt June asks.

"I'm just gonna suck it up and move back in here. I figure

I can help around the house a little and get some jobs babysitting and maybe a part-time gig in town. I can piece it together, I know I can," and then I look up at Aunt June, who has tears in her eyes. "What's wrong? Is that . . . are you okay?"

"Baby. We're fine, it's just . . . we were planning to leave town once summer is over."

"What? Why?"

"What's left for us here? Your mom and dad are gone again. I saw him yesterday and both of 'em were headed back to the city for something they can't find here. And when you told me you were getting the money to go to California, I just decided not to sign the lease. Figured we could head South. I've been wanting to get to Asheville or Charlottesville—some kind of mountains that don't hold so much history. I just figured without all of you here, then what was I holding on to?"

"Oh . . . you're . . . both of you are just . . . that's it? No more Monument?" I start to cry all over again, as if I'd been holding back or on to those tears for way too long, just keeping them stored up inside. "It's good . . . that's not why I'm crying. It's good. I wanna leave too. There's too many memories here and too much drama and chaos, it's just . . . How do I fix it? How do I make it right?"

"Listen, is this thing you have really serious? Is it really as good as you're telling me?"

"Yes. Yes, I have never felt this way. I know it's wild and doesn't make any sense, but I can see myself when I am with him. Some whole other part of me comes alive and I wanna hold on to that, but . . ."

"Then take a risk. Do something unexpected. What do you have to lose?

SUNDAY

JP

It seems unlikely that I'm going to see Mia Malik today, or any other day again, for that matter. It's even more unlikely that I'll be able to parse why I lied about everything this summer and why she lied right back at me. *Dear Mia,* I write on a sheet of heavy hotel stationery. *I have no idea how to start this letter. I want to explain things. I want to ask questions. I'm not sure if any of this comes from a good place.*

I pause for a beat, tapping my pen against the heavy stock. Beats stack into longer moments, moments into extended minutes, and before I know it, I've been sitting alone at breakfast for the better part of an hour. It's past 9:30 and my mother is very late to meet me. This is nothing new or surprising, but it's shitty all the same. I see her entering the dining room, scattered. She passes the weirdo quartet, who have figured out a way to make "Be My Baby" sound like haunting classical music.

Any second now, she's going to sit down at the table and—through her dark sunglasses—gaslight me about getting the time wrong. In spite of everything that happened last night, she'll only want to talk about college and my future career.

"Good morning, John Paul," she says before ordering sausage, eggs, and French toast. I politely accept a refill on my coffee. I've already had two cups but can't seem to pump any life into my body. She acts amazed that I'm "early" to breakfast. I tell her we were supposed to meet an hour ago, and she explains to me all the ways that I am wrong.

This conversation is one-sided. My mother is speaking at me in rapid-fire hits. As expected, I'm given a list of things I'll need when college starts. To my surprise, she references last night, advising that I not date anyone seriously until I have "graduated from college and med school and finished residency at a hospital."

I don't tell her that I'm never going to study medicine or that her dreams of me being a doctor are so far off that there's not even a multiverse version of John Paul Reyes, MD. I don't tell her that I'd really like to try and write comic books or get up the courage to audition as a backup dancer for touring artists.

I don't tell her that my relationship with Mia is the best thing that's ever happened to me. I don't tell her that Mia is the only person I've ever had these deep feelings for. I feel my heart swell. I told Mia that I loved her last night. I've never told anyone anything like that before.

I don't tell my mom any of this because it goes against that cardinal rule I already broke with Dali—the elders are always right.

What they're right about, however, is as sprawling and disconnected as the dots between Luzon and Mindanao.

Eating the fisheye will help you see into the future.

Playing violin will get you that scholarship.

White people have the cleanest kitchens because they don't cook in them.

A good haircut should not touch your collar.

Stir-fried vegetables in pork fat is still perfectly vegetarian.

I'm gripping my hands so tightly under the table that my thumbs are about to explode. She's telling me my entire future. I hear this fairy tale every summer.

"You will be a famous surgeon in Los Angeles or a sports medicine doctor in San Francisco. You will marry a nice girl and she will stay at home with all five of your children—four boys, but the youngest a girl. As a lola, I will live with you in your mansion or in the guest cottage out back. Perhaps the cottage would be better for your privacy. But I will live with you all the same—"

"Mom," I say, interrupting. "You're never going to live with me. You don't want to live with me." *So much for not telling my elders the truth.*

"Why do you say that, John Paul?"

"We haven't lived together since I was a little kid," I say plainly. "I think you like your work. I think you like the freedom of moving around. Maybe one day you'll retire in Baguio, but I really think you like to stay in motion."

"We're not talking about me," she dodges quickly. "We're talking about you."

"Okay," I start. "Let's talk about me. You always tell me about the life that I'm going to have one day—what I'm going to do and how I'm going to live. It's been a hard year, Mom. I miss Dad. I miss Jackson Heights. And after everything that's happened, I don't think anyone can see very far into the future. I've got a little money saved up to start college. I'll try City College next year. I'm going to see what that's about. But I don't want to get into crazy debt. I don't want to stay in a career that I hate to pay off a degree that I never really wanted."

For the first time in all my eighteen years, my mother is actually listening to me. And then we talk—really talk. About jobs—all kinds of nonmedical jobs. And we talk about Jackson Heights—restaurants from back in the day and how hard it is to find good Filipino food anywhere but the coasts. She tells me that she started construction on the house in Baguio, and that she hopes Dali and I will come and visit her when everything is up and running.

I tell her that I've been thinking about moving back to Queens, even though I need four or five roommates to afford the rent. It's all worth it though. Being home costs money, but the cost of not knowing where home is, is even harder to bear.

Before we know it, we've outstayed the children's buffet, the string quartet, and everyone on the morning service.

"I have to go now, John Paul," she says softly. "I'm working down in Kentucky this month."

"Fly safe, Mom. Maybe I'll see you at Christmas."

"Oh! One more thing," she says, standing up from the table. Reaching into her shoulder bag, she pulls out a vintage Air Jordan box tied up in a bow with the golden sun and three stars of the Filipino flag. "Your dad wanted you to have this."

"Original Jordan 4s!" I exclaim. My excitement dips slightly when I notice the size. "Ah, these are Dad's size. I think they're gonna be a little small for me."

"Trust me, JP," Mom smiles. "They'll fit you just fine."

"These shoes are crazy heavy, Mom," I say, almost dropping the vintage black box.

I slide the bow off the red jump man and flip the smooth, one-piece lid to the back. I gently move the vintage Nike tissue paper to the sides, revealing a mint condition pair of OG black and gray Jordans. Released back in '89, these were some of the lightest basketball shoes you could buy. *Why do they feel so heavy?*

I read a small card Scotch-taped to the inside of the lid.

John Paul—

Go on an adventure! Wander and wonder,
have yourself a ball—

Love you so much, Baby Boy Reyes—

Dad

Just then, it all makes sense. Stuffed inside and all around the shoes are rolls and rolls of tightly wound cash.

"Your father saved all this for you," my mom explains. "He sent me money for you every month. He was afraid if he kept it in New York, he would spend it." She starts laughing her happy laugh.

I slam the lid shut, remembering another important FilAm rule—never count money in public.

"There's a lot of cash in there," my mom whispers. Then she hands me an envelope of large bills. "This one is from me. Between your father's box and my envelope, maybe you can go to college for more than a year. And maybe you can just have one or two roommates instead of four or five."

Go on an adventure . . .

I walk my mother to meet her cab at checkout and start looking for Mia. I run everywhere. The docks, the lake, the trails around the Mountain House. Jasmine looks at me with pity at the Kids' Club. "Let it go, dude," she tells me. "There's nothing more to say."

I see Ellis in the hallway of family portraits. He ignores my existence.

"Ellis," I say as he walks past me. He pauses and reluctantly turns.

"JP, all your lying was real messed up."

I pause and take a breath. "I know. If I could do it differently, I would, but I can't."

"Why can't goats just be straight-up about who they are? You all lie all the freakin' time about freakin' everything—money, family, *everything*."

"Wait, what's a goat? I'm not a . . ."

"It's what we call the guests who treat us like we don't exist. The ones who act like our only job is to serve them."

"But that's not me."

"I didn't think it was. But now I'm not so sure. Are you even a *real* X-Men fan?"

"Yes. Yes I am. But, full transparency—I think X-Force is the better team."

Ellis hides an honest chuckle.

"Yeah," I say. "I think you think that too. Look, I'm just trying to find Mia. I don't want to hurt anybody. I just want to tell her what I was trying to tell her last night. It's important to me. I think it might be important to her too."

"*You* want to talk to *Mia*?" he asks, puzzled.

"Yeah, you know where I can find her?"

"She got fired, man. After last night, Layla had her pack her bags and head off the mountain. She went to her aunt's house."

"But what about the bet? What about leaving town? I gotta see her before we leave."

"You could just text her?"

"No, no . . . I have to see her in person. How do I do that? Where does she live in town?"

"Talk to Caloy at the front desk. They always know where folks are."

I nod, feeling some slight relief about things with Ellis.

"What kind of rich are you, JP?" he asks.

"Money wise? I'm doing great. I have enough cash in this shoebox for a year at City College. I have two pairs of functional shoes. I'm looking for a roommate in New York, if you know anybody."

"Manhattan?"

"Nah, I can't afford all that. Outer borough—*Queens*. You thinking about a move?"

"I'll keep you posted." He smiles. "But you didn't answer my question. What kind of rich are you?"

"I found out I have more love with someone than I could have ever imagined. So yeah, I'm rich. I'm freakin' filthy rich. I don't want to lose it."

With that, we nod our goodbyes, and I head down the stairs to the front desk.

"Caloy!" I say excitedly. "I'm so glad you're here. I'm looking for Mia Malik. Do you know where I can find her?"

"I'm sorry, JP. She's not on the mountain today."

My heart sinks. I look at the ground—*as if there's some sort of answer down there.*

"Caloy, can you do me a favor?"

MIA

"Baby, wake up!" Aunt June calls, knocking on my bedroom door. "You said you don't have too much time."

I open the door already dressed. I waited until the sun was fully in the sky, but now it's time to move. "You sure this is gonna work?" I ask.

"Only way to know for sure is if you try. What do you have to lose? You sure you don't want a ride?"

"It's okay. It's just . . . this is something I wanna do by myself. I gotta see this through on my own."

I take my old bike out of the shed. Check the tires to make sure they're working and then I ride. My legs pump wild and reckless through town. Heat radiates fast through my body. I push ahead, circling and circling, to find my way through all those same alleys and back roads. The Mountain House is only five miles away but feels like a whole other world. I steel myself for the journey. It's all uphill from here.

Aunt June said I needed to take a risk, and I know she's right. I know it's time, so I do not look back once. I forge ahead. I look straight in front of me and pedal until my heart feels like it might firework right out of my chest. I do not think about Mom and Dad and their struggles and addictions. I know it is not my fault that they are sick, and push the guilt and the shame I feel for that down too.

There's no forgiveness for what I did to JP, but I go ahead and try to be softer with myself. Give it grace, give it time. Keep moving, keep steady, keep ready for whatever comes next. Sweat is pouring down my face. I swipe it away and push faster. I get out of town and the past starts to shake off from my body. Each movement brings me closer to whatever is supposed to come next. Get through town and over the bridge and ride through fields and fields of wildflowers.

I can hear JP describing the orchids in the woods and I can feel his hands all over my body, the way he made me catch my breath, and my heart is gold now and beating so heavy inside of me. He made me feel caught up, shimmering, glowing, all soul winding and warm, caught up and lost at the same time. Keep going stronger, pushing deeper, finding strength to do the thing I said I would do.

The road up is steep, but I do not stop. I pass cars coming down the mountain. For these guests, vacation is over. I do not falter or pause. I just keep my head down and keep my legs tumbling around each other. Pushing, aching, barreling up until I finally see the beginnings of the resort. I am not supposed to be here. I was fired last night, escorted off the grounds, and I know I should stay away, and maybe old Mia Malik would have. Maybe she would have just played it safe. But I am not one to follow the rules anymore. I know that about myself now. I know what I want, and I ask for it. I guide it. Give it directions. I don't stand for anything less. I am scared of what's to come. I need to see JP. I need to make this right. And most of all, I need him to still be there.

I am flush coming off the bike. I stop at the bunkhouse, hoping no one will notice since today is changeover day and most of the staff is helping with the load out and the load in. I rush into the bathroom and try to salvage what I am looking at in the mirror. I look like the chaos that I started, but I freshen up. Wash my face, under my arms, and behind my neck. I can do this. I have to.

I run out of the bunkhouse and make my way to the main lobby. I need to see Caloy or Ellis. One of them will know how to find JP. In the meantime, I text: can i see you? it's important. Nothing returns to me. I run through the main house, dodging the dozens of families moving out with their loaded suitcases, and race up the front steps to the Abrigo suite. I bang my fist on the door. I don't care who opens it. I don't care what his aunt and uncle or mom or whoever is with him thinks. I don't worry about what they'll say to me or how I am supposed to act. I just bang and bang. "JP! Cass! Tiffany? Anyone?" One of the new members of the hospitality staff opens the door.

"Excuse me?" she says. "Can I help you?"

"I'm Mia," I say, realizing that she doesn't recognize me and must think I am a guest. "Is . . . do you know if they all packed to leave?" I ask. It's still early. They can't be gone already.

"I'm so sorry. I was told this room was ready to be turned over."

"Shit. They're gone. Okay, thanks!"

I run out and head toward the dock, which is where most families go for a final goodbye to the Majestic Mountain House or a last picture of vacation. On the way, I rush into the Kids' Club.

"Mia!" Jasmine gasps. "What are you doing here? I've been texting you. Layla said they let you go. What's happening?"

"Is JP still here?"

"How would I know? I'm so over him and how he treated you and . . ."

"Jasmine, please. I have to see him. Where's Ellis?"

"He's working the café today. But why? He lied to you."

"Come on. We all know I lied too. And if I wanna get out of this, I have to find him to tell the truth. Can you please just text Ellis for me? Ask him if JP left yet? Please? I'm gonna check the docks. Tell him to text me if he hears anything!"

My legs are gummy and uneven, and I feel like I might just pass out. When I get to the docks and they're not there, panic starts to set in. What if I totally messed this up for real? What if it's over? What if I really do lose my one good thing? What then? And then I remember. Everyone goes to the front desk to sign the guest book before they leave. They go to hold on to the memory of this place, as proof they were here, that they mattered, that they existed, and so I stay moving and get to the front of the Mountain House. I see Caloy walking into the back room, and in front of me there's a kid standing at the guest book. I don't have time for this. I have to make my move. I have to make this happen. Trust myself. Move ahead. Do the thing I have been thinking of. What is this kid waiting on? Is he thirteen or eighteen? Is he a teenager or an adult? What is even happening? And then I see him move to take his hat off and that messy head of hair comes piling out and then I realize exactly who it is.

JP

I'm standing alone under the Guest Services sign at the front desk. Tita Dali, Tito Alvin, Tiff, and Cass are all waiting at the valet for the electric SUV. I'm feverishly trying to finish writing out a message to Mia Malik. Just then, a familiar voice calls me from behind.

"JP . . ."

That sounds exactly like Mia. I turn. It *is* Mia. "Hey," I reply, shocked to be standing here at the exact right moment.

"You're still here. I was . . . I was worried you'd already left."

"No, I didn't want to leave without seeing you, without saying goodbye."

"Me too."

"But then Ellis told me you were fired, and I didn't know what to say or how to say it, so . . . I'm writing you a note."

"A note?" Mia questions. "What does it say?"

"You want me to read it?"

"Yeah, please. Read me the note."

"Okay, okay, yeah . . . I'm gonna read it." I clear my throat, take a deep breath, and start.

Dear Mia,

You'll never know how sorry I am for not telling you the truth about myself. A lot has happened in my life over the last handful of months. That's not an excuse for me lying. Some true things about me—I love hip-hop and dancing. I like all foods except peanut butter crackers. My dad made these as my lunch from fifth grade through ninth grade and I just got really burned out on them. My Tito Alvin (the guy that everyone thought was my dad but isn't my dad) is really rich and paid for me to be at Majestic Mountain House this summer. I've been living with him, my Tita Dali, and my cousins Tiffany and Cass since my dad died. Today, my mom gave me a shoebox stuffed with a bunch of money from my dad. She gave me some other money too. It's enough for me to live on, with a sensible number of roommates, and pay for school for at least a year . . .

I lower the paper, looking up at Mia.

"That's it?" she asks pointedly.

"No, no. It's just . . . that's all I have right now. I was writing more . . . *I'm going to write more.*"

"Why don't you just tell me what you wanna say."

I fold the heavy paper in half and look Mia right in the eyes. "This year started as the worst year of my life. My dad had a heart attack in December and he just . . . died. I don't think it hurt him too much. It happened really fast. I spent winter and spring trying not to remember anything or feel anything. Then, this summer, I met you and . . . You're not afraid of anything, Mia. You're not afraid to walk to the edge of a cliff or swim across a lake, you're not afraid to tell jerks what's what, you're not afraid to take a goat through the Garlic Press, and you weren't afraid to tell me the truth about your family. You're not afraid to chase your dream to somewhere you've never been before. I met you, Mia, and I started to feel everything. I love you."

"I love you too. I wanted to tell you last night," she says.

"Me too! It's just . . ."

"It's just we were on a jumbotron?"

"Yeah. We were on a jumbotron. You were winning some kind of lottery cash prize. Everyone was cheering you on and I had no idea what was happening. It was bad."

"I'm not keeping the money, JP," she says honestly. "It's right here." She pulls it out of her bag. "My next stop after finding you was gonna be dropping this with Caloy and then trying to win over Layla so I can get my job back."

"What? No! You have to keep the money!"

"Why? It was a crappy bet and the only way to win was to make you lose. And once I got to know you, I didn't . . . didn't mean to hurt you, and I did."

"I'm still here," I say. "Look," I stretch my arms out wide. "I'm okay. And you need to keep the cash."

"Why? What is it worth now?"

"Oh, I don't know . . . Maybe it could cover living expenses once you get to the West Coast?"

"I'm not going out West . . . Don't you understand? I'm staying here. Right here. This is the end for me."

Just then Caloy returns from the back office holding a folder of papers. They give it to me. I look down at it and smile. I asked for the printed copy for proof, to be able to hold some part of the future with Mia Malik. I hand it over. She studies the page in front of her.

"One-way ticket to Los Angeles," she says with a smile in her voice. "You didn't?!"

"I did. I had to figure out something to do with that whole shoebox full of cash. It was just burning a hole . . ."

"In your future!" Mia says. "You can't use up all your money for me."

"I didn't spend all of it," I say, and pull out a second piece of paper with my ticket printed on it.

"Nooo . . . Are you serious?"

"Whoa! We're sitting right next to each other. That's wild," I say, smiling so hard my cheeks hurt.

Mia smiles too, and then starts laughing—hard, her voice echoing off the high ceilings.

"I told you I'd follow you anywhere, right?"

"You're positive?" Mia asks.

"Yeah, I am. It's time to see what's out there for me . . . for *us*."

"And that's the truth?"

"That's the truth. We've already told each other every lie."

ACKNOWLEDGMENTS

With love for our family—

Gianina Hagan, Patrick Hagan, Michael Hagan, Jen Hagan, Jake Hagan, and Lisa Hagan

Marsha Dehne Flores, Dominador Alverez Flores, Kevin Flores, and Melissa Johnson

Thank you to the brilliant community of artists and friends in our lives—

Grisel Y. Acosta, Stephanie Dionne Acosta, E.J. Antonio, Lisa Ascalon, Jennifer Baker, Melanie Ballard Sewell, Julia Berick, Dan Bernitt, Berry, Leslie Hibbs Blincoe, Tokumbo Bodunde, Marc Boone, Cheryl Boyce-Taylor, Lori Brown-Niang, Susan Buttenwieser, Moriah Carlson, Kate Carothers Smith, Esther Castillo, Daniel Choate, Becca Christensen, Cheryl Clarke, Megan Clark Garriga, Olivia Cole, Athena Colón, Angie Cruz, Brandi Cusick Rimpsey, Matthew D'Alessio, LeConté Dill, Mitchell L. H. Douglas, Jason Duchin, Dana Edell, Kelly Norman Ellis, John Ellrodt, Kathy Engel, Maria Fico, Rajeeyah Finnie-Myers, Lisa Forsee Roby, DuEwa Frazier, Asha French, Tanya Gallo, Catrina Ganey, Sandralis Gines-Gonzalez, Aracelis Girmay,

Nanya-Akuki Goodrich, Lisa Green, Andrée Greene, Rachel Eliza Griffiths, Ysabel Y. Gonzalez, Karen Harryman, Daniel Heffernan, Lindsey Homra, JP Howard, Amanda Johnston, Parneshia Jones, Carey Kasten, Caroline Kennedy, Michele Kotler, Britt Kulsveen, Nikita Ladd, Todd Lesousky, Rob Linné, Veronica Liu, Mino Lora, Tim Lord, Will Maloney, Alison McDonald, Chad McTighe, Caits Meissner, Stacy Mohammed, Yesenia Montilla, Andrea Murphy, Christina Olivares, Willie Perdomo, Lisa Perez, Andy Powell, Sarina Prabasi, Danni Quintos, Emily Raboteau, David Reilly, Carla Repice, Kate Dworkoski Scudese, Pete Scudese, Matt Scherer, Vincent Toro, Natalia Torres, Alondra Uribe, Edwin Velasquez, Jessica Wahlstrom, Renée Watson, Jenisha Watts, Kelly Wheatley, Alecia Whitaker, Crystal Wilkinson & Marina Hope Wilson

Renée Watson & Kelly Wheatley—thank you for your early readership, thoughtful guidance, and enduring support.

Bex—thank you for bringing Mia and JP fully alive on the cover.

Sarah Shumway Liu—thank you for believing in this book, believing in our voices, and all of your thoughtful care in bringing this love story to life.

Thank you to the team at Bloomsbury: Erica Barmash, Alexa Higbee, Beth Eller, Lily Yengle, Alona Fryman, Jeanette Levy, Donna Mark, Diane Aronson, Laura Phillips, Lara Kennedy, and Helen Armalas—for all the work you do to get our books ushered into the world.

Rosemary Stimola and our family at Stimola Literary Studio—Allison Hellegers, Erica Rand Silverman & Adriana Stimola—thank you for nurturing stories and voices that matter.

From David Flores—Ellen, I'll follow you anywhere.

From Ellen Hagan—I'll let you.